He Falls First

JILL SHALVIS

Copyright © 2025 by Jill Shalvis
Cover and internal design © 2025 by Sourcebooks
Cover design by Kari March Designs
Cover images © nj_musik/Adobe Stock, Baranovska/Adobe Stock, irina11998877.gmail.com/Depositphotos
Internal design by Tara Jaggers/Sourcebooks

Sourcebooks and the colophon are registered trademarks of Sourcebooks.

All rights reserved. No part of this book may be reproduced in any form or by any electronic or mechanical means including information storage and retrieval systems—except in the case of brief quotations embodied in critical articles or reviews—without permission in writing from its publisher, Sourcebooks.

No part of this book may be used or reproduced in any manner for the purpose of training artificial intelligence technologies or systems.

The characters and events portrayed in this book are fictitious or are used fictitiously. Any similarity to real persons, living or dead, is purely coincidental and not intended by the author.

All brand names and product names used in this book are trademarks, registered trademarks, or trade names of their respective holders. Sourcebooks is not associated with any product or vendor in this book.

Published by Sourcebooks Casablanca, an imprint of Sourcebooks
P.O. Box 4410, Naperville, Illinois 60567-4410
(630) 961-3900
sourcebooks.com

Cataloging-in-Publication Data is on file with the Library of Congress.

Printed and bound in the United States of America.
PAH 10 9 8 7 6 5 4 3 2 1

TO ANYONE WHO HAS EVER WISHED ON THE
STARS FOR THEIR SOULMATE, THIS ONE'S FOR YOU.

PROLOGUE

Ryder

"FASTER! *DON'T LOOK BACK!*" I yelled to Caleb and Tucker as we scrambled across the rocky bluffs and windswept cliffs high above the river, breath heaving, terror in our veins.

The Colburn siblings lived by one rule: if you poke the bear, run like hell. At twelve, I was the oldest and fastest, so I should've had a huge lead. After all, if we got caught, I'd be the one he'd go after first.

But since my baby sister, Kiera, had been the one to crash her bike into good old dad's precious truck, leaving both a dent and a chip in the paint, I had her by the hand, ruthlessly dragging her along with me to keep her safe.

The going was tough thanks to the uneven, choppy terrain that made up the rugged Sonoma, California coastline. Dirt, sand, and jagged rocks shifted dangerously beneath our feet as we scrambled through wild grass that came up to our navels, and it didn't help that the night was pitch black thanks to a sky churning with an incoming late spring storm.

Hopefully it made us hard to see.

Except...nope. Over the distant roar of the crashing waves that met the end of the river, I heard pounding footsteps behind us.

"Captain Asshole's gaining ground!" my brother Caleb warned, right on my heels. "*Shit, how is the old man still so fast?*"

I knew exactly how. Hank Colburn, aka Captain Asshole, aka Dad, was military born and raised, and tough as nails to boot, not to mention mean as a snake. My heart pounded in my ears from dread and panic. To our left, the land stretched out to a sharp ledge that pointed over the sea. Straight ahead were the hidden caves we'd found years ago, where we stood a chance of losing him, since for all his physical agility, Hank suffered from claustrophobia as a part of his post-traumatic stress. We flat-out hauled ass toward those caves, the horizon rising and falling away, an illusion thanks to the hills all around us.

But then Kiera slipped, her hand yanked from mine as she hit her knees. "Ry!" she cried, and in that split second, I knew.

We weren't getting away.

But I also knew exactly how furious my dad was. He loved his truck, certainly more than us, more than *anything*. Twisting, I scooped up my now sobbing sister, tossed her to Caleb and Tucker, and then shoved all of them ahead of me...

Just as a heavy, sweaty hand snatched the back of my shirt with a grip of iron. I didn't fight. But, heart thundering in my chest, I also didn't turn to face Hank, not until I watched my brothers and sister slide past the massive moss-lined boulders designating the caves' entrance and vanish from sight.

CHAPTER 1

Penny

Present day

THE GROUND RATTLED THE bones of grandma's 1928 red brick Queen Anne Victorian house and I jerked awake with a gasp. My bed was still rocking and rolling as I threw myself out of it and into the hallway, yelling a warning.

"*Earthquake!*"

Grandma Nell appeared at the bottom of the stairs in a candy apple-red silk nighty—wielding a hammer. "Sorry, sweetheart, it's just me. But good news, I got the old generator right where I want her."

At seventy-four, her confidence was impressive. She'd survived a lot in her lifetime. Two mild heart attacks and the same number of bad husbands. It was the curse all the Rose women bore; when it came to love, we *always* chose poorly and I was no exception.

"Why are you working on the generator at…" I padded barefoot down the squeaky stairs past five-decades-old flowery wallpaper and squinted at the antique grandfather clock against the far living room wall. "Three forty-five in the morning?"

"Well, when you're old like me, you sleep like crap. I needed something to do." Grandma fondly patted the pink and white wainscoting closest to her. "Luckily, our old house is always happy to provide me with work."

No lie. The hard oak floors were scarred, the walls and dramatic high-vaulted ceilings and intricate crown moldings needed attention, the furniture was hopelessly outdated, but to me, this was home. The place meant everything to us—cranky pipes, rickety stairs, leaky roof, and all.

"You couldn't have picked something quieter to do? Like, I don't know, demo our hopelessly outdated kitchen?"

Grandma chortled. She liked my sarcasm. I'm pretty sure she was the only one who did.

"And didn't we talk about you not pushing yourself too hard?" I asked. "Not to mention, wearing actual clothes in the common area so we don't scar my little brother?"

"*You* talked." But Grandma grabbed her thick, terry cloth robe from the back of a chair. The robe was the same pink as the wainscoting and possibly as old. "And no need to worry about Wyatt. We both know a twelve-year-old boy will sleep until we drag him out of bed. And even then, he wouldn't take his gaze off that gaming console of his, earthquake or zombie apocalypse."

Fact. "You actually got the generator running?" I asked. The thing was nearly as old as Grandma, but since we couldn't afford a new one anytime soon, I had my fingers crossed on a light winter in Star Falls this year. Sonoma County was famous for its lush coastline and wineries, but in recent years we'd had extreme weather with wildfires and more rain than Noah's Ark had ever seen, which meant rolling blackouts. And it'd actually *snowed* two winters running.

"I sure did get the generator running," Grandma said proudly. "For ten whole seconds."

I drew a deep breath, then nearly leapt out of my skin when someone screeched out in a sing-song voice, "*Goooooooooood mornin'!*"

I flicked on a lamp and eyed Pika-boo, grandma's green and yellow parrot. The budgie blinked sleepily at me, the tuft of feathers on top of his head sticking straight up like he was coming off a three-day bender.

Spreading his wings to show off, he said, "I'm so pretty. Did you poop?"

That was the thing about budgies. They had an extensive vocabulary and were usually far too smart for their own good. But Grandma just cackled, amused by Pika-boo's propensity to repeat back whatever phrases he'd heard that would get him the biggest reaction.

"You're *very* pretty," I said to the preening bird, who was doing a little morning gig routine. "But maybe we could cut down on asking people if they've pooped."

"Hi," he said in an exact replica of my voice. "How are you?" He paused. "Did you poop?"

Smart-ass. Not that I dared say it out loud and teach him yet another new word. I yawned so wide, my jaw cracked. "It's too early for this. I've got a few minutes left before my alarm goes off. I'm going back to bed." I pointed at Pika-boo. "Be a good boy."

He bobbed his little head. "Be a good boy."

In the warm glow of the lamp, Grandma tenderly cupped my face with both of her weathered palms. "Sorry I woke you." One of her thumbs gently skimmed over the bandage at the curve of my jaw. Her eyes filled with sorrow and grief. Unable to face the reason for that, I shook my head and gently stepped back.

She simply gave me a warm, loving smile. "You need to drink more water, honey. You look pale. And eat more. I'm going to get dressed for work." She headed up the stairs in that red nightie and pink robe.

You had to admire a woman who didn't care what anyone thought. I'd always cared too much, which was probably why my life was currently circling the drain. I needed to be more like grandma—formidable and fearless.

I touched the bandage at my jaw. I'd been back home for six months now. Before that, I'd been sharing a rental house with a few roommates in Seattle and running my own ready-made meals business while navigating a bad relationship (was there any other kind?). Mitch had presented himself as one of the good ones, and I'd bought it hook, line, and sinker. I hadn't seen the red flags in time to get out unscathed by the sneaky emotional and mental abuse, but the important thing was that I had gotten out.

Leaving him had coincided with my half brother, Wyatt, calling me in a panic. Mom had taken a job as a lounge singer on a cruise line in the Bahamas, abandoning him and grandma.

So I'd come home, gotten a job at a local catering company. It hadn't been easy. I'd had to remind Mitch several times that we were never ever getting back together—a message he hadn't fully accepted until a week ago, when I'd made a quick trip back to Seattle for some more of my things.

The bandage under my fingers hid the reason Mitch now had a restraining order against him. It was temporary, but I couldn't see Mitch further risking his career for more trouble. Or so I told myself on the nights I couldn't sleep.

I climbed the stairs and crawled back into bed, whimpering at the soft, warm bedding, needing these last few moments of peace more than I needed anything in my life. I eyed last night's half-eaten bag of cheese puffs calling my name from my nightstand and remembered Grandma telling me to eat more. No problem. I popped a few in my mouth before lying back, sighing with bliss as the trans fats hit my system. *Ahhhh—*

Beep beep beep…

Damn. I slid out of bed—again—grabbed my water bottle, and headed down the hall to get a quick shower before work, taking a long swig from the bottle as I…

Bumped into a brick wall that didn't belong to the house.

I sucked in a breath and choked on the water as it went down the wrong pipe because…*not a brick wall.*

But a man.

A tall, built, shadowy man.

Still coughing up a lung from accidentally waterboarding myself, I went into a *hi-ya, I'll-kick-your-ass* stance. I didn't know karate from a waltz, but I knew it was all in the attitude—which I had in spades.

"*Easy,*" the shadow said in a low, husky voice as a disembodied hand patted me on my heaving back.

Eyes streaming, throat burning, I jerked back. "I'm going to 'easy' my foot right up your—"

The hall light flicked on. Blinking rapidly to adjust my vision, I caught sight of an imposingly built man who was… *not* a stranger. Nope, it was Ryder Colburn, a client of Hungry Bee, the catering service where I worked. All I knew about him was that he had brooding eyes, an athletic way of moving that drew my attention, and a gruff voice, though he always nodded politely at me on the rare times our paths crossed—which was a good thing since I'd given up men, especially the hot ones. Well, at least my brain and heart had. My body was still in dispute on the subject.

His eyes lit with an annoying smirk, and I realized I still held my karate chop pose. Awesome, because why humiliate myself once, when I could do it twice? Dropping my hands to my sides, I straightened, and a cheese puff fell out of my shirt.

We both stared at it. "Well, that's not embarrassing at all," I muttered.

Ryder snorted. I tried not to stare, but my eyes had a mind of their own. His wavy, sun-kissed brown hair was tousled, like he hadn't bothered to do more than run his fingers through it. The ends curled around his ears and the collar of his perfectly tailored suit that probably cost more than my car. He was sans tie today, with the top two buttons on his shirt undone, revealing an alluring hint of dark ink. He had some nerve looking so good this early in the morning.

He hadn't said anything since his soft but commanding "easy." As usual, his expression gave little away. I'd been delivering food to his building for six months now and I still didn't know much about him other than he'd turned being enigmatic into an art form.

"What are you doing up here?" I asked.

"Dropping off Hank."

Right. Grandma was Hank's daytime caregiver, and Hank was Ryder's father. I had no idea why Ryder always used his dad's given name in a tone that suggested aggravation instead of calling him "Dad." Personally, I thought Hank was a sweetheart, and he kept Grandma busy. She loved taking care of people, so the job was a natural fit, and her paycheck went into an account for Wyatt's future education.

Assuming, of course, that we got the kid through middle and high school first. "It's early," I said. Usually the drop-off happened long after I was at work.

"Yes."

That was all he said. Apparently, he didn't like to waste words, which was frustrating for someone like me who had the opposite problem. But I knew he was quiet. Not shy, not even close. I'd seen him direct a large, rowdy crew with ease, speak to a conference room full of suits, and once I'd watched him wade into a vicious traffic fight in front of his building, breaking it up with only a few words.

"This might be hard for you to believe," I said, "but I'm going to need more than 'yes.'"

Ryder almost smiled, I could tell, but then his gaze caught on the bandage just under my jaw. Lifting my hand to cover it was utterly involuntary.

He met my eyes, quiet for a beat, during which I silently requested that he not ask. Finally, he said, "I have an early meeting in Petaluma. Nell said she didn't mind, but if Hank's any sort of problem, please let me know."

Wow. That added up to more words than he'd spoken to me in the whole time I'd known him. "So you *can* speak in full sentences."

The corner of his mouth twitched. Maybe amusement, maybe annoyance.

"And Hank's never a problem," I added.

Something came and went in his eyes. Doubt maybe? I had no idea. All he said was, "Let me know if that changes."

I nodded, then shivered from the water I'd spit down the front of myself. I wanted to hop into the shower, but the thought of doing so while Ryder was only two feet from the bathroom door made me feel uncomfortably vulnerable. This was a relatively new anxiety for me. I no longer seemed able to like someone, much less *trust* them, until I'd seen them lose their temper. And I was willing to bet no one ever saw gruff, imperturbable, stoic Ryder Colburn be anything except perfectly composed.

Which meant I could never like him.

Not that it mattered, since there was that whole gave-up-men thing...

His gaze slid down my body and his almost smile reappeared, making me realize I'd somehow forgotten I stood there in my pj's, which consisted of my baggiest, oldest pair of sweatpants and a long sleeve tee with Wonder Woman swinging her golden lasso over her head.

Correction: a very wet tee, now plastered to my skin. Great. "I'm feeling self-conscious."

"That's not what I'm feeling."

I met his hazel eyes, and it wasn't humor I caught, but a surprising heat, which both unnerved me and caused an answering thrum low in my belly.

Stupid belly.

I reminded it that I didn't want to feel *anything*, but apparently Ryder, who embodied an island-of-one stance with a side of fuck-that, could make a dead woman come back to life.

Along with my nipples.

It was ironic, really, because my choice in sleepwear should've been…well, a walking/talking advertisement for abstinence. Personally, I loved Wonder Woman, who was everything I only wished I could be—strong, fierce, brave. *Yes, hi, my name is Penny Rose, and I'm twenty-seven years old and want to be Wonder Woman when I grow up.*

A corner of Ryder's mouth twitched, so I did what I do—went on the defensive. "You have a problem with Wonder Woman?"

He gave a leisurely shake of his head. "Nope." Then he gestured with his chin toward my chest. "She goes with your attitude."

"I don't have an attitude."

"*I don't have an attitude!*" Pika-boo yelled, imitating me from the living room below. "Did you poop yet?"

Ryder's lips twitched.

I grimaced. "Last month he ate something he wasn't supposed to and plugged himself up, so for a week or so we were constantly asking him if he pooped yet, and now he likes the reaction he gets when *he's* the one asking that question."

Another lip twitch and I tossed up my hands. "*What?*"

"Cute." His gaze slid to my shirt once more before murmuring, "And fighting doesn't make you a hero."

I blinked. "Did you just…" *Quote my absolute favorite Wonder Woman saying to my face?*

But he was already walking away, jogging down the stairs and out the front door, without another word.

CHAPTER 2

Penny

TWO HOURS LATER, I stood in the industrial kitchen of Hungry Bee Catering. Each chef had their own individual station, and at this time of day, most of them looked like a natural disaster had occurred at Williams Sonoma. Everything was chaos—pots and pans and utensils scattered on countertops and in sinks, the scent of myriad spices filling the air, and the easy chatter between the cooks.

I'd just cleaned my station and was loading up the food for delivery. At the station to my right, my best friend and fellow cook, Violet, was still putting the finishing touches on her meals while she recounted her blind date from the night before.

"...he ordered steak and lobster, and *two* bottles of wine," Vi said, waving a spatula. "A total cliché, but whatever. And then, when the bill came, he patted down all his pockets, making a big show of looking for his wallet—which he didn't find, by the way. After letting me cover the whole thing, he trailed me to the parking lot, where had the nerve to come in for a kiss. I mean, I did my hair for this date. I even put on a bra for this date."

I stopped in the middle of boxing up the food and slid her a look. "Is he still alive? Do you need help burying the body?"

"Eh, it wasn't worth jail time. I told him the only thing he could kiss was my ass. But definitely worst date of all time."

"And yet you keep bugging me to join a dating app."

Renee, who was Hungry Bee's bookkeeper and Vi's sister, stopped on her way through the kitchen. Unlike us cooks, who were all dressed in black pants, white tops, and aprons if we were cooking, Renee wore a fitted maxi dress that I couldn't have pulled off for a dozen reasons, not the least of which was because I was five foot four—if I had shoes on and stretched my neck.

"My sister wants *everyone* to join a dating app," Renee said. "Even though I keep telling her I do *not* want to meet the woman of my dreams online."

"Well, how else are you going to meet her in a small, one-bar town like Star Falls?" Vi asked, hands on hips.

"Right now I prefer TV and books anyway." Renee eyed their stations hungrily. She liked to pop by just after we loaded up, in case there was something good left over. Today she nabbed the sole mini quiche left on Vi's stovetop.

"Well, one of you has to get a life," Vi said, transferring her dirty pots and pans to her sink. "I need to hear someone else's horror stories for a change."

"Hard pass," I said. "Been there, done that, zero stars, do not recommend."

"What if you're missing out on finding The One?"

This made me laugh. "I've got better odds of flying to the moon."

Renee pointed to her own nose and nodded sagely.

"You'll get lonely," Vi said.

"I've got a vibrator and excellent batteries," Renee said. "Way cheaper than dating."

We were all still laughing when a voice broke into our amusement. An icy voice that belonged to our boss, Kiera Anderson. "Am I paying you all to sit around and reminisce?"

Vi, her back to Kiera, went wide-eyed, looking like maybe she'd swallowed her tongue.

Renee squeaked and rushed back to her office.

I gulped. I needed this job, badly. I loved Star Falls, a charming, quirky little town that was like The Little Engine That Could, serving local winery and ranching communities, along with river and beach tourism. But as far as my particular skill set went, unless I wanted to make the two-hour commute to San Francisco every day, Hungry Bee was what I had to work with for now.

"We were just heading out," I said, smiling at the petite brunette dynamo who had zero tolerance for bullshit of any kind.

I used to be good at the whole smiling thing, but I was clearly out of practice because Kiera didn't look impressed. Instead, she scanned our counters, frowning at Vi's—who hadn't yet cleaned.

"Our clients do not want to hear excuses. Nor do they pay us to be late. Get moving."

Vi and I scattered like mice.

My heart was still pounding as I headed outside and loaded up the Hungry Bee van. My first client of the day was Colburn Restorations, specialists in high-end renovations of historical buildings far and wide. Ryder was the CEO.

Oh, and fun fact, also Kiera's brother.

Twice a week I cooked three days' worth of food and stocked the staff kitchen for his employees. I could only hope Ryder wasn't here after this morning's nipple-gate.

And it wasn't just that. We'd had an actual conversation. Sort of. And there in that dark hallway, before even the crack of dawn, something had happened. I wasn't sure what exactly, but there'd been a dark, alluring spark. Dark being the key word because I didn't want to be allured.

I had one need—financial security so I could take care of Grandma and Wyatt. Okay, make that two needs, because I also could also use a nap. Driving these needs were my fears—failing my family, and (this one I kept buried deep) that I'd never free up my heart and soul enough to find a life for myself.

So I should be immune to such a thing as a hot guy, darkly alluring or otherwise. Theoretically...

Shaking my head at myself, I loaded up and got on the road, giving in to my favorite pastime—overthinking. I liked to stick with my strengths. At least the scenery was incredible. Rolling green hills, a tapestry of wild grass dotted with colorful wildflowers and cypress trees, their dark forms stark against a stunning azure sky. Beyond the fields, the Pacific Coast unfolded dramatically, the rugged cliffs sculpted by the crashing waves. The only thing that could top off this view would be this view *and* pancakes.

At this time of day, I rarely hit traffic, but of course today, a train was stalled on the tracks and I started sweating the tardiness and what Kiera would say if she found out.

And she would. Kiera always knew everything.

Fifteen minutes later, which felt like fifteen years, I turned onto Star Falls Drive. The main drag welcomed me with a charming combination of Victorian, Craftsman, and American Colonial Revival architecture that housed an eclectic mix of local specialty shops selling everything from wine and baked goods to handmade candy and jewelry.

Colburn Restorations had parking in the back of the building, but for ease of unloading, I usually pulled up at the front curb by the main entrance. The only available spot was across the street on a blind turn, and at this time of morning, with the sun beginning to peek over the trees, it could slant right into the windshield, making it impossible to see past the glare.

But late was late, so I rushed to load my cart then tried to jog across the street, but of course two of the wheels decided this was the morning to fight me. Every few feet, I had to stop and kick a wheel back into place.

"Come on, come on," I muttered.

The story of my life. My epitaph would probably read: She Was In A Hurry.

A horn blasted, and I looked up to see a truck barreling right for me. Before I could so much as open my mouth to scream, someone plowed into me, sending me flying out of the way.

Brakes squealed as I fell to my hands and knees. My savior hit the ground right next to me, but was up in a flash, scooping me up, dragging the both of us to the sidewalk as the truck finally skidded to a halt—right where I'd been standing.

Craning my neck, I stared at the man who'd just saved my life.

Ryder Colburn, mouth dialed to grim, eyes dark with anger.

Reflex had me shrinking back, and he stilled, lifting his hands as if to say I come in peace.

His fury wasn't directed at me, I realized, but at what had nearly happened.

Knees suddenly wobbly, I sat down hard on the sidewalk.

"You okay?" he asked, his voice a low, rough rumble.

Was I? I had no idea, but I nodded and made to get up. Because that was what I did when I got knocked down. I got back up. Always.

But Ryder crouched at my side, balanced on the balls of his expensively shoed feet. "Give yourself a minute."

"I'm fine." My eyes locked on a faint scar slashing through his right eyebrow. I opened my mouth to ask about it, but running footsteps came from the truck, and then the driver stared down at me in dismay and dread.

"*Oh my God, lady, are you okay?*"

"You nearly fucking killed her." Ryder's voice was quiet, *deathly* quiet, but also still deeply furious. And yet no yelling, no sense of a temper out of control…

The driver swallowed hard, still staring at me. "I didn't see—the sun slanted right into the windshield, blinding me." Pale, he swallowed. "You came out of nowhere. You all right?"

I took mental inventory and found everything to be attached. That had to be a good sign.

"You need an ambulance?" he asked. "A doctor?"

"No," I said quickly. My insurance was crap. The out-of-pocket expense alone would kill me. "I'm fine."

Ryder gestured the driver back a step from me, then met my gaze, voice quiet steel when he asked, "Do you hurt anywhere?"

Only my pride. "No."

Nodding, he held out a hand, giving me the choice to take it or not. Seeing as my knees were knocking, I put my hand in his.

His touch was shockingly gentle as he helped me up. "Take a minute."

"Really, I'm good." I drew a breath, then gasped in horror. The food! I whirled to find my cart on its side like roadkill, the boxes spread across the asphalt. "Oh my God. Kiera's going to kill me."

"This wasn't your fault." Ryder slid the truck driver a look, and the poor guy blanched, then pulled out a business card and thrust it at me.

"Call me if you need anything."

Ryder was already at my cart, righting it with an easy show of strength, before helping me gather the fallen boxes. A handful of employees had rushed out of the building to help. I knew them by name, and by their favorite foods.

Caleb, Ryder's brother, was built like the professional hockey player he'd almost been, and had the appetite of one. He claimed to live for my breakfast burritos. Ryder's other brother, Tucker, reportedly the family rebel, was lanky, even though he could inhale a dozen of my chorizo street tacos in one sitting. Bill, mid-fifties, gruff but fair, round as a barrel—he liked my lunch wraps, all of them. Daniella, I think she was the operations manager, always wanted my breakfast casseroles. Each of them was putting out pissed off vibes.

For me.

It both made my throat tighten and my tummy jangle. "I'm fine," I kept saying, proud that my voice wasn't shaking like the rest of me.

When everything was loaded back onto the cart, the group got a single nod from Ryder and vanished.

"I'm really okay," I said for maybe the fiftieth time.

Ignoring this, as he had every other time I'd said it, Ryder began to push the cart toward the brick-and-glass building with one hand, the other firmly entangled with one of mine. I was still shaking, I realized, and even as I thought it, he glanced at me with concern.

I smiled, but it wasn't real until I stepped inside the building, and as always, my blood pressure immediately lowered. Tools and equipment from a long-past era hung from the open-beamed ceiling three stories above—wagon wheels, saw blades taller than any man, and a collection of antique construction tools. Complementing the brick-and-mortar walls were black steel posts and open staircases that led to a large mezzanine filled with work spaces broken up by glass walls.

Ryder was watching me carefully, his tension stirring a need in me to reduce his stress.

"I love this building."

"Me too." He looked around like he was trying to see it from my eyes. "A hundred and twenty-five years ago, it was a lumber mill. A few decades ago, someone turned it into a furniture warehouse. Then I got my hands on it."

And he'd modernized it, while also somehow romanticizing its past. "Being here feels relaxing, even though I'm working."

Those hazel eyes of his warmed. "Same."

We made our way with my cart to the staff kitchen. The large room had rustic wooden countertops, cream cupboards, and a center island with barstools. I loved all kitchens, but especially this one.

"And speaking of work..." I tried to push him from the cart so I could inspect the food, but instead, I found myself nudged into a chair that he pulled out from one of the employees' lunch tables. Worried about the time, especially if I needed to go back and remake the food, I could feel my anxiety kick into gear. "I really am fine."

"I know. You're Wonder Woman."

I snorted. "I need to—"

"You're bleeding." He gestured to my palms, and then the ripped knees of my black trousers, revealing torn skin.

I hadn't registered the sting until I saw blood. Huh. And ouch.

Ryder's gaze touched briefly on the bandage just beneath my jaw. "Your lip's bleeding, and you scraped your chin just above and to the left of that bandage on your jaw—"

"It's nothing. I need to—"

"This first." Pushing off from the counter, he pulled a first aid kit from a cabinet above the industrial-size refrigerator and set it on the table between us. "Can I see your hands?"

Seriously, where was a big black hole to swallow me up when I needed one? Grandma had once told me the only way out of a situation you don't like was straight through. Going around never worked.

Straight through…

So I flashed him my torn-up palms that now burned like a bitch. "Just a little road rash."

He looked unconvinced. "Needs to be cleaned out. Your knees as well." He'd remained a respectful few feet back, hands in his pockets. "Can I take a closer look?" His voice was quiet. Calm.

I could feel his need to step in and fix, like it was an essential part of him. When I nodded, he came close and lifted a hand, keeping it inches from my face, another question in his eyes, silent this time.

I nodded again and my skin tingled as his rough, calloused fingers whispered across my temple, tucking a strand of hair back before tipping my face up so he could see my chin.

I shivered.

He frowned. "Cold?"

I was a whole bunch of things, but cold wasn't one of them. All this time, I'd thought his eyes to be a swirling, intriguing mix of green and browns, but there was some gold swirled in there too—

He ran his finger just below the bandage along my jawline, his voice a quiet rumble. "Is this covering stitches?"

I closed my eyes. "Yes, but they're almost dissolved now."

"Could you have torn open the injury?"

Again, I had no idea. "No."

He blew out a long breath. "And your knees?"

The holes in my trousers didn't reveal much. But if he was expecting me to pull my pants down and let him play doctor, he couldn't be more mistaken.

Clearly my expression told him that much, because his eyes flashed amusement. "Happy to assist."

"Over your dead body."

A corner of his mouth twitched. "There she is…"

Not being anything close to a trusting soul, I crossed my arms, but I ruined the stare down by wincing as my palms brushed against the material of my shirt. "Don't you have an empire to run? Aren't you busy?"

"Yes and yes."

He confused me, and I didn't like being confused. Plus, there was an odd…crackle in the air between us. I knew what it was, and I didn't want it. I eyed the suit that fit his leanly muscled body to perfection, relieved that while he had some gravel and dust on him, there were no obvious injuries. "You're clearly on your way to an important take-over-the-world meeting. You should go. It's okay—I've got this."

"Sure. Soon as you either let me clean your wounds or…" A tinge of amusement hit his eyes when my own flashed a death glare his way. "You do it so you don't get an infection."

Door number two it was. I grabbed the kit and stalked past him, heading to the employee bathroom down the hall. I cleaned everything that was bleeding, bandaged my knees and palms, and then stared at the woman in the mirror. Torn black trousers, dirty white button-down, thick light brown hair more out of the ponytail than in, my matching light brown eyes, wide with something that I couldn't name.

My skin wasn't quite white, nor quite brown, but something in between, a shade my grandma always said came from her Brazilian mother and the Italian man she'd cheated on her husband with. I'd never met any of them before they passed but was grateful for the genes because my life might be difficult, but I could tan just walking to the mailbox. Got to celebrate the little things…

I fixed my hair, but there was little to be done for my swollen lip or my chin, which had turned the color of a ripe raspberry. I both looked and felt like a complete wreck.

Nothing new there. I opened the bathroom door and stopped in surprise. Ryder stood leaning against the opposite wall, arms crossed over his broad chest.

Waiting for me.

Pushing away from the wall, he stepped close, his gaze sliding down my body, missing nothing as he handed me a small, soft ice pack.

"I don't need it."

"Okay," he said with a shrug. "But if you don't get the swelling down, your clients are going to ask you what happened."

Ugh. I snatched the ice pack and pressed it to my lip first, sucking a breath in through my teeth as the cold hit.

Ryder's "I told you so" was silent, but I rolled my eyes again anyway.

"I'll call your work and tell them you're going home for the day," he said.

"No!" I drew a deep breath and lowered my voice with some effort. "I'm good." I'd already taken a day off this week to go hunt down Wyatt when he'd played hooky from school. "I'm okay."

Before he could object, I strode back to the kitchen, going still when I realized the cart had been emptied and had been set by the door. The chafing dishes were filled and ready to be consumed. I knew the woman who worked the reception desk here always refilled everything as necessary, but she didn't come in this early, so she hadn't done this.

I whirled to face him. "What did you do?"

"I believe it's called helping."

"Nothing was ruined? Are you sure?"

He lifted a shoulder. "Don't worry about it."

Narrowing my eyes, I inspected the spread again, more closely this time, then opened the trash. I couldn't stop the sound of distress that escaped me at the sight of some of the breakfast casserole mixed in with a few breakfast burritos.

"There were a few casualties," he said calmly.

Oh my God. Kiera was going to kill me. "I'll make more and come right back—"

"There's plenty."

"Thank you," I breathed with such relief my stinging knees nearly collapsed. "And for making sure I didn't turn into a human pancake."

His mouth quirked. "I'm very glad you're not a pancake."

This morning at the house, I'd been irritated at the sight of him looking—and smelling—like a million bucks, while I'd stood there with bed head and Cheetos falling out of my pj's. But it sure as hell wasn't irritation I felt now warming me from the inside out. Dumb. I was so dumb.

"I owe you."

"You don't."

"I do. I insist."

Those eyes of his lit with something that looked a whole bunch like an undeniably sexy playfulness, and he murmured, "What did you have in mind?"

A shiver went down my spine, and I had no idea if it was a thrill or trepidation.

No, that was a lie. Trepidation had nothing to do with it and I knew it.

He smiled one of those knee-buckling smiles. "You've got panic all over your face."

I covered my hot cheeks and he gave a low, throaty laugh. "Have a good one, Wonder Woman."

My ensuing hot flash lasted all the way to my next client, damn him.

CHAPTER 3

Penny

ON FRIDAYS, I DIDN'T have to get to work until seven, but my body never seemed to get the message. I still woke up before sunrise, already needing a nap. I took a shower, dressed for the day, then headed downstairs.

Pika-boo saw me coming from where he stood on the coffee table, tap-dancing in excitement on a stack of Grandma's *Star* magazines. "I've lost my fucking keys again, dammit, shit, hell!"

I laughed. "Been listening to Grandma again, have we?" I gave him a cracker, then found Grandma sitting on our back porch with Delia, our next-door neighbor. The two of them were sipping coffee while watching the sun come over the horizon.

Delia, in her fifties, was sweet and warm and had a contagious belly laugh. She'd never met anyone she hadn't immediately charmed, which probably explained why her house was stuffed to the gills with her husband, their three adult children, those adult children's significant others, and four grandchildren under the age of five.

Sometimes Delia came over just to hear herself think. With a blissed-out smile, she stood and stretched. "Back to my circus," she said on a laugh.

When she was gone, I took her place and smiled at Grandma, who looked tired. "Everything okay?"

"Always."

Gee, and she wondered where I got the island-of-one attitude from…

She passed me her mug and I took a sip.

"You know the Legend of Star Falls," she said.

Anyone from Star Falls knew the Legend, which said that if you caught sight of the rare phenomenon of three falling stars arching together across the sky, your soul mate would enter your life. As if.

"What about it?"

"Delia said she heard on the news that because of how the planets and stars are aligned this month, there'll be more shooting stars than usual. People are going nuts, hoping to see the Legend. They're organizing star gazing parties and sleepover camp-outs. My book club's one of them. They met last night at midnight. I couldn't go since I'm working today, but it's just as well. They drank too much wine and fell asleep. Not a one of them caught the Legend. *Rookies.*" She smiled. "But I did some research of my own. Just before dawn is a better time to see anything. I didn't see it this morning, but it's just a matter of time."

"You're looking for a soul mate?" I asked in surprise.

"Is that so odd?"

I turned my head and studied her upturned profile. I knew my grandfather hadn't been a good match for her, just as I also knew she'd dated here and there over the years, but never anything serious.

"Not odd at all," I said softly. "Everyone deserves love."

Without taking her eyes off the sky, she smiled and reached out for my hand. "Including you."

I didn't know how to explain to her that it wasn't that I thought I didn't deserve love. It was that I didn't trust myself to choose wisely. Big difference.

I was still thinking about that as, on my way to work, I veered off route to hit up my favorite stress relief—Al's Diner for breakfast. Once upon a time, Al's had actually been a McDonald's. I'd been in middle school when the franchise restaurant had moved to a bigger location. Al had been a cook for years at McDonald's, and when they'd vacated the building, he'd decided at sixty-two years young it was time to become his own boss, and he'd opened the diner. He'd put his decades of skills to excellent use. The diner was always packed, but he preferred locals and took care of us. I parked and got in line at the take-out counter.

"Hey, darling," Al greeted when I reached the register. He had a huge family, and most of them worked for him. His wife cooked, as did his eldest son, Austin, who in high school had been voted most likely to win the lottery and lose the ticket, but he made the best pancakes on the planet. Al's other five sons served, bussed, or handled the money side of things.

Al leaned on the counter, in no hurry. "Tell me you're here to finally marry my Austin."

"No, but I am here to eat his pancakes."

"Good enough. What can I get for you? The usual?"

A few minutes later, I had my drug of choice—coffee and the pancakes in a bag to go. Minus the one pancake already in my hand. I'd narrowed down the fine art of buttering and rolling them, eating each like a burrito while driving. Taking a big bite, I turned to head out of the diner's side door when I saw him.

Ryder, sitting at the back booth.

He wore another of those business suits that did funny things to my insides, things I didn't want to put words to. He had two adorable toddlers in his lap, a boy and a girl, and was simultaneously trying to cut pancakes while keeping the kiddos from drinking the syrup.

"Okay, here you go," he said, handing each of them a plastic fork. "Remember, forks are for food, not for poking each other."

The little girl, three years-old tops, giggled so sweetly, staring up at him with big adoring doe eyes. "But Unca Ry Ry, he poked me first."

"Did not," the little boy said. The kids were near exact replicas of each other—*and* Ryder.

"Did so!"

"Did not!"

Ryder wrapped an arm around each toddler and said only one word. "*Eyes.*"

The chaos stopped immediately as both turned their faces up to his, meeting his gaze.

"Whoever is the least sticky when you're done gets a prize," he said.

This caused a chorus of squeals.

"Disneyland?" the little girl asked with enough exuberance that the entire place looked over.

"Nice try," Ryder said. "I was thinking a quarter for your piggy bank."

"Can I has two?" the boy asked.

"Only if you're double clean." Ryder tapped his little nose lightly with his finger, smiling down at the kid in a way I'd never seen. He looked...younger somehow, and softer, and my ovaries rolled over and exposed their underbellies.

The kids laughed and threw themselves at him, surely spreading syrup on that pristine suit, not that he seemed to notice.

Because his gaze had landed on me.

I waved my coffee at him in greeting. "Hey," I managed casually, like I hadn't been caught staring. *Again.*

His mouth twitched. "Hey back. We've got an extra spot."

I smiled at the kids. "You look pretty busy."

"This is Abi and Alex," he said. "My niece and nephew. Kidlets, this is Penny."

Abi smiled shyly and buried her face in Ryder's chest. Alex grinned at me and ate a bite of pancake, syrup dripping down his chin.

Ryder jerked a chin to the available spot in the booth, and I was tempted. Far more than I wanted to be. "I'd love to, thanks, but I've got to get to work."

"I full," Alex announced to the whole restaurant.

"You had one bite," Ryder said.

Alex shoved a piece of pancake into his mouth. And then another. When he tried to get a third in, Ryder said, "No."

The kid eyed the bite in his hand, then stuffed it in Ryder's mouth instead.

"Yum," Ryder said, while grimacing over Alex's head at me, making me laugh.

Abi had a piece of pancake on her fork, syrup dripping down her entire arm as she offered it up to me. "Bite?"

"Oh, I'd love one, thank you, but I've got mine right here." I waved my neatly rolled-up pancake at them.

"Coward," Ryder murmured.

"Unca Ry Ry, Alex stuck his tongue out at me!"

Ryder looked at Abi. "Are we pretending or lying?"

She just blinked those huge eyes up at him, and he sighed. "Baby, we talked about this. No lying allowed."

Abi huffed out a breath. "'K."

Alex tapped Ryder on the shoulder. "Unca Ry Ry, Unca Ry Ry, Unca Ry Ry—"

"Yes?"

"I didn't stick my tongue out."

"I know."

"Can we go to the park again? The one with the slide that Unca Cal Cal got stuck on 'cause he's too big?"

Ryder grinned. "That was fun, but it'll have to be another day. You've got preschool."

"Awwwww." Abi flung her arms around his neck. "I wuv you, Unca Ry Ry."

"No, *I* wuv him," Alex yelled and threw himself at Ryder as well, the two of them hanging from his neck. Somehow he managed to clean them up, and the table as well, and then stood, a kid in each arm.

He took in my expression and sighed. "This is going to ruin my reputation, isn't it?"

"In a big way." I smiled. "*Unca Ry Ry.*"

He merely flashed me a grin. "Have a good one."

I watched him walk away. He teased me about being Wonder Woman, but he was the superhero. A superhero in a sexy suit. "You too."

HE FALLS FIRST

The day was long, and I was exhausted by the time I pulled into Grandma's driveway. Delia was in her yard watering, her grandchildren racing over the lawn. One was buck naked and squealing as she ducked under the spray of the hose. Another was chasing a bunny. Two more played in a puddle, muddy from head to toe, only the whites of their eyes visible. Delia, not at all bothered by the havoc, merrily waved at me. Behind her, her freshly painted house looked cheerful and welcoming.

I waved back and walked up our front path. Our house hadn't been painted, though it was in desperate need, and yet something about this place never failed to feel like home to me, more than anywhere on earth, its weathered red bricks and pale stone gingerbread trim a slightly faded beacon guiding me back every time.

Heading inside, I took a deep breath of the familiar pine and lavender scent that was all Grandma. From his perch in the corner, sandwiched between a massive picture window and built-in shelves shoved full of Grandma's entire life, Pika-boo was bebopping to some tune in his head, but he stopped to make kissy sounds at me. His version of affection.

I returned the kissy sounds, then realized Wyatt sat on the couch, his back to me, headphones on, playing a game on the TV.

"Hey to you too," I said. "How was your day?"

Nothing.

"Wyatt?"

Not so much as a glance. Adjusting the bags to one hand, I pulled out my phone, accessed our internet app and changed the password, signing everyone out while I was at it. Then I counted backwards in my head: three, two, one...

"Hey, what happened to our internet?" Wyatt yelled, still not looking around.

I moved to stand between him and the TV and waved at him. "Hi. Remember me?"

Wyatt pulled his headphones off one ear to say, "Internet's out."

"Internet's out!" Pika-boo repeated.

I snorted but kept my eyes on my brother. "Don't you mean 'hi, sis, great to see you, how was your very long day?'"

He sighed. "Hi, sis, great to see you, why is our internet out?"

"Oh, it's not. I just changed the password."

He gaped at me. "Seriously?"

I gave him a smug smile. "Maybe I just wanted to remind you that I'm still your big, and therefore annoying, sister."

His eyebrows bunched together. "Mission accomplished," he muttered.

"Homework?"

"Did it in class," he said. "New password?"

I raised a brow.

Wyatt sighed dramatically. "*Please?*"

"Aw, look at that—you *can* remember the magic word." I ruffled his hair. "Pretty fly for Wi-Fi, no spaces."

"Pretty fly for Wi-Fi, no spaces," Pika-boo sang.

Wyatt just rolled his eyes. He was a smart-ass but also smart as hell. I knew he got bored in school, but there were definitely worse things he could be doing in class than his homework.

"You eat your lunch today?"

This got a vague almost-shrug from scrawny shoulders that were slightly hunched. This too skinny, surly, sullen teen who I loved with all my heart had faced way too much heartbreak in his short life. I wanted to see him happy. See him smile like he used to, because his smiles, when he chose to bestow them, could light up a room and make my deeply buried heart sing.

Unable to help myself, I leaned in and pressed a kiss to the top of his head. "Love you."

"*Love you, love you, love you,*" Pika-boo sang.

Wyatt gave a great suffering sigh.

"To the moon and back," I added.

"Ew." But there was the teeniest tinge of affection in his voice.

I'd take it. I wanted to hug him, but I'd already pushed my luck. Instead, I headed into the kitchen to find Grandma attempting to fix the dishwasher, even though I'd *begged* her not to. I opened my mouth to ask her to please stop, and—

The dishwasher door fell off.

"Huh," she said. "Who saw that coming?"

I raised my hand. "Me, myself, and I! And stop tinkering. I don't want you to get hurt."

"Hey, I'm tougher than I look. And I think we need a renovation."

Truth. "Just waiting on Santa to come through with a bucket of gold." I got a good look at her. Her pink t-shirt read: STAND ASIDE BOYS, THE EXPERTS ARE HERE. "That's new."

"Hope you like it." Grandma grinned. "'Cause yours is in the mudroom, along with your tool belt." She patted hers—pink leather—and it nearly slipped off her skinny hips. "I've been watching YouTube videos. We've got this."

Oh boy. I set the bags of food on the table, not even trying to argue. Somewhere in her sixties, Grandma had decided life was too short to waste a single second and had turned into a teenager.

Who was I to judge? I gestured to the bags. "Dinner."

Wyatt appeared in the doorway, beelining right for the food. "Did you say dinner—Aw, man," he grumbled, pawing through the bags. "Leftovers again? You used to cook."

"I *did* cook," I said indignantly. "At work."

He sighed.

"What our dear boy means," Grandma said, "is that you put *extra* love into your home cooking versus your work cooking. I really hope you're not letting this job destroy your secret dream of having your own café."

I wasn't sure I trusted myself with my secret dream anymore, but that didn't seem to stop me from having it... "It's hardly a secret if you keep talking about it."

Grandma shrugged. "Keeping secrets ages you. Why do you think I don't look a day over thirty-nine?"

Wyatt, who'd just taken an unfortunate sip directly from the orange juice container he'd pulled from the fridge, choked.

"I hope it went up your nose," I said. "And for the millionth time, stop drinking straight from the container." I turned back to Grandma. "I still love cooking." I did. Now, did I love my job? Not...fully. I got to see Vi and Renee every day, and also create some fun menus, but Kiera was perpetually grumpy and the hours sucked.

Wyatt, still digging through the to-go boxes as if he hadn't seen food in a year, came up for air with a piece of roasted chicken.

"Utensils!" I said.

HE FALLS FIRST

"Utensils!" Pika-boo yelled from the living room.

Wyatt rolled his eyes again.

"They're going to fall right out of your head one of these days." Dear God, I sounded like an old woman. But when *I'd* been Wyatt's age, I'd been struggling to keep up with schoolwork while always scheming a way out of having to go off with my mom for some lounge singer position that she wouldn't be able to hold on to.

Those years were in my rearview now, but sometimes I still felt like that kid who had too much on my shoulders, knowing that any financial security for my family would have to come from me. I've spent a lot of hours robbing Peter to pay Paul, and I was eager for that to be over with.

I grabbed a piece of chicken.

"Utensils," Wyatt said, heavy on the sarcasm.

After eating, I spent the rest of the evening setting up bill payments online, while continuously checking the water level in the bucket in the laundry room from our leaky roof since it was raining again. Every time I emptied it out, I groaned at the dishes still in the sink. Much, much later, I finally fell into bed so that I could get on the hamster wheel and do it all over again tomorrow.

I'd no sooner fallen asleep than I heard Wyatt whisper my name from the doorway.

I sat straight up. "What's wrong?"

"Are you going to leave and go back home?"

"This is home."

"I'm talking about Seattle. Where you lived before you came back to take care of us."

I turned on my bedside lamp to find him standing there

in his pj's, hair wild, eyes worried, looking so young my heart squeezed. "Wyatt...where's this coming from? I've got no plans to leave."

"Yeah, but Mom'll show back up sooner or later." He shrugged a bony shoulder. "And you'll leave. Like Mom always does."

I drew a deep breath. "I'm not going anywhere, not as long as I'm needed."

He scowled. "That's one of those adult answers, and it's bullshit."

"*Wyatt.*"

"No, it is. You think I'm a kid and because of it, you don't tell me the truth. Maybe because as soon as you think we're good, you're out." He stormed off.

"Hey," I called after him. "I'm not going anywhere!"

In answer, his bedroom door clicked shut. He didn't believe me. I dropped my head back to my pillow. Was he right? After being here the past six months for "family obligations," would I walk away once my mom showed up again, as she inevitably would?

I thought of Grandma, getting older, trying to do too much on her own. Wyatt, only twelve, constantly abandoned by our flaky mom.

They needed me.

No, that wasn't quite right. My life had detonated, and I was trying to make a comeback, but I still didn't fully trust myself or my choices at the moment.

Which meant *I* needed *them* far more than they needed me.

CHAPTER 4

Ryder

I HATED BEING BEHIND A desk with the same passion I reserved for broccoli and flip-flops, but someone had to catch up on the paperwork, even if it'd already been a long-ass day. Caged and restless, I nearly growled when my personal admin, Grif, came to my office with one of his famed smoothies he liked to make me drink, along with that damn iPad of his that was undoubtedly filled with more shit for me to do.

He held out the smoothie.

I grimaced.

He grinned. "You're such a big baby."

Not many talked to me with the irreverence that my brothers did. Grif had been a street kid when I'd first met him a decade ago, having been kicked out of his house for the audacity of being gay. I'd given him a job and a place to stay. He no longer lived with me, but he'd kept the job, for which I was grateful.

Suspiciously, I eyed the smoothie he insisted on making me at least weekly. "Why do they have to be green?"

"Come on now, what did green ever do to you?" He held out the glass. "Remember it tastes good, yeah?" He wiggled it a little, knowing I hated drinking anything green, but *not* knowing that it reminded me of military Hank forcing us kids to drink disgusting vegetable juice in the mornings.

"Hell." I sipped cautiously at first as always, but as promised, it tasted delicious.

Grif laughed at me, then nodded to the iPad. "Quarterlies are due tomorrow and there's a list of stuff the accountant needs from you by end of week. Also due tomorrow…employee reviews." And then he was gone.

I latched on to the most important word he'd said—tomorrow. Tomorrow was not today. So I stood, needing out of the building more than I needed air. We currently had more projects than we could handle, and I'd spent too many hours this week staring at a screen. The only bright spot had been the twenty minutes yesterday morning when Penny had been here, stocking us up on food and setting up a birthday party for Bill in the conference room.

I was leaning against the huge table when she'd walked into the conference room, my excuses lined up for why I'd been there—an early meeting, I needed caffeine… But truthfully, I needed to see her simply because, more often than not lately, she was the best ten minutes of my day.

She'd walked in and met my gaze, her brows raising sassily.

I'd laughed. My first laugh for the day. Her hair was, as always, slipping out of its ponytail and flying around her pretty face. I knew it drove her crazy, but I loved it. I wanted to sink my hands in that hair. I also loved that small crease that formed between her eyebrows when she frowned in concentration. Or at me. Especially at me.

Clearly, I was a very sick man.

She'd wanted a second table for the food. We dragged one in from the storage room, the two of us getting stuck in the doorway, and for a beat, we'd been pressed together from shoulders to knees.

Best half second of my entire week.

Knowing nothing was going to top that, I headed out of my office. I hadn't even gotten to my truck before Caleb called.

"Hey," he said when I answered. "You want in on the office bet?"

"What is it?"

"Whether or not anyone will get the Legend of Star Falls on camera this week."

"You mean the Legend that doesn't exist? No." I paused. "You?"

"Hell, yeah. I'm betting no one will record proof. It's easy money, man. You sure you don't want in?"

"Very sure."

"Your loss. Where you off to?"

"To relieve Nell of Captain Asshole."

"Oh. Right."

I could almost hear the smile fall off Caleb's face as he hesitated. "Need any help with him this weekend?"

Yes. "No. It'll be your turn soon enough."

"Yeah, can't fucking wait."

My gut churned with regret and concern. Being the oldest had meant being the protector. And that hadn't gone away just because we were no longer kids. I would shield my siblings as much as I could, but Caleb had taken nearly as much of Hank's temper as I had.

"You don't have to—"

"I do."

"You don't," I insisted, trying to sound like I meant it. But I was exhausted. I'd never intended to end up running a company with a hundred employees, spending all day managing people, reading contracts, and schmoozing clients. All I'd ever wanted was to work with my own hands. I wanted to take on old, decrepit buildings that no one else saw the value in and bring them back to life. But somehow, life had gotten complicated, and it no longer mattered what I wanted.

"How's he been?" Caleb asked quietly.

I exhaled slowly. After Hank's first stroke two years ago, the guy had leaned on his Captain Asshole personality hard, getting himself kicked out of every single assisted living place within two hundred miles of Star Falls.

Quite the feat. "Not himself."

Caleb gave a soft, mirthless laugh. "Yeah. That second stroke changed everything."

After that second stroke, he'd required a craniotomy. And that time, to our collective shock, Hank had woken up a completely different person—no longer verbal, not really, but neither was he Captain Asshole. This man who looked and walked like Hank Colburn now smiled, hugged, even laughed, always just happy to be.

It was a complete mindfuck.

Even so, after rehab, none of the assisted living facilities would take him back. So Caleb, Tucker, and I had looked at the calendar and divided the year into three. Three, not four, because we'd left Kiera out of all of it for many reasons, the biggest being that she was still grieving the loss of Auggie, her husband.

That Auggie had also been my best friend and business partner didn't play into this. I was Kiera's older brother, and it was my job to make sure she was okay. Auggie would want me to do whatever was necessary in order to ensure that.

I was taking the first shift with Hank, and then I'd pass him onto Caleb, and then Tucker, and we'd do our best, various childhood traumas and triggers and all.

I'd taken the first rotation, and he'd been with me for a month now. It'd felt like ten years.

"This probably isn't a good time to tell you," Caleb said reluctantly. "But..."

I stopped in the middle of the parking lot and pinched the bridge of my nose. "I really hate sentences from you that start that way."

"Hey," he said, "I hardly ever start sentences that way."

"You *often* start sentences that way. Alarmingly often."

"Name one."

"Okay," I said. "How about that time you put blue Gatorade in a Windex bottle at school and walked around drinking it until a teacher caught you and called 911? You called me in a panic from the ambulance racing you to the ER to get your stomach pumped."

"Okay, well, that was my bad," he admitted.

"And then there's the time that your asshat college friends dared you, the biggest college hockey star in the country at the time, to walk into a fast-food joint and say, 'Dude, the M&Ms are coming and they have guns.'"

"Well, how was I supposed to know he'd call the cops? And then TMZ."

I tipped my head back and stared up at the pink and purple

sky, heavy with dusk as it chased the sun over the hills. "Why are we having this conversation?"

"Tucker discovered trouble on the Millbrook job. Materials went missing to the tune of $13,500. Bill's investigating."

"Shit." It happened, and it wasn't a huge number in the scope of the job's ten million dollar budget, but it was enough to put a strain on everyone while we got to the bottom of things. In the past when this happened, sometimes it turned out to be an inventory or accounting error. Other times we followed the trail straight to the thieves, who could be anyone from stupid teenagers looking for a thrill to someone making a living stealing materials off jobsites and then reselling them. And sometimes we never found out what happened, and our insurance kicked in. I hated all of those scenarios.

"I'll talk to Bill." And file a police report. And contact the insurance company... "Gotta go."

"Over and out," my smart-ass brother said.

Fifteen minutes later, I parked at Nell's house. Because my mind apparently has its *own* mind, I looked for Penny's car, but she wasn't here. Refusing to acknowledge the flash of disappointment, I headed up the walk.

The door opened and Nell stood there in an orange track suit and matching lipstick, looking like a pumpkin latte. "Hey, hon, come on in. Your dad's working on a puzzle on the back porch while I try to fix a leaky faucet."

I followed her to the kitchen. A worthless lightweight hammer and one of those tiny screwdrivers people used to fix glasses lay on the counter next to the sink—neither of which were going to fix a leaky faucet.

"Be right back," I said, and returned with tools from my truck.

HE FALLS FIRST

Nell eyed them when I returned. "What's all that?"

"Allen wrench, spanner wrench, slip-joint pliers, utility knife, and a real screwdriver."

"I need to get me some of these," she said.

"It's okay, I'll fix the sink."

"You should know I've called a bunch of plumbers over the years, but no one's ever been able to fix it. You think you're the man for the job?"

"Yep." I'd just popped off the faucet handle to access the mechanism when Nell tapped me on the shoulder.

"Honey, maybe you're new at this, but it's leaking from the faucet part, not the handle."

"See this ridge that goes over the valve seat? Inside's a washer that presses against the valve seat to create a tight seal. It gets a lot of wear and tear from repeated use. That's your leak." I showed her where it was cracked and all stretched out. "You just need a faucet repair kit. I'll bring one tomorrow." I eyed the ladder leaning against the countertop. "What's that for?"

"Penny borrowed it from a neighbor. The lights are flickering and giving us headaches, but she hasn't had a spare second to look yet. Thought I'd have a go."

I frowned. "You're not going to get up on that ladder."

"Of course I am. Penny works herself half to death on an easy day. I can't let her do everything around here too." She patted my shoulder again. "Don't worry, when I was a kid, I wanted to be in the circus, so I got good at tightrope walking. I've got incredible balance."

I squelched a grimace. I adored Nell, but she wobbled on her bony legs when she walked. "I've got it." Before she could protest, I was on the ladder, tightening each of the nine bulbs in the room.

The lights stopped flickering.

"Aren't you the one." She stared up at the ceiling. "You're hired. All I need is a new kitchen."

"Maybe tomorrow." I lowered my voice. "Hank was okay today?"

"You always ask me that with dread, but he's great. He's a sweet angel of a man."

What did it say about me that I still didn't quite believe the transformation, that I kept waiting for him to revert? Probably I didn't want to know what it said. For now, it was a miracle. Actually, it was Nell who was the miracle, and I'd never stop being grateful.

"You're a life saver, and I owe you big."

She beamed. "You don't. You already pay me way too much money."

"It's not enough. If you ever need anything, please just name it."

She angled her head, eyes flashing interest. "Like...a favor?"

"Yes, like a favor."

She stared at me for a long beat, the sweet little old lady gone, in her place a sharp negotiator. "Hmm," she said.

Maybe I should've been worried, but what could she possibly want that I couldn't provide? "Name it."

She peeked out at Hank, who was still bent over a puzzle, then pulled me into the living room.

Damn. Maybe Hank had found his old personality after all and Nell was having trouble telling me. The doctor had assured us more than a few times that most likely this new Hank was here to stay, but I had never quite been able to believe it. If he'd hurt Nell's feelings, I'd—

Hell. This was the crux of my mental torment. There'd never been any closure for me and my siblings' childhood. No apologies, no talking things out, no nothing. The man we'd hated with every ounce of our being was gone.

And yet still here, torturing us in a new way.

Nell craned her neck, looking out the front bay window that gave us a view of the street.

"You waiting for someone?" I asked.

"Yes, so I've gotta make this quick." She looked me right in the eyes, which probably gave her a neck cramp since she came up to my elbow. "Listen," she said. "You know my granddaughter. She's got a heart of gold. For years, she's supported me from Seattle because the pay was much higher there. But she lost her job when Covid hit, and became her own boss, selling ready-to-go meals that she home-cooked. Then she had to come home."

She paused to clear her throat, like this was hard to talk about. "She deserves more than what life's dealt her. She deserves a life that's more than just heartache and hard times. She deserves *fun*. I want to help her there, hopefully with a little assist from you."

Why did I suddenly know I wasn't going to like this? "Assist?"

Once again, she took a quick peek out the window, then turned back to me. "Penny recently really went through something, something really hard…"

Aaaaaand she had my full my attention.

"Her mom's one of them free spirits," Nell went on. "Hard to tie her down. Six months ago, she took a job on a cruise ship without much notice. That's why Penny gave up her life and came back to Star Falls. She knew I'd need help with Wyatt. But something's off. She hasn't spoken about it, but I can see it in her eyes. She's...not okay. She's not the same happy-go-lucky girl she's always been."

Worry filled me for this woman I barely knew and yet cared about on a level I didn't quite understand. "You don't know what's wrong?"

"She won't say, but it doesn't matter, a grandma knows these things." A flash of pain crossed her face. "I think she had...man trouble."

Instantly, I thought of the bandage along Penny's jaw, the one that had appeared a week ago, and how she'd flinched away from my touch. My stomach tightened as I read between the lines.

"Did that trouble follow her here?"

"No." Her eyes darkened. "But something happened during her quick trip back to Seattle. She's retreated into herself, even more than usual." Nell's mouth was tight. "She's done so much for me, supporting me and Wyatt since she was a teen, always having our backs. It's my turn to help her now."

If there was one thing I understood, it was helping family. "What do you need from me?"

She drew a deep breath. "I think Penny's problem is that she no longer trusts herself. I think if she could have even a single night off, a night *out* with someone. A certain someone who'd bring fun and laughter with no pressure..." She met my gaze, hers hopeful. "Just one teeny tiny little night out."

I understood where she was coming from, because we Colburns, for all that we gave each other shit, had each other's backs. Always. But this...this "little favor"...I couldn't. Not when I was attracted to Penny, *far more than I wanted to be,* if I was being honest. But I wasn't in a place in my life to date.

I just wasn't. And yet there was Nell, looking at me with such hope.

"Look," I said gently, "Penny's lovely and sweet—" Nell snorted, and I had to smile. "She is." Well, sometimes. She was also sharp as a tack, funny as hell, feisty enough to keep me on toes, and effortlessly and cluelessly beautiful, all of which were incredibly sexy to me.

"She's amazing."

Nell nodded. "Now *that* I buy. So you'll ask her out?"

I knew a date with Penny would be a lot of fun, but I couldn't do that to either of us. "Nell, I can't."

Her smile faded. "Oh. Okay."

"I'm sorry—"

"No, I get it. Lots of people say they owe you a favor but have no intention of ever following through."

Fuck me. Had I thought Nell a sweet, gentle, little old lady? Because behind those rheumy blue eyes lay a sharp, laser-focused mind and she'd just walked me right into her trap. I rubbed my jaw, desperate to come up with a good reason I couldn't do this. Even if I was stupid enough to agree, which I wasn't, Penny would hate this. Hate *me*.

"I blame myself for what she's going through, you know," Nell said, looking out the window again. "Her grandpa was a horse's patoot, excuse my French. And then Penny's mom's taste in men has always been lousy. Poor Penny never had a chance of landing in a healthy relationship. She wouldn't know a good man if he stood right in front of her and set the world in the palm of her hand. So really, it's no wonder she got hurt. And now, she's given up a personal life, stopped doing anything but working and supporting this family, but worst of all, she's given up on love."

I'd heard nothing after "she got hurt." Drawing a deep breath, I then let it out slowly. "Nell—"

"She'll never ask for help. She'll just suck it up, go on less sleep and push herself too hard. She's always been like that. She doesn't want anyone to know when she struggles."

I knew what that was like as well, more than I wanted to admit. It'd been my life too, always watching out, always the caregiver, never having the luxury of letting my guard down. And suddenly I wanted, with shocking, gripping, desperate intensity, to go find Penny and make sure she was okay.

Nell flashed a small smile, rounding the bases, coming in home with her closing argument. "Now, do I also think Penny is amazing? Yes. Beyond. Does she additionally have an attitude problem? Also yes. *But*," she said earnestly, "under all that tough skin, she's loyal and caring, and she'll go to the end of the world for the people in her life."

I happened to love *all* of those traits, especially in Penny. But that didn't mean this was a good idea. And yet…she'd been hurt. She'd retreated into herself. And Nell was worried enough to ask me for this favor.

"Shit."

She patted my arm, smiling sweetly in her victory. "Thank you. I'll never forget this."

"You'll never forget what?"

We both turned to find Penny in the kitchen doorway, having come in the back door. She set three bags down on the kitchen table, but left her purse slung over her shoulder, like maybe she wasn't staying. Her eyes were narrowed in on me, honey-colored strands half in and half out of her ponytail, her shirt untucked, exhaustion revealing itself in the purple smudges beneath her eyes.

And I wanted to wrap her up tight in my arms.

In the past two years, I'd stayed out of relationships. Any encounters had been casual. I couldn't even remember the last time I'd felt the urge to pull a woman in with the sole purpose of comforting her. But that's what I wanted to do right now with Penny. Wrap her up and hold her tight.

"I'm a good boy," Pika-boo announced to the house, apropos of nothing. "I'm the goodest of all good boys."

"You are," Penny said and pulled a cracker from one of the bags on the table, feeding it to the bird, who danced merrily on his tiny little feet in thanks.

Penny was watching me watch her. I could usually get a read on a person quickly, but this woman defied my talent. Even so, I could've sworn her expression was both irritated at finding me here, but also a little excited. Hell, maybe the excitement was the reason for the irritation. She was attracted to me, but didn't want to be attracted to me.

Join my club...

The scrape on her chin from nearly being run over by that delivery truck was fading. The bandage along her jaw was gone, in its wake an inch-long scar, fresh and shiny pink.

I had to draw a deep breath and force a lightness into my voice that I didn't feel. "How's it going?"

"It's going." She glanced at her grandma. "What's going on? What won't you forget?"

Nell gave me a look that said *you see what I'm dealing with here?* She turned to Penny. "Just going over Hank's care. Nothing to worry about, honey. How was your day?"

Penny eyed us both for a minute. "Peachy."

I fought a smile and lost because damn, she had me wrapped

around her finger with that attitude. And suddenly I knew two things with absolute clarity. One, crazy as it seemed, she had the power to hurt me. And two, I was pretty sure I had the power to hurt her as well. Only she'd already been hurt, and I wouldn't add to her pain.

"I brought dinner," she told Nell.

"Do we have enough for two extra?"

Penny glanced at me again, pensive this time. Maybe even… worried. "Yes. But it's probably what he's been eating at his office all week, so I doubt he'd be interested."

"He" was far more interested than he should be. But I knew how to read a room. "Thank you, but I've got to get Hank home. He's got his weekly visit from his home-health nurse in a bit."

Nell met my gaze, her own filled with gratitude. A gratitude I did not deserve. This "teeny tiny night out" she wanted me to instigate would come back to bite me in the ass, I knew it. Just as I knew I wasn't going to say no. I was going to do as she'd requested and ask out the first woman who'd fascinated me in way too long. Me, the guy who hadn't been able to access his emotions in an even *longer* time.

What could possibly go wrong? Only everything?

CHAPTER 5

Ryder

"WORTHLESS WASTE OF TIME POS..."

Bill had been on this tirade about yesterday's missing materials for so long I'd stopped listening as we walked out of the police station the next morning. "Let it go."

He gaped at me. "You can't be serious."

A few months ago, Bill had suffered a silent myocardial infarction. The mini heart attack and subsequent procedure to clear a partial blockage of his coronary artery had been a success, and he'd been back at work for weeks. He wasn't supposed to stress, but given the way his eyes were about to pop out of their sockets, he was doing just that.

"I'm as serious as that heart attack you had."

He waved this off dismissively. "I'm fine now. I've told you a million times. I can't believe you're willing to write off 13,500 bucks. This is our third theft this year. It's adding up. What's wrong with you?"

"A lot, and I'm not willing to write this off."

My superintendent stopped in the middle of the lot, hands on hips. "So what are we going to do about this?" he demanded.

"Investigate. I'm going to pull in Caleb." He'd been learning the ropes the past few years, fitting into wherever he was needed. He had a way with people, but he was just as good on any of the jobsites getting shit handled. "He's observant and thinks outside the box."

Bill snorted. "You mean he's nosy as shit, and beneath that affable smile, he's got the nose of a hound dog."

All true. And not for the first time, or even the hundredth time, I wished I could keep my brother onboard. But he deserved to find his own path. Didn't mean I wasn't going to utilize his talents until he left.

Bill's phone rang and he answered with a "you okay?" and an unusual worry in his voice. "I'll be there right after work—" He listened, brow furrowed, but it wasn't until he put a hand to his heart that I figured out who he had to be talking to—his daughter Hazel.

Hazel had gone to high school with Tucker. They'd been best friends, and she'd been a pseudo-Colburn sibling—until she'd left Star Falls without a word shortly after graduation and hadn't looked back.

She'd been gone for years in radio silence, only to reappear a few months ago. It'd been great to see her but awkward as well, trying as adults to reconnect to the relationships we'd had as kids. All of it made harder by the fact she refused to talk about the past.

I understood that.

Caleb understood.

But she and Tucker, who'd always been the closest, hadn't

yet found a middle ground and were currently, mysteriously, ignoring each other whenever their paths crossed. Which happened frequently because Hazel, a master carpenter, ran her own custom woodworks company. Bill, always a cranky closed book, hadn't said much, but I was guessing father and daughter—oil and water on the best of days, and the reason I could never hire her—were having some growing pains getting reacquainted as well.

"Everything okay?"

"Is it ever?" he muttered, then got into his truck and drove off.

Huh. I called Tucker.

"Yo," he answered breathlessly, odd noises in the background.

"Am I interrupting something?"

"Yes, but don't let that stop you." Tucker shut a door and then it was quiet. "I sent you a text. I'm at the fire station, working out with some of the guys."

Tucker was a volunteer firefighter paramedic, had been for years. His dream was for Star Falls to get the funding for permanent staff so he could get paid for the only job he'd ever wanted. Since that hadn't happened, he worked at Colburn Restorations for a paycheck, and I was grateful to have him. He was, and always had been, the heart of our family.

"Have you talked to Hazel?" I asked.

A beat of silence, heavy on wary. "Why?" he finally asked.

Not an answer. "She just called Bill," I said. "It didn't sound good."

Tucker snorted. "Have you met them?"

"So...you're not worried?" I asked.

"I didn't say that." And then he was gone.

Shit. I called Hazel's phone next.

"Hey, Ry."

"Hey back. You good?"

"Where's the fun in being good?"

I laughed, because true.

"I've got an idea to run by you though." She paused. "I'll give you a ten percent bro deal if you hire me for your finish carpentry contracts."

"To risk the watery grave your mom promised me if I hired both you and your dad at the same time, I'd need a whole bunch more than ten percent off."

She was quiet for a moment. So was I. We both knew I couldn't hire her. We both knew why. I cared about her deeply, but Bill had been with me for years. Shit, I hated this. If she was asking, she needed help.

"You really okay?" I asked.

"Always. You?"

I drew a deep breath. "Always."

After a few seconds of dead air, she chuckled mirthlessly. "We're both so full of it. Buffalo wings and darts at the Cork and Barrel this week?"

"Yes. And it's Caleb's turn to buy."

"Nice. Leave Tucker's grumpy ass home. Twenty-five percent off for a carpentry contract. Final offer. Think about it."

"You know I can't fire your dad."

"And you know I can't stop trying."

She was joking, but I could read between the lines. Even though she'd told us her business was doing great, she needed the work, and that had my stomach sinking. And what was up with her and Tucker? My brother, good-natured and easy-going, was the *last* person on the planet I'd call a grumpy ass.

HE FALLS FIRST

Later. This was a later problem, and I had plenty of now problems to deal with. In fifteen minutes, I was at Nell's house. I never got tired of admiring this place—the red brick walls that perfectly contrasted with the pale stone detailing, the curved windows unique to an early 1900s Queen Anne Victorian, the decorative arches, the steeply pitched roofline with fish-scale slate shingles and large dormers. The fact that the structure was showing her age in cracked and broken bricks, chipped paint, and broken trim made me ache to get my hands dirty giving the old girl some TLC.

For once, Hank wasn't here. Once a week, my neighbor Teresa "borrowed" him when her dad came to visit. Charlie could talk anyone's ears off, and since my dad couldn't talk at all, it was a match made in heaven. Plus Teresa always made Hank his favorite foods, meatloaf and potatoes. Just the thought made me shudder. I hated meatloaf and potatoes with the heat of a thousand suns. It reminded me of the military food we'd lived on. To this day, I start twitching if I have to eat anything that resembles cafeteria food.

Kiera used to tease me that I had such a lame trauma trigger. And I suppose, compared to her and my brothers' various triggers, it was. Kiera was an over-planner who became anxious and bossy if things didn't go the way she'd orchestrated, making everyone around her miserable. Caleb—big, burly, tough as hell—would step in front of a bullet train for someone he loved, but if the conflict became emotional, he walked. Always. Tucker couldn't handle seeing someone he cared about getting hurt. I'd once fallen while rock climbing when the guys I was with hadn't properly belayed me, and he had suffered nightmares for months after.

None of us needed a shrink to know where the triggers came from.

Shaking off the memories of how screwed up we all were, I grabbed the faucet repair kit I'd brought to fix Nell's sink along with the necessary tools and knocked at the back door.

Penny sat at the kitchen table with her laptop, a very large glass of wine and a plate of what looked like her own mint chocolate chip cookies at her elbow. I'd probably kill for either, especially since there was still that matter of the favor Nell had asked of me. I'd spent far too many hours when I should've been sleeping trying to decide just how stupid I was for actually considering asking Penny out.

The thing was, I wanted to do it for me, not for Nell.

Penny was muttering to herself, which reminded me so much of Bill that I snorted.

She turned her glower my way. "*What?*"

Her hair was piled on top of her head, held there by a clip that wasn't quite doing its job containing those wild waves of hers. No makeup, and near as I could tell from her *Bite Me* t-shirt, no bra either. I loved the look, to the point that all of my stress promptly melted away. The power of nipples…

She narrowed her eyes.

I had zero idea why her attitude both cracked me up and turned me on, and even less of a clue if she felt any of that back, but I smiled.

"Hello to you too."

She sighed. "Sorry, paying bills makes me cranky."

I knew what it was like to struggle with not enough money, and seeing her stressed out pinched my heart. "Anything I can do?"

"Gift me a winning lotto ticket?" She popped a whole cookie in her mouth and gestured to the rest, along with the wine. "Help yourself," she said around the large bite.

I picked up her glass, holding her gaze while I took a sip. When I swallowed, she bit her lower lip. I tried not to let it go to my head as I inhaled two cookies.

"Good?" she asked, amused.

"Amazing." I took one more. "I skipped lunch."

She stood, went to the fridge, and pulled out two wrapped sandwiches. "Turkey or roast beef? I made them this morning and no one here has claimed them yet."

I ate both. She poured me a glass of wine as I did.

"What's up?" she asked when I finally filled up.

I gestured to the faucet repair kit I'd set on the counter and rolled my sleeves to my elbows.

Her gaze drifted to my forearms. "What are you doing?"

"Promised Nell I'd fix the sink."

"You don't have to do that."

"I know." I opened the kit and headed to the sink, and two seconds later, felt Penny breathing over my shoulder. I turned my head and our mouths nearly collided.

She inhaled sharply, but interestingly enough, didn't pull back. "I want to be able to do this myself next time," she said while staring at my mouth.

"Good idea," my mouth said while wondering what hers would taste like, and how her legs might feel wrapped around my hips—

"So…show me?" she murmured.

I blinked, for a split second thinking she wanted me to follow through on my fantasies. But then she smirked.

"That's cruel," I muttered.

She laughed, the sound contagious, and the way she gestured to the sink, silently demanding I get on with it, made me laugh too. I showed her what to do, how to pull off the bad part and replace it.

She reached into the sink to do the work, our arms brushing, her hair in my face, but neither of us shifted away. Not surprisingly, she followed my instructions to the T, her nose adorably scrunched in fierce concentration.

"How did you learn to do all this stuff?" she asked, leaning against the counter as I gathered up the tools.

I shrugged. "Growing up, we lived in a lot of places that were…not new. I got good at taking things apart and putting them back together again." I was pretty sure she was listening, but her eyes were on my mouth again.

"How do you still smell good after a long day at work?" she whispered.

I couldn't help the grin, and she blinked as if she hadn't meant to ask that out loud.

I laughed. "You think I smell good."

Tossing up her hands, she went back to the table.

Knowing now was the perfect time to ask her, I instead gathered my stuff and moved to the door, because I really wished I'd told Nell no so I could do this just for me.

"Ryder."

I turned to find Penny holding out a baggie of her cookies.

"Thank you," she said softly. Genuinely. "How much do we owe you?"

I took the baggie. "Consider the debt paid, and thanks for lunch." *Ask her, ask her*, a little voice inside my head said.

She tilted her head. "What are you having for dinner?"

I just stared at her. She made a sound that clearly meant I was an idiot before going to the freezer and pulling out a container that she carefully packed into a cold pack–style lunch box.

"Chicken enchiladas. Enough for you and Hank. Warm them up in the oven, not the microwave."

Two things. One, she'd said Hank, not "your dad," which meant she'd picked up on my complicated feelings about the man and didn't seem to judge me for it. And two…I might've just fallen in love right then and there.

At war with myself, I didn't ask her.

The cookies were gone five minutes into the drive to my last stop of the day, one that had my heart aching. Twenty minutes later, the smile Penny had put on my face was long gone as I navigated the narrow, two-lane road. I passed through rolling hills and vineyards dotted with pockets of ageless redwood groves, the towering giants piercing the sky. Above, the last beams of sunlight filtered through the dense canopy, dappling the road in a mosaic of light and shadow.

When I pulled into the parking lot, a gorgeous sunset sat in my rearview, the evening sky now streaked in moody, bruised blue and purple swaths across the horizon.

It matched my state of mind.

I locked the truck, breathing in the earthy scent of redwood and fresh, rained-on dirt before I began walking across the grassy rolling hills. All too soon, I stood before a gravestone, and as I did every time I'd been here in the past two years, I crouched low and swiped my hands over the granite, dislodging fallen leaves and pollen.

Grief battered me, just as heart-stopping and soul-crushing as ever, making it nearly impossible to breathe. "Hey, Auggie."

The trees overhead immediately rustled, and I could've sworn I felt a warm breeze. I let out a rough, low laugh, pressing a hand to my aching chest. I wasn't sure what I believed when it came to the afterlife, but it was hard to deny that I always felt my best friend's presence here.

We'd met when we were just two punk-ass kids on a Coast Guard base. Over the years, we'd each moved a lot, but occasionally ended up at the same station, and it was always like no time had passed. We stayed thick as thieves despite the miles, past rough family lives, through getting into colleges on opposite coasts, becoming business partners, and then brothers-in-law when he married Kiera.

All to have him shockingly die two years ago, on his thirtieth birthday.

I wished Kiera had come with me, but she still couldn't be here with any of us, only alone. Alone was her favorite state these days, and we tried to honor that. Meaning the schedule we'd created to keep an eye on her and the kids was a secret because we enjoyed breathing. Either myself, Caleb, or Tucker checked in with her every few days, leaving food, filling her gas tank, handling her honey-do list, hanging out with her three-year-old twins Alex and Abi, whatever we could think of to make sure she knew, like it or not, that she wasn't on her own.

Kiera had gone from resenting the intrusions to being... *almost* glad she had siblings. We were slowly wearing her down.

Well, Caleb and Tucker were.

She was still mad at me. She never said so—she didn't have to. And though I didn't blame her, not after how Auggie had died, it still broke my heart.

"Hey, man, brought you a chair."

I'd heard the footsteps of two people coming up behind me,

but hadn't turned because I knew who they were, even before the one with the uneven gait had given them away.

Tucker appeared first, the youngest Colburn brother, our rebel and resident rule breaker, and while he was undoubtedly the least serious of us, he was also the most feral and adventurous. I had lost years of my life trying to rein him in. Thankfully, he'd left his feral years behind him. Well, mostly.

Caleb was the classic middle child, wild, reckless, fearless, and...enjoyed his role as the family screw-up. I narrowed my eyes at him as he strode unevenly across the grassy knoll thanks to that long-lasting, brutal, career-ending college hockey injury.

"You better not have hacked my phone again to find me," I said.

Caleb, six foot two, tatted up, both of those things endearingly at odds with his thick-rimmed glasses that he couldn't see without, rolled his eyes.

"Where's the trust?"

I turned to Tucker, who didn't look the least bit apologetic.

"Of course we hacked your phone. If you don't like it, answer a fucking text once in a while." He set up the three beach chairs he carried in a semi-circle facing Auggie's gravestone.

Caleb held out a large pizza box and a six-pack of beer.

I sighed, which they took as permission to stay.

CHAPTER 6

Ryder

FLANKED BY MY BROTHERS, both of their mouths shut for once, I stared at Auggie's gravestone and let out an irritated breath. "I don't need a babysitter."

"No shit, o-grumpy-one." Tucker gave me a not-too-gentle shoulder check, shoving me into a chair. "Babysitting was *your* role. You always, and I do mean *always*, covered our asses." He sat too. "Today we've got yours."

I accepted a beer, but didn't speak. Couldn't. When we'd first lost Auggie, I'd spent those early days and weeks and months as a shadow of my usual self. These two had pushed, nagged, and bullied me back to the land of the living.

Something Auggie hadn't had the luxury of.

Caleb opened a beer for himself and lifted it in a toast to the headstone in front of us. "Hey, Aug. Happy birthday, man. Wish you were here so I could rag you about being old now."

I slid him a look. "You're only two years younger."

"The key word there is younger."

HE FALLS FIRST

Today would've been Auggie's thirty-second, which made my chest tighten. Too damn young to be gone. We were silent for a long moment, and it was only when Tucker suddenly sucked in a breath and pointed at the sky that I was brought out of my grief.

When had night fallen?

And even as I wondered that, I caught what Tucker saw—three falling stars arching in unison across the moonless sky.

Caleb pushed his glasses closer to his eyes, then let out a sound of surprise. "Is that…"

"Three falling stars," I murmured in stunned surprise, watching them arc in perfect unison.

"Hell, no." Tucker slapped his hands over his eyes. "I don't see anything. And I damn well don't see the Legend of Star Falls."

"It's just a myth," I said, somehow unable to take my eyes off them. "Like Loch Ness and Elvis being alive."

Caleb's eyes were closed. "It's not real, it's not real," he whispered to himself on repeat.

I watched the trio of stars slowly blink away as if they'd never been. I knew the lore went that seeing the stars meant a soulmate would enter your life—whether you wanted such a thing or not. And for the record, I did not.

"You guys don't really believe that three little stars can determine our fate."

"Nope, just yours," Tucker quipped. "Since you're the only one who looked. Right, Caleb?"

Caleb was quiet for so long, we both turned to him.

"Bobby Ramirez," he said. "Our electrical subcontractor. Remember when a few years back he claimed to see the Legend of Star Falls? He went straight to his girlfriend's house and proposed."

"And now he and Mindy have three kids." Tucker shuddered in horror. Without opening his eyes, he jabbed a finger in my direction. "Make sure you drive straight home instead of asking some rando woman to marry you."

I rolled my eyes. "You can look now. The stars are gone."

"What's gone?" Tucker asked. "I saw nothing."

Caleb knocked their bottles together. "That's the spirit."

We fell quiet after that. I stared at Auggie's gravestone, my airway constricted with grief. "I can't get used to him being gone."

"Yeah, well, whoever said time heals all wounds was full of shit," Tucker said.

"True that." Caleb cracked open the pizza box to reveal a fully loaded pie. "I'm starving."

He'd been born starving. The family joke was that he had a gut of iron and a hollow leg. He gestured for me to take a slice.

I shook my head.

"Come on. It's a birthday party." He took a piece. "Auggie loved pizza. The least we can do is let him smell it." Then he turned to me, no smile on his face. "Eat. You've lost some weight." His voice was uncharacteristically solemn.

I shook my head, ignoring the long look they exchanged.

After a long moment, Tucker turned to me. "Ry."

I knew he probably intended to have a well-meaning conversation about my feelings, but I could think of nothing I'd rather do less. "No."

Caleb blew out a breath. "Fine. I'll shut up. Soon as I say one more thing."

"Please don't."

"Oh, I'm going to. I'm going to keep saying it until you

finally get it through your thick skull. Auggie's death on that mountain wasn't your fault."

I tipped my head back and again stared up at the night sky, each star so sharp and perfect that they looked like diamonds scattered across a bed of black velvet. It didn't seem real.

Just like Auggie being gone still didn't seem real.

I drew in a careful breath, remembering Kiera's anxiety before that fateful trip, so worried about Auggie's safety. And what had I done? I'd blithely told her that sometimes you had to push yourself, that life was about exploring. So, yeah. *Not my fault, my ass.*

"Did you tell him to go skiing alone?" Caleb asked. "Off trail, no less?"

I ground my back teeth. "I encouraged the trip."

"Yeah," Tucker said. "You encouraged someone you cared about to go after his dream, and you know better than anyone there are no guarantees when you're going after a dream. In fact, you do that for all of us all the time, encourage us to follow our heart."

I shook my head. "Not talking about this."

"Then just listen," Caleb said. "Because when it comes to your dreams, you've given them up. You've gone from the guy who was always the first of us to take a risk to being the guy who cuts the corners off your bread because they're too sharp."

I slid him a look.

"Oh, you know what I mean. I know we were young when Mom died, but I very clearly remember her telling me that not only was I her favorite, but also that I was never wrong."

I rolled my eyes, and Caleb smiled, proud of himself.

"Why are you here?" I asked in my best asshole-boss voice.

"Did your team finish fixing the problems with the contract for the Escobar job?"

"Just about." Caleb took another piece of pizza.

"Just about?"

He made a show of chewing slowly, then swallowing before answering. "You going to micro-manage me?"

"Here we go," Tucker muttered.

"The contract is coming along," Caleb finally said, licking some sauce off his thumb.

It was a huge job, a renovation of a historical landmark, a 1920s tenant house on fifteen acres along the Russian River, to be turned into a retail space. But there'd been nothing but problems with every agency in town approving the plans. The owner of the property, our client, had given us the job knowing that we excel at solving problems.

"What's happening with it? I'm happy to help," I said.

"Like you have the bandwidth right now."

"What the hell is that supposed to mean?" I asked.

Not stupid, Tucker snagged the pizza box from Caleb's hand and scooted his chair back from us a bit.

Caleb rolled his eyes. "You nearly walked into a wall twice this week because you were busy staring at the cutie pie who cooks like an angel."

I drew a deep breath. "The job. Say more words about the damn job."

He sighed, like I was being an unfathomable pain in his ass. "It involves permits, Caltrans, and Bill. They all had a meeting that nearly ended with fists in faces."

Shit. Bill, brilliant as he was, also had the shortest fuse on the planet, and it had cost us over the years. "What happened?"

"The city planner got involved. He's a class A asshole, and—"

"Just tell me you didn't inform him of that fact to his face. Again."

Caleb grinned. "Do I look stupid?"

"Don't answer that," Tucker muttered to me.

Caleb looked at the gravestone. "Auggie, man, how did you do it for so long, dealing with this guy's do-as-I-say-and-not-as-I-do bullshit? Oh, and let's not forget his daddy issues."

Tucker grimaced. "It's like you *want* to die."

"You about done?" I asked Caleb.

"Oh, not even close."

Tucker sighed dramatically. "We don't have enough alcohol."

Caleb slid me a smug-ass grin. "Someone saw you two getting cozy in the staff kitchen early one morning over a week ago now."

I choked on my beer, then cursed myself for the tell. The last thing I needed was for my stupid little brother to know just how thoroughly infatuated I was.

"*Someone?*"

Caleb turned and eyeballed Tucker.

Who groaned and stared at his beer. "Definitely didn't bring enough alcohol. And I told you that in confidence, dickwad."

"What's her name again?" Caleb asked. "Payton? Pheobe?"

"*Penny*," I said through clenched teeth, and when the idiot cackled and clapped his hands in glee, I wanted to chuck the pizza at him.

But Tucker hugged the box tight to his chest like it was a precious baby. "The girl who lives with dad's caretaker," he said helpfully.

"She's no girl," Caleb said. "She's all woman. Gutsy, sharp-witted, pretty—"

I nearly growled. Or maybe I did, given how Caleb smirked. "Oh, did I hit a nerve?" he and his big, fat mouth asked innocently.

"Seriously though," Tucker asked him. "Are you tired of your front teeth?"

I drank some beer and took a deep breath. "Whatever you think you saw that morning between Penny and me, it wasn't that. She nearly got run over, I was just helping her patch herself up." Every time I thought about that morning and what could have happened to her, my heart stopped. It'd stopped that morning too. The way she'd taken the whole incident in stride, like maybe her life was as questionable and as uncertain as it'd been in that heartbeat when she could've been killed, had done something to me.

And then there was how I still couldn't forget the way she'd reacted when I'd reached out to touch her. That recoil. Not the usual reaction I got from a woman...

She got hurt...

Yeah. Nell's words still haunted me.

"Penny," Caleb said.

My head jerked up. "What about her?"

"Nothing. Just wanted to see how fast you'd look up." He grinned. "Like a moth to the flame."

"Here we go," Tucker muttered, tipping his head back to stare up at the stars.

Caleb just grinned. "You two played doctor. *Adorable*."

"We're not talking about this."

Tucker took another bite of pizza and then choked dramatically, a hand to his chest like an old woman clutching her pearls.

"What?" I nearly broke my neck trying to see what had spooked him.

"It's the Legend," Tucker said. "The Legend of Star Falls. You saw them, and now you've officially met your soulmate."

"We *just* saw them. Even the universe can't work retroactively."

"Maybe the Legend somehow knew you'd see the stars tonight and started working ahead of time," Caleb said helpfully.

"That's the stupidest thing I've ever heard."

Caleb managed to be quiet for ten whole seconds—an amazing feat—before he said, "But what if it's not?" The amusement was gone from his tone. "Stupid, I mean. What if it's real? You, of all of us, Ry, deserve to find someone. You know that, right?"

"No." I shook my head. "We all deserve happiness, yes, but—"

"It's your turn," Tucker said. "You never put yourself first. You took the initial shift with Captain Asshole, and you keep saying you don't need help, that you're fine—which we know is a lie. What if it's your time to meet your person, and maybe that person is, say, a funny, feisty, pretty brunette who cooks like heaven on earth?"

Dangerous territory. Especially since I had a feeling about Penny that I couldn't shake. Like she was different, special.

And I didn't deserve to find happiness with her.

Caleb jabbed a finger at me. "I know what that look means, you bastard. You're going to be stupid about this."

I smacked his finger out of my face. "Not stupid. Practical."

"How is it practical to deny yourself something good?"

"He thinks he doesn't deserve it," Tucker said quietly, and maybe also angrily.

"That's bullshit," Caleb said.

"Yeah, it is." Tucker didn't take his eyes off me. "We owe you."

"You owe me nothing."

"We owe you *everything*," Caleb snapped. "Every damn thing that we are today, it's because of you."

Unbearably moved, with a stupid lump the size of a regulation hockey puck in my throat, I couldn't do more than shake my head.

Caleb wasn't having it. "You've always shielded the people you love, taking everything on your shoulders. When Mom died. Whenever Dad was out for blood. And I know you think you didn't shield Auggie, but he was his own person, and he made a choice. That isn't on you."

I looked away.

But then Caleb took my hand in his—something he hadn't done since we were kids—and gave me a serious look.

"You're ugly and were found under a rock."

I choked out a laugh through my burning throat. "Love you too, you prick." It'd been a while since that particular Colburn sibling insult had been deployed.

Caleb leaned past me and glared meaningfully at Tucker, who blew out a breath and reached for my other hand even as he muttered, "We look like three little girls."

"Hey, girls love this shit," Caleb said. "Being with a guy who can access his feelings? Gold. And that bad attitude of yours is going to keep you from getting laid."

"Hasn't so far," Tucker replied smugly.

I looked at Auggie's grave. I appreciated the company, I did. And I knew they'd always be here for me if they thought I needed them—whether I liked it or not. They only wanted to help, but I needed to bandage my invisible wounds in my own way.

I squeezed their hands. "No more words."

Tucker shrugged, easily accepting that. "Then eat."

So I took a piece of pizza and we ate, keeping Auggie company.

CHAPTER 7

Penny

ON SUNDAY MORNING, I once again jerked awake to the house shuddering, and it was déjà vu as I leapt out of bed. It was still dark, and I had no idea what time it was as I flew down the stairs.

"Grandma? Is that you and the generator again?"

The smoke alarm suddenly went off and I whirled around in a circle, looking for the fire, knocking a lamp off a side table, barely catching it in time to save it.

No fire.

I stilled. "Pika-boo, is that you?"

"Meow."

I ripped the blanket off his cage to find him looking very proud of himself. I pointed at him, then turned at the sound of a chuckle.

Hank sat on our couch holding the remote, pointing it at the TV. Tall and broad, he always carried himself like he was a five-star general. That was, if a five-star general was nonverbal, wore a white t-shirt and sleep pants with little hearts on them, and had the sweetest disposition I'd ever seen. He was hitting a button on the remote with his thumb repeatedly to no avail, but at the sight of me, he waved cheerfully.

"Morning," I said, skidding to a halt, breathless, wondering why he was here on a Sunday.

He gestured to the remote.

We'd been here before, so I moved to his side and turned the remote right side up. "Try that."

"Ahhhh." He hit the button again. The TV went on and he gave another "ahhhh," smiling at me and doing something with his face that looked like he was having another stroke, but which I now knew meant he was trying to wink. So I winked back.

Grandma appeared in the kitchen doorway, dressed in jeans and a pink t-shirt that said: COUGAR OF THE YEAR.

I narrowed my eyes at her feet, which for as long as I could remember, had never been in anything but beat-up blue Keds sneakers, but now were in brand-new work boots. And just as pink as her shirt and tool belt.

"What was the banging? You're not killing the generator or dishwasher again, are you?"

"I've got a surprise for you."

"Poop?" Pika-boo asked.

Budgies had the capacity for a vocabulary of two thousand words, and ours just wanted to talk about poop...

"No." Grandma looked at me. "Guess."

Oh boy. Her last surprise had been trading in grandpa's ancient junker truck for a slightly less old 4Runner, a manual, which she'd never used before. She'd promptly crashed it into our mailbox.

"Do I need to call the insurance company again?"

"Haha, and no." She grinned. "I'm giving our kitchen a little makeover. Who knows, maybe you'll love it so much that you'll stay," she said carefully.

"Grandma, we can't afford to renovate."

"We'll start small—with the kitchen."

"That's the opposite of small!"

She waved this off. "I wanted to do it so you can go back to working for yourself, making home-cooked meals, working toward your dream of opening that café—"

"But that's the thing about dreams...they're not really meant to come true. Not for people like me."

"You're wrong." She put her hands on her hips. "*No one* deserves it more than you."

"Ahhhh," Hank said, nodding in agreement.

The truth was, a kitchen remodel would be amazing. "Two problems. One, we're so broke we can't pay attention, and two, neither of us knows the first thing about renovating our *lives*, much less a kitchen."

"But...we both know someone who's learned a few things about renovations. And, surprise, he's willing to help us. We'll be his worker bees."

A very bad feeling settled in my gut. "He who?"

Ryder poked his head out of the kitchen. He wore army-green cargos that emphasized his long legs and fit his body in a way that left my mouth dry. There were a lot of pockets for his goodies, although I was pretty sure not all of his goodies were relegated to the pockets. His black t-shirt stretched taut over broad shoulders and was loose over his abs, and dear God, he wore a tool belt low on his hips—not pink. His ball cap was on backwards, that sun-kissed, multifaceted brown hair curling out from beneath it.

He was a walking Taylor Swift song, and I was shockingly here for it.

I'd never seen him in anything but a suit before, which had only hinted at a leanly muscled body, but today's look shorted every circuit in my brain.

"Morning," he said.

I rolled my tongue back into my mouth. "I don't know how she conned you in this, but you're not obligated—"

"He's here because when he picked up Hank a few days ago, he found me trying to check the smoke alarm battery," Grandma said.

"On a ladder about to electrocute herself via screwdriver," Ryder said, giving me a *yeah, I couldn't believe it either* look. "She said she was working on the kitchen next. Without any knowledge or the right tools and equipment."

"Hey," Grandma said. "I got *some* of the right equipment. Have you seen my new boots?"

"Grandma, the astronauts on the space station can see the boots."

"Well, I'll have you both know I watched a bunch of YouTube videos on kitchen remodels," she said. "But now I don't have to know everything because Ry stepped in to help. Don't you love a man who can take charge *and* work with his hands?"

Ryder looked like maybe he was regretting getting out of bed that morning.

"You don't have to do this," I told him.

"I'm happy to."

That was hard to believe, but Grandma smiled at him.

"Actually, he said he'd do whatever needs to be done only if I promised *not* to help, and when I said I really, really wanted to help, he said only if I did exactly what he said. No going rogue."

Dear God. My grandma had emotionally blackmailed Ryder Colburn. I now had an eye twitch *and* my brain was firing on zero cylinders, and not simply because he was leaning against the doorjamb, posture relaxed and easy, commanding the room with a confidence I couldn't have managed on my best day.

Okay, maybe that was exactly why my brain wasn't firing. But why did he rev my engine? I was supposed to be on empty! Except with him standing there in that damn tool belt slung on his lean hips, I didn't feel empty. I felt a whole bunch of things I shouldn't, like how that stubble on his jaw would scratch against my skin, and the shocking desire to feel his calloused palms gliding over my body—

"Pen? Honey?" Grandma waved a hand in front of my face. "You just got all flushed. You're not having hot flashes already, are you? You're a little young for that. You okay?"

No, I was most definitely not okay. I'd just swallowed my tongue and had possibly just gotten pregnant as well.

Ryder's lips curved into a small smile, as if he knew exactly what he did to me. Smug bastard.

"Anyway," Grandma went on before I could further embarrass myself, "Ry's going to come by either in the mornings when he drops Hank off, or in the evenings when he has spare time. I mean, think about what you might do with a newly renovated kitchen, Pen. You could even open that café..."

All very tempting. But I couldn't let her rope Ry into this. "I don't think—"

"He's going to take down the cabinet doors today to refinish them. Can you imagine how wonderful that will look? He's also going to check out our appliances to see what needs upgrading."

Okay, yes, I moaned about our avocado-green stove and sunshine-yellow fridge on the daily, but—

"Did you know that as a general contractor, he can get appliances at a deep discount? I'm so excited! I've been wanting to do this forever. All I needed was someone with the knowledge to be the boss—"

"I'm not anyone's boss," Ryder said. "I'm just helping out."

I let out a short laugh. "You do remember you've got something like a hundred employees, right?"

He swiped a hand down his face, and I was fairly certain he sighed. I'd be willing to bet he'd never been a sigher in his life. Not surprising that I brought it out in him, I had that effect on men.

"The bottom line is we aren't going to take advantage of him, Grandma. He's a busy man—"

"I've got the time," he said.

I stared at him, wondering why he would do this for us.

He stared back, giving nothing away.

"I just ordered everyone pink tool belts," Grandma exclaimed, waving her phone. "Team Pink!"

"Ahhhhh?" came from the couch.

"Don't you worry, sweet cheeks," she yelled out to Hank. "I got you one too."

Ryder looked pained, whether at the nickname for his dad or just the morning so far, I had no idea. But I felt...confused. "You already work a gazillion hours. Why would you give in to her?"

He shrugged. "It's a way to do something I love."

"Which is?"

"The work," he said simply. "I miss it."

I tried to read the lie, but I was pretty sure there wasn't one. He actually *wanted* to do this, and I had to admit, the thought of an updated kitchen, where maybe we could use the toaster and the dryer at the same time without blowing fuses, made me nearly as giddy as Grandma.

"Are you sure?"

"Yes."

Okay, so maybe I needed to stop looking a gift horse in the mouth. "Thank you," I said quietly.

His smile softened in a way I'd never seen as he looked into my eyes—

"Please turn the fuckin' TV down!" Pika-boo yelled cheerfully.

"That one's on you," Grandma said, pointing at me.

"Shit, damn, hell, hot balls on a stick, cocksucker!" the bird replied.

I gave Grandma side-eye.

She winced. "Okay, yeah. I'll work on it."

Ryder fought a smile, and we stood there staring awkwardly at each other. Well, okay, I was the awkward one. He looked perfectly at ease with himself.

Hank pushed himself up from the couch and shuffled toward the doorway to the kitchen, pointing to the coffeepot.

"I'll get it," Ryder said. "Sit."

Hank shuffled back to the couch, and a minute later Ryder brought him a mug filled only halfway. He'd added ice cubes. "Careful."

Hank nodded and smiled at his son. "Ah."

Ryder hesitated, then patted the guy's shoulder before

turning back to the kitchen. I adjusted to let him pass, but his body still brushed mine. I tried not to make eye contact, but his gaze was locked on me the whole time and I couldn't look away. I had no idea what was happening. My face heated as if I hadn't been touched in years. Which, since I'd self-combusted in the shower just last night, made no sense.

"We're going to pay him," I said to Grandma without taking my gaze off Ryder.

"Of course we are."

"Even if he argues about it."

Ryder's lips twitched.

"Which he will," she said. "Don't worry, I'll be keeping track of his hours. I'm going to write him a check, which he's *going* to take, even if I have to drag him down to the bank and watch him deposit it."

The image of her even trying made me snort. "No one takes checks anymore. You can use Zelle or Venmo."

Grandma blinked. "I don't know either of those people, and why wouldn't Ryder take a check?"

Both of my eyes twitched now, and I met my new contractor's amused gaze from where he'd been watching the Nell and Pen Show. "Can I talk to you?" I asked. "Alone?"

He bowed his head once and headed out the back door into the early dawn light. The sky was a kaleidoscope of colors, dark purple to the west, streaked with a lighter purple and then a swath of brilliant red and oranges toward the east ahead of the sun. A massive storm cloud churned in the north. It'd rain soon, which was good as I hadn't watered the yard this week.

Ryder eyed the two flowerpots on either side of the back door, both filled with dead foliage.

"Just establishing expectations for all the other plants," I said.

He chuckled, and I absolutely did not immediately want to make him chuckle again.

There were two towering oaks just off the patio, and I stood between them, staring anywhere but at the man at my side.

"It's nice out here," he said.

"I love it," I admitted. "Especially in the summer. When I was younger, an owl befriended me. She'd hoot softly outside my bedroom at night." I smiled. "I'd leave her food, and she'd leave me a pile of dead mice."

One side of his mouth curved. "I bet you were a handful."

"I bet you were worse."

The almost smile turned into a grin. "I was."

I drew a deep breath, wrapping my arms around myself in the early chill, and *dammit*, once again, I stood before him in my pj's. And yes, it was the Wonder Woman top.

His eyes sparkled.

"Not funny," I said.

"Am I laughing?"

I took a closer look, and whoa, he was right. That light in his eyes wasn't laughter, it was…damn.

Heat. I had to look my absolute worst, but that was actual, honest desire on his face, and the knowledge of it flipped a switch deep, deep inside me.

"Why are you doing this?" I whispered.

"Standing here with you? You wanted to talk to me," he said innocently.

Innocent as the devil. "You know what I mean. You just let yourself get bamboozled by an old lady. I want to know why."

"Your grandma saves my ass five days a week by watching Hank."

Okay, I could maybe buy that. "I've got more questions."

"Shoot."

"Is this a pity job? Because we aren't a charity case. Plus, you already work so hard. Why would you do manual work when you don't have to? And why do you call your dad Hank?"

He rocked back on his heels, his hands in his pockets. "Not a pity job. Not a charity case either. I meant what I said. I sincerely owe your grandma, who just wants someone to update her kitchen for the granddaughter she loves with all her heart. As for the other two questions—I don't get to do the actual work much anymore and I miss it, and…because he wasn't much of a dad."

His voice had been quiet, calm, emotionless really, but somehow I heard the hurt in the words, and it made me feel ashamed of myself for questioning his motives. Blowing out a breath, I stared down at my toes for a beat, then stepped closer, tipping my head back to look into his eyes.

"I shouldn't have assumed bad intentions."

He shrugged like he was used to it, and that made it worse somehow. "Ryder—"

He raised a brow. "Penelope."

I snorted and relaxed. "Thank you for doing this for my grandma."

"Who is doing it for you."

I closed my eyes against the truth because sometimes being loved also hurt. "I know."

"She loves you."

My eyes flew open. "I know that. She and Wyatt…they're

the only two people I've ever been sure of." I started to turn away. "And now that I'm done apologizing, I've got to get going."

"Are you?"

I faced him again. "Am I what?"

"Done apologizing."

I paused. "You didn't hear me?"

"No, because you didn't say it."

I opened my mouth, then shut it. Dammit. He was right. I hated that. "Okay, fine. I truly am sorry for misjudging your intentions."

"And?"

I narrowed my eyes. "And what?"

He shrugged, looking like sex on a stick. "Thought maybe you wanted to also apologize for jumping down my throat."

Was that humor lurking at the corners of his mouth? "Don't take it personally. I do that to everyone with a penis."

He chuckled, and dammit, that sound... "You're not annoyed at me?" I asked.

He shrugged those broad shoulders. "Most people 'yes' me, tell me what they think I want to hear."

I found a laugh. "Well, no worries on that count with me."

He studied me for a beat, like he was trying to figure something out, but couldn't. So I was completely caught off guard when he suddenly said, "Go out with me."

I stopped breathing. "Um, what?"

He smiled. "You looked like I just suggested flying to the moon without a rocket ship."

Why was my pulse racing? Impending stroke, maybe? He wanted to go out? On a date? With me? Was he nuts? Who in their right mind would want to date me? And then there was the fact I'd given up dating. "You know it's not a good idea to mix work with pleasure—"

"Of course not. But..." He gave her a cat-in-cream smile. "We're not at work right now."

I looked around, including behind me, on the off chance I was being punked. Then I gestured to myself. "You can't seriously want to date..." I waved at myself. "*This*."

That smile of his went positively filthy and positively leaked testosterone and pheromones. "Oh," he said in a sex-on-a-stick voice. "I most seriously do."

At that, my body was utterly onboard, no questions asked. My brain not so much. "But...why?"

Ry closed the space between us, then tilted his head as he slowly took me in from my bare feet, up my legs—did he just slow down at their juncture?—to the strip of bare belly exposed by my cropped tee, before meeting my gaze. A slow smile curved his lips.

"Who wouldn't want to go out with Wonder Woman?"

My pulse pounded in my ears so loudly that surely he could hear it. And why was my heart threatening to secede the United States of Penny? "I don't actually...date."

"Do you eat dinner?"

"I mean..." I had to laugh. "Yes."

"So let's call it...just dinner."

"Just dinner."

"Just dinner," he repeated in a soothing voice I knew could persuade a nun to sin. "Your choice of when and where."

Okay, I could do "just dinner." Right? *Oh my God, was I listening to myself?* My mind was getting on board now too? What the hell. I had valid reasons to fight this, a whole bunch of them, even if I couldn't think of a single one at the moment. Yes, I'd been burned. Yes, I'd sworn off emotional attachments. But the thought of just one night, no expectations, no promises, where I could have fun and let my guard down and just be…

I wanted that. I wanted that bad.

"Louder, please!" Grandma yelled from the small downstairs bathroom window.

Dear God. "*Grandma, what are you doing?*"

"Taking my constitutional."

I grimaced. "Stop eavesdropping!"

"Sure thing, honey!"

"And shut that window!"

Ryder was smiling when I turned back to him. "Not funny," I said.

"Agree to disagree." He tilted his head. "So…is there a night that works for you?"

"Tonight," Grandma yelled out the still opened bathroom window. "She's free tonight. She's actually free every night. She's cute, but she don't get out much."

"Thanks, Grandma." But I shook my head. "I'm sorry, tonight's out." I had plans with Vi and Renee to eat our weight in chocolate and bitch about life. "And tomorrow night I'll be busy with Wyatt, who's got a science project due the morning after that, which he probably hasn't started, so—"

"I'll help Wyatt," Grandma said, thankfully this time from the kitchen window. "I'll just be here staring up at the sky for the Legend of Star Falls anyway."

Ryder smiled. "Your grandma will help him."

"She's fibbing. She hates science." All I knew was that this venture felt like something I needed to obsess over for at least a week first. "Maybe next weekend?"

"Next weekend then," he said, calm, patient, but also… smiling.

"Maybe."

He knew I was stalling. What he apparently *didn't* know was what a terrible, no good, very bad idea this was. "For *just* dinner," I reiterated

"Just dinner," he said comfortingly.

Which had the opposite effect.

"Anywhere you want to go," he added.

"Anywhere?"

"Yep." Then he smiled the sexiest, most trouble-filled smile in the history of smiles.

Okay, maybe this would work. All I had to do was remember I wasn't on the Man Train, and no matter how good he looked—and smelled, dammit—or what his smile did to certain body parts that I was not speaking to, it'd be fine.

Fine.

And maybe if I kept repeating it to myself, I'd actually believe it. "I'll think about it."

"Take as long as you want."

Since overthinking was my true superpower, I had no doubt I'd think of little else.

CHAPTER 8

Penny

OPENED MY EYES AND realized I was on the floor, jagged pieces of broken glass all around me, something trickling down my neck. Blood. And it was staining the rug. Not my rug, but Mitch's.

I sat up with a gasp in my own bed and hit the light.

No blood on me anywhere. Nothing but a scar from the memory of that night. It'd been just a dream. I let out a shaky breath and touched the scar on my jaw.

It was over. I was far away and free. I was fine.

I repeated this mantra to myself until I stopped trembling, then got into the shower and stood there so long I ran out of hot water. I got out and firmly told my pale, trembling reflection in the bathroom mirror that I was a kick-ass, strong woman who'd left her past in the past.

A kick-ass woman who'd left her past in the past and…was not ready to do anything as official as "just dinner." And then I went to work, because even a kick-ass, strong woman needed to eat and put a roof over her head.

HE FALLS FIRST

An hour and a half later, I drove out of the Hungry Bee kitchen in a heavy downpour and parked at Colburn Restorations. Still feeling a little shaky, I pressed a hand to my quivering belly and promised myself homemade chocolate chip cookies if I made it through the day without falling apart, at least not publicly. So I pulled up my proverbial big girl panties and stepped out into the crazy rain. I'd been so busy talking myself off the ledge before leaving the house that I'd forgotten my raincoat.

There were worse things, so I loaded up my cart and pushed it into the reception area, taking a minute to shake off like a wet dog, which did nothing since I was already soaked to the bone. But good news, now I couldn't tell if I was trembling because of the cold or the dream, which meant I could pretend it was the cold.

I knew what Mitch had done to me wasn't my fault, but I hated that I'd fallen for a pretty face and pretty words. I'd been completely infatuated—and completely intimidated—by him and his success. He was powerful and respected and, as everyone had kept telling me, a huge catch. I'd ignored many, many red flags, so much so that the gaslighting and bullying had crept up on me. In fact, I'd never seen it coming, and I hated that too. He'd been bad for me, in so many ways, but the worst part had been the utter loss of my own self-worth and confidence.

A very kind therapist had gently helped me come to terms with that, and I liked to think that I could avoid falling into the same trap next time, but that didn't mean I trusted myself enough to dive back in. I'd gone out a few times since Mitch, just to see what would happen. And what happened had been utter disinterest on my part. So I'd stopped trying.

And yet I'd just committed Wonder Woman to going out with Ryder Colburn.

What had I been thinking? I mean, I couldn't get hurt in a relationship if I wasn't in one. But...this wouldn't be a relationship, my perky nipples argued. It wasn't even a date. It was Just Dinner.

With the first guy to make you feel...anything.

Gah.

I should cancel.

I *would* cancel.

I was nodding to myself as I looked around, realizing the building was very quiet this morning. I saw no one as I pushed my cart down the hall. At the doorway to the staff kitchen, my phone vibrated an incoming call from Wyatt.

"Bro," he said.

I'd given up asking why he called me that. I'd decided to take it as a compliment. "Wow, I'm impressed you're up so early—"

"It's raining," he said.

"You're awake on time *and* you've looked up from your game long enough to know it's raining? Okay, who are you and what have you done with my baby brother?"

"Har-har. The bucket in the laundry room's filling up."

Oh, shit. I used to think being a grownup was one crisis after another. I was wrong. It was multiple crises. Concurrently. All at once. All the time. Forever and ever. "I forgot to check it when I left," I said. Busy morning having anxiety and all that... "I need you to empty it."

"Do I have to?"

I resisted knocking my head against the kitchen doorway. "If it's filling up, yes, please."

"I don't think it's *that* full."

I drew a deep breath for patience. "Wyatt, just empty the damn bucket before the kitchen floods again."

"But—"

"You like eating, right?" I asked.

"Well, yeah—"

"So let me spell this out for you—if the kitchen floods again, I can't cook."

"You guys are in the middle of redoing the kitchen. Which means you can't cook here for a while anyway."

"Just empty the damn bucket!" I had never felt more adulty in my life. "*Please*."

"Okay, okay, jeez. But I need you to sign some stuff. There's a dumb field trip. And then there's that soccer tournament in South Bay. Coach said to tell you we need drivers. Also, I'm supposed to bring in a check today. Oh, and Tommy got an iguana and I want one too."

I hit mute to snap out a word that I didn't allow Wyatt to say. Then I put the phone back to my ear. "Would've been helpful to know about the school stuff last night. You know, when we were in the same place at the same time."

"I forgot. I also forgot that there's a birthday party tonight I want to go to."

"You're twelve."

"Birthday party, not a drug drop."

I rubbed the spot between my eyes. I suppose now I knew why parents always had stress lines there. "Whose birthday?"

"You don't know her."

"Her?" I squeaked.

"Cindy Martine. She's my math teacher's daughter. There'll be annoying adults chaperoning. Kenny's mom is going to drive us there and pick us up."

"You swear?"

"I swear."

"Do you like her?" I asked. "This Cindy?"

"For once, can you just be normal and say yes?" he grumbled.

"Yes, but we need to talk."

"About what?" Wyatt asked warily. "About me getting an iguana?"

"The birds and the bees."

There was a stunned, and possibly horrified, silence. "You've given me that stupid talk like a bazillion times. Plus I'm not..." He blew out a disgusted breath.

"You're not having sex yet, I know. I'm hoping you don't until I'm dead, but there're a lot of things that lead up to it—"

"Please don't name them, not ever again."

"Fine. Then tell me the rules."

He sighed dramatically and lowered his voice, like I was torturing this out of him. "I get verbal consent before so much as touching anyone. I respect personal boundaries, even the nonverbal ones."

"And...?"

I couldn't see him through the phone, but I knew he rolled his eyes so hard he probably saw his own brain.

Radio silence.

"Tell me," I said. "Or no party."

"Don't be a fool, wrap your tool."

I grinned. Gotta get your kicks where you could... "Text me when you get there *and* drop me a pin, and text again when you leave. Be home by ten."

"Midnight."

"Nine-thirty," I said.

"Ten it is."

Okay, so he was calling only because he needed stuff. I'd like to say I'd never been such an annoying, thoughtless, heartless teenager, but I'd be lying through my teeth. I probably owed my mom an apology. But then again, she hadn't exactly mom'd me much, so maybe we were even.

"I'll come by the school between my deliveries. Don't forget to remind grandma before you leave that Hank's got a doctor appointment today, okay? I scheduled them an Uber."

"She says she's driving. Soon as she finds her keys."

"She won't. I hid them."

"Where?" he asked.

"Where I hid the alcohol from you, and I'm not telling."

"I told you, it was Tommy who drank the vodka in the freezer. Not me."

"Which is why Tommy's not allowed over anymore. Don't forget to brush your teeth."

"Aw, man."

"With toothpaste," I added.

But he was already gone. Of course he was. I let out a long breath and whispered my favorite four-letter word again.

A rough, quiet laugh had me jerking my head up. I couldn't see another soul, so I rounded the corner of the island and nearly tripped over the man sitting on the floor, his back to the sink, his long legs out in front of him.

Ryder. Wearing another baseball cap, black cargo pants this time, battered work boots, a white Colburn Restorations t-shirt with...

A whole bunch of blood soaking through the cotton.

CHAPTER 9

Penny

RACED INTO THE KITCHEN, dropping to my knees at Ryder's side. "*What happened?*"

"Nothing, I'm fine."

Fine, my ass, but I met his gaze. "I'm getting a sense of déjà vu."

That got me an almost-smile. "At least *I* didn't almost get run over by a truck," he said. "This was just my own stupidity." Closing his eyes, he leaned his head back against the island, exposing his throat.

I'd let myself wonder later why a man's throat was so sexy. For now, I could see pain in the grim set of his mouth.

"Why are you drenched and shivering?" he asked.

"Forgot my coat."

He started to shift, like he was going to get up and take care of me, but I put a hand on his chest. "Stay."

With a chuckle, he opened his eyes. "I'm not a dog." He took in my concern and his expression softened. "I'm okay, Penny. I just need a moment."

On my first day of delivering food here, six plus months ago now, Ryder and his guys had been doing some sort of team bonding warrior ninja obstacle course that had been set up in the parking lot.

It'd been dawn and pouring rain then too, but I'd been able to pick him out of the crowd, up on a high rig, effortlessly and gracefully swinging from ring to ring while dodging nunchucks and massive bouncy balls. As I couldn't do more than one pull up at a time, I'd been fascinated by his easy show of strength. I'd still been watching when one of those huge balls had taken him out.

He'd crash-landed on a thick mat, but not before also taking a nunchuck to the head. He'd gotten to his feet, bleeding but smiling—because he'd gotten farther on the course than anyone else.

"Why are guys so dumb?" I asked the room.

He gave a low laugh. "Comes with the equipment."

Not impressed, I gave him a deadpan look. "Do you need an ambulance?"

"No."

"Ryder—"

"I don't. I'm okay. I just had a little mishap with a ladder and a chain-link fence on a jobsite. I came in to patch myself up and needed to sit down for a minute. No big deal."

I stared at him. No use asking if he was still dizzy, he'd just deny it. "If it's no big deal, then let me see."

He hesitated.

"Hey, I let you see mine."

This earned me a lip twitch, but not a peek at his injury.

"Also, I owe you," I said. "My excellent nursing will make us even."

"Hardly. I threw myself in front of a truck for you." His eyes took on a mischievous gleam. "But, *maybe,* if you were to wear a naughty nurse uniform..."

"Keep dreaming, perv." I tugged on the hem of his shirt. "Off."

"You didn't have to lose your shirt."

"Maybe next time."

He smiled. "Now you're just teasing me." He removed the baseball cap, leaving his dark hair sexily tousled. Then, very carefully and slowly, he pulled his t-shirt over his head.

I didn't know whether to drool or gasp in horror. His side was black and blue and had a three-inch gash running horizontally between his belly button and his ribs. "Looks like you tried to give yourself an appendectomy."

He choked on a laugh. "It's just a scratch."

"Yeah, and I'm the Easter Bunny." I ran back to my cart, grabbing two clean towels off the stack I'd brought with me. I stopped to thoroughly wash my hands, then dropping back to my knees at his side, I pressed one of the towels against the injury.

He hissed in a breath.

"Hold this," I demanded. "Is the first aid kit back in its place above the fridge?"

"I don't need it."

"Answer me or I'm calling 911."

A barely there exhale escaped his lips, which from another man would've been a huge sigh. "Yeah. But first go into the closet behind the door. There's a black hoodie hanging there. Grab it for me?"

I brought the big, cozy sweatshirt to him, but he shook his head. "Put it on."

"What?"

"Humor me. Please," he added when I didn't move.

Blowing out a breath, I pulled on the deliciously soft and warm hoodie and sighed. I hadn't realized how cold I was.

He smiled. "Better."

"Thank you," I said, but also rolled my eyes because I never knew how to deal with someone doing something for me. To get the first aid kit, I had to climb onto the counter, and he watched me with a small smile.

"How is this funny?" I asked, shoving up the too-long sleeves.

"Just admiring the view. You're strong."

"Do you have any idea how much the trays I carry around weigh?" I flashed him a body builder stance, flexing my arms.

"Wonder Woman." He held my gaze, the jade of his eyes streaked with melted honey. "Inside *and* out."

Nope. I wasn't going to let that go to my head. Not even a little bit. So instead, it went to my belly, making it quiver.

"It's a stupid place to keep a first aid kit, up so high like that," I grumbled, trying to get down off the counter without dying.

"You're the only person in this entire building who can't reach it."

I slid him a look. "Was that a height joke?"

"I wouldn't dare."

With a snort, I came back to him, pulling on a pair of medical gloves I found in the kit before beginning to carefully clean around the injury. He didn't make a sound, but his abs twitched, giving away his pain.

"I'm sorry," I whispered, and he shook his head.

I was so focused on not meeting his gaze while touching him that I just kept staring at his torso, which seemed made entirely of lean muscle. His skin marred by the occasional scar, and swirls of dark ink ran over his shoulders and chest in a sexy pattern that made my mouth water.

"And I'm not short," I said apropos of nothing. "I'm five foot four."

His mouth quirked. "I stand corrected."

"I'll have you know," I said in a playful tone meant to distract him from the pain. "There are plenty of advantages to being… height challenged."

"Do tell."

"Well, since I fit into tight places, I'm an expert at hide-and-go-seek."

"I'm sure that comes in handy all the time."

"It does when you're trying to turn a raised-by-wolves cub into a human twelve-year-old boy." I pulled out some gauze and antibiotic cream. "Once I cover up the wound, I'll drive you to the ER."

"No need. Find the skin glue I've got in there."

I gaped at him. "You need a doctor."

"Pass." He started fumbling in the kit himself, and I slapped his hand away. "Are you always this stubborn?"

"Takes one to know one."

"Uh-huh. I thought you handled the business side of things, not the actual physical labor. Why didn't whoever was working with you take you directly to the hospital without passing Go?"

"I keep telling you, I like to get dirty." He flashed a mischievous smile when I bit my lower lip. "And as for this morning, something came up on a job that had to get done right away, and no one else was available."

"So you went alone? Even I know that's against your own rules."

He shrugged, then tried unsuccessfully to hide his wince. "I'm the boss."

"Ah. Which means you get to be stupid, but no one else does."

He rubbed the spot between his eyes. "Up until two years ago, I spent most of my time in the field. I miss it. It gives me balance. And I do know what I'm doing." He paused. "Usually."

I found the skin glue. "So you really aren't renovating our kitchen out of pity."

"If anything, pity me for being stuck inside an office for the past two years."

Still on the floor, our faces were close, our bodies even closer with him leaning back against the island, and me on my knees at his side. He hadn't shaved and I liked the dark scruff, a lot.

Around us, the world was still quiet, giving the moment an intimate feel, so I dared to ask, "What changed two years ago?"

"I had a partner. Auggie managed the day-to-day running of the business side of things, and I handled everything in the field. When he...died, I had to shift my attention to management. It's been long enough that I should be used to it by now, but..." He shook his head.

My heart sank at his loss. "I'm so sorry." Stupid, useless words, but I hoped he heard the genuine sentiment beneath them.

"He loved numbers, loved managing this place, just as much as I loved working with my hands." He drew a deep breath. "People thought I was the funny one, but they were wrong. It was Auggie. He had a wicked sense of humor and could prank the shit out of anyone, but he was also quiet, unassuming, and so chill you had to check him for a pulse to make sure he was still breathing. He liked quiet evenings at home with his wife and kids. He liked vacations where he could sit by the pool and watch over his family and read a good book. He was..."

"Your virtual opposite?"

He gave a half smile. "Yes, and also my best friend. I'd been after him for years to live a little. To pick even one thing outside his comfort zone. Just one damn thing, something he's always wanted to try, something new, something thrilling. I helped him plan a backcountry ski trip with a group of our friends."

He paused and swallowed hard, like memories were bombarding him. "Two days before the trip, I broke my ankle rock climbing and needed surgery. I couldn't go. We talked about rescheduling, but he ended up still going because the trip wasn't refundable. On the second day, Auggie skied off trail and lost control, hitting a tree at full speed."

My mouth fell open in shock. "Oh my God."

"Yeah." Ryder knocked the back of his head against the island, staring up at the ceiling as he let out a small, baffled laugh. "I'm sorry. I don't know how we got here, with me spilling my guts, both literally and figuratively. I don't talk about this, ever."

"I'm glad you told me." I couldn't imagine the pain he'd been through. "So is you taking on Auggie's job your penance then? You have to suit up and move the pieces on the chessboard instead of doing the work you love so much?"

He didn't answer. Which was an answer in itself.

"Ryder, how's what happened your fault?"

He waved a hand. "How is it not? I set up the trip." He shoved his fingers through his hair, a frustrated gesture. "He went off trail, alone. What was he thinking?" He shook his head. "I should've been there."

Just the thought of him having died with Auggie made me tremble, and I shocked myself by reaching out for his hand. "You feel guilty."

"Every fucking day."

I could hear the pain in his voice, just as I'd heard the hesitation to even say Auggie had *died*, like putting that word out into the universe made it too real. I met his hooded gaze, his eyes dark and tormented. He'd filleted his side and hadn't so much as blinked, but grief had taken him down.

"No one could possibly blame you."

"*I* blame me."

I shook my head. "I'm so sorry you lost him. It doesn't seem fair."

"Life isn't fair." His gaze searched mine, still dark, still hurting, but somehow his expression gentled. "You know loss."

I nodded. "My dad's been gone a long time now, since I was a kid, but you never forget."

"How old were you?"

"Nine."

He winced, as if feeling my pain as his own. "Nell raised you?"

"My mom at first. Well, more like we raised each other." I smiled, even though it wasn't funny at all. "And then later on, yeah, my grandma."

"And now you're raising Wyatt. He must be your...half brother?"

"Hard to believe I'm the adult in charge, but yep." My smile was more of a grimace. "Guess we have some things in common after all—both of us stuck living a life we hadn't planned on."

"You don't have to be stuck," he said. "You could still follow your dreams. Maybe open that café your grandma mentioned."

I snorted out a laugh as I finished with the skin glue and went back into the kit for gauze. "Pipe dream."

"Doesn't have to be."

"Oh, I'm sorry, Mister Perfect Crafted-For-Him Suits that probably cost more than my car," I said on a laugh, "but some of us barely make ends meet."

The kitchen door opened and Bill strode in, heading directly for the coffeepot, muttering a string of obscenities while he was at it, something about stupid fucking thieves picking the wrong fucking company to mess with, and how if he caught them, he was "going to shove his fucking foot up their—"

He stopped short at the sight of Ryder and me on the floor, along with the bloody gauzes, and froze. "Jesus. What happened?"

"Nothing," Ryder said.

"Yeah, right. Should I be concerned?" Bill asked, looking preemptively concerned as he eyed Ryder.

"Negative."

Bill took in our positions, our closeness. The concern faded, replaced by a brows-up expression. "Am I…interrupting something?"

"Yes," Ryder said, at the exact same time I said, "No."

Bill's scowl turned upside down. In fact, he laughed out loud, even slapped his own knee. "I knew I liked you," he said to me, and then he winked. "And not just because you just won me a lovely pot of cash."

Ryder's eyes narrowed, irritation seeping from his pores.

"Tell me I'm not paying you and a bunch of nosy-ass busybodies to bet on my personal life."

"Have you met us nosy-ass busybodies?" Bill snorted. "We bet on everything. But this one wasn't my idea."

"And yet you still put money down. See that it doesn't happen again."

Bill saluted him. "You got it, boss."

"*Oh, and make sure* Penny gets the winnings. All of it."

Bill opened his mouth, clearly to balk, but Ryder cocked his head.

Looking pained, Bill nodded. "Will do."

When he was gone, Ryder shook his head, like he couldn't believe he actually paid these people. Our gazes met. "So," he murmured. "What's next for you?"

"Oh, um…" I struggled to think when my brain kept whispering in my ear to lean in a little closer and press my face to the crook of his neck and inhale him… "Work, grocery shopping, and then laundry."

He flashed a smile, and it became my immediate goal to make him do that more often. "I meant," he said on a chuckle, "what's next in your life plan. Why not the café?"

"You're hilarious." I pretended we were done with that convo, searching for medical tape to hold the gauze to his injury. "Hold still," I murmured when he went to straighten and sucked in a breath through his teeth.

"I'm fine."

I met his gaze. "Do men ever admit when they're hurt or scared?"

"It's just a scratch."

No tape, but I found a wrap to hold the gauze in place,

faltering when I had to lean into him to wrap it around his torso. It put us nearly mouth to mouth. Annoyingly breathless, I sat back, pretending to look him over as if I hadn't been doing just that for ten minutes.

"No other injuries?"

"No."

"Swear?"

The very corner of his mouth quirked. "You're good in an emergency, you know. Cool head." He paused. "You've done this before."

I found a mirthless laugh. "Oh yeah."

"As a job?"

"No."

"For…people you care about?"

I shrugged. "You'd be surprised how resourceful having crappy insurance can make you."

A ghost of a smile crossed his face but faded quickly. "So who takes care of you?"

"Me." Feeling oddly exposed, I started to gather the trash from the supplies I'd used. "Have you had a tetanus shot lately?"

"How old are you?"

I slid him a look. "Always answering a question with a question."

"Bad habit." Cocking his head, he looked me over. "Twenty-four? Maybe twenty-five? So young to be so serious."

"I'm twenty-*seven*, and if you ask Wyatt, that's ancient. Now answer my question. Have you had a tetanus shot?"

"Yes." He smiled. "You worried about me?"

"Well, you *are* adjacent to the biggest portion of my paycheck."

"Pragmatic and brutally honest," he said with a nod. "I like it."

"Yeah, well…" I gave him a shoulder check. "Give me some time. It'll grate on you soon enough."

His warm hand caught mine as he looked into my eyes. "You know that for sure, huh?"

I was finding it hard to think as he gave me a light squeeze, his calluses sliding against my own. "I do." Cold hard facts and my own past had taught me that. But…in the time I'd known him, he'd never treated me with anything but respect.

Working in a service industry, I'd learned that in general, I was mostly invisible. So I wasn't sure exactly sure when my bar had been set so low that I'd stopped expecting to be treated well. It'd been a long time since I'd felt seen, like *really* seen, and I never would've guessed it'd be this man to do it. I realized we were staring at each other again, the air practically crackling around us.

He flashed that smile of his, more than a little naughty now. "This thing seems to be getting stronger."

"You mean *worse*," I corrected.

"You think so?"

"I know it." I was still hovering over him, our mouths lined up, and the urge to close the distance shocked me. "I mean, what are we even doing?" I whispered.

He gave a slow shake of his head. "Whatever you want to be doing and nothing more."

I absorbed the words, the meaning behind them, and warmed from the inside out. "I…need to tell you something."

"Anything."

I closed my eyes. "I thought about the whole…just dinner

thing. And I'm not ready." When he didn't say anything, I opened my eyes and found him still looking at me, no bad temper, no annoyance, no irritation.

"Too soon?" he asked softly.

I nodded. "I'm sorry."

"No, don't." He shook his head. "You don't owe me an apology."

"I really want you to understand…" I bit my lower lip, let out a nervous laugh, then bit it some more. "But I don't quite understand myself. It's just that the thought of purposefully going out on a date, it's a step to a relationship, and…I'm not ready for that. But…"

"But what?"

There was a physical ache in my chest at the thought of going back to just delivering food and not seeing him, not talking and laughing… "This…talking, laughing…flirting." I gestured between us. "I like this. All of it." Especially the flirting. I couldn't explain it, but somehow it gave me back some power. "I just don't want to lead you on or anything."

"I understand. And you're not." He smiled, eyes warm. "Because I like it too."

Relief made it hard to breathe, much less speak, so I just nodded, hoping he got it.

"So how about this," he said. "We keep doing…this." We both smiled. "Nothing has to change," he said. "Not until, or if, you want it to. It's your move, Penny. Always."

I felt the smile curve my mouth. "You're putting me in the driver's seat?"

"You've always been in the driver's seat."

My smile got wider. "I do like driving."

He laughed, and then winced. Sobering, I went back to being Nurse Penny.

"Pain level from one to ten. Where you at?"

"I'm good."

"That's not a number." The waistband of his cargos had slipped low, revealing that vee cut of muscles that some guys had, the ones that made women stupid. He reached for his discarded shirt, his lean stomach folding in on itself. Mine had never done that a day in my life.

He cleared his throat, and I realized it wasn't the first time he'd done so. Caught red-handed ogling. "Hey, I'm just making sure the glue is holding and that you won't bleed out on my watch," I said.

"Uh-huh." Given the canary-eating grin on his face, he was enjoying the attention. "Hey, Penny."

"Yes?"

"You're cute when you blush. And I like when you look at me like that."

Flustered, I picked up the first aid kit. "Debt now officially paid. Be careful today."

A real smile curved his mouth. "Where's the fun in that?"

I snorted. "Fun's a luxury." I started to move toward my cart.

He slid his hand into mine, stopping me. "When I was little, my grandma always kissed my boo-boos to make me feel better." His voice was guileless, his eyes not so much.

I snorted with as much sarcasm as I could muster, but on the inside, my stomach went squishy. "Did she now?"

He nodded solemnly. "She said kisses given with care were magical and healing."

I was pretty sure I was getting a glimpse into just how much of a player he could be when he wanted. He'd probably made seduction an art form, and why shouldn't he? He was all calm confidence with a hint of bad boy swagger, and let's not forget those washboard abs. Or all the testosterone and pheromones he exuded by just breathing.

And I loved that he'd not skipped a beat at me turning him down for a date, but he'd made me feel safe when he'd listened to what I'd wanted, that I still wanted to play. And he was game. So...I didn't back down. It was my greatest character flaw, I knew this, but I also knew without a doubt that this man liked it when I played with him. And somehow, in some way I hadn't realized, I needed that. I needed to know I could go toe to toe with him, that he liked my snark, liked my challenging him.

He could have no idea that he was helping me regain some of my inner power that I hadn't felt for too long. It filled my empty tank to the brim, allowing me to access emotions that I'd locked away, things like curiosity and desire. And in the moment, just this once, I wanted to be selfish. I wanted something for myself. And to my great shock, what I wanted was him.

So in the spirit of messing with his head the way he so effortlessly messed with mine, I smirked and slowly lowered my head to his injury, absorbing and smiling at the rough sound of surprise he let out, watching as I put myself into position to make him a very happy man, and...

...brushed a chaste kiss to the bandage before straightening and shooting him an innocent smile.

A low groan rumbled from his chest. "Cruel, cruel woman."

I laughed. "Is that not how your grandma did it?"

"Funny. Come here, Wonder Woman." His eyes, heated now to a near molten gold, never left mine as he slipped one hand into the hair at my nape, the other cupping my face, tilting it the way he wanted before pressing his mouth—God, his hot mouth—over the still fresh scar just under my jaw.

If the air between us had crackled before, it burst into flames now.

Slowly he pulled back, and we stared at each other in shock at the seductive, erotic chemistry vibrating between us. I knew what he could do to me with just a look, but somehow I always forgot until I found myself whimpering on the inside for more.

"I think it's safe to say that wasn't a grandmotherly kiss," I whispered.

"No, it was not." His voice was deliciously whiskey smooth and rough at the same time. "You okay?"

"Very." I stared at his mouth. "Maybe...maybe we don't need a label for...this."

"Label, schmabel."

With a breathless laugh, I leaned into him again. "Tell me if I hurt you."

"You won't."

Guy code for: *he'd die before admitting to it.* "I mean it," I said. "I don't want to make this too hard."

"Too late," he quipped.

We were both laughing when I touched my mouth to his.

CHAPTER 10

Ryder

My heart skipped a beat when Penny kissed me, her lips warm and sweet on mine. I held still, wanting her to decide where to take this, because I already knew where *I* wanted it to go. Hell, I'd always known. Had I wanted to go out with her? Yes, but not because Nell had asked me to do so. Now that Penny had turned me down, I was off the hook.

And we had a fresh start, just her and me.

When she was ready, that was.

Her mouth hovering over mine, she hesitated, and just before she pulled back, she very gently nipped my bottom lip, tugging a groan from deep in my chest.

When her eyes fluttered open, I stared at her while my thumb slid lightly over her lips, wondering if they tingled like mine, wondering if she had any idea what she'd just done to me with that one kiss.

The memory of those three falling stars flashed in my head.

It was just a silly legend, and yet... When was the last time I felt like I was dying from a single barely there kiss? Never.

"Sometimes I look at you and I can't breathe," I murmured. Shit. Clearly, I'd hit my head instead of filleting my side—

"You probably just need an allergy pill."

Such a beautiful smart-ass. I chuckled, loving her irreverence, how she challenged me so effortlessly, reminding me that beneath all the hats I wore, all the balls I juggled, I was just a man.

A man who hadn't opened up to anyone since Auggie had died. Hell, I'd barely let my own siblings in, not really. And yet somehow, in a shockingly short amount of time, this woman had slid beneath all my brick walls, bringing me out of my own head, dragging me back to the land of the living. Being with her was easy and...fun. And if anything was missing from my life right now, it was that.

I had the feeling that Penny might feel the same. That maybe I could be the one to bring some fun to her life as well. Maybe even more than fun. The thought gave me something I hadn't felt in a while.

Hope.

And with that thought, I caught her hand and tugged her close again, my mouth aiming for hers just as Caleb stuck his head into the kitchen. "Ry?"

I considered banging the back of my head against the island some more. "Go away."

Did he? Of course not. He rounded the corner as if I hadn't spoken, eyes locked on the tablet in his hands. "The meeting's sitting around waiting for you, man. Since when are you ever late—"

He finally caught sight of me on the floor and Penny on her knees at my side, our hands still on each other.

She straightened and clasped her hands together, like "nothing to see here."

A slow smile crossed Caleb's face. "Interesting."

"Goodbye," I said.

His smile turned pure trouble, the level of trouble I'd been bailing him out of all his life—only at the moment, I didn't feel like bailing him out at all. I felt like punching him in his big, fat mouth.

"The last time *I* dared to be late," my dumbass brother said to Penny, "I had to wash all the trucks in the yard. And Tucker had just thrown up in his, due to a hangover he wouldn't admit to."

I gave him the *keep talking and die* look, which he merrily ignored. "I can only assume you accept your punishment for the tardiness. Oh, and Daniella had a vagrant climb into her truck earlier to take a nap, and let's just say you might have to wash that one *twice*." Then, with a wink at Penny, he left, sauntering down the hall whistling, the ass.

"I think I just ruined your reputation," Penny said.

I didn't tell her that she'd only enhanced it. I also didn't tell her that we seemed to be dancing to a song that didn't exist, playing a game that had only two rules. Hers. And mine.

And neither of us had a clue what those rules were.

CHAPTER 11

Penny

SEVERAL DAYS LATER, I was at my workstation, which currently looked like the definition of organized chaos: all burners going, prep table crowded with ingredients from the seven different meals I was working on simultaneously, sink stacked with used utensils, pots and pans, the air sizzling as I flipped strips of carne asada in the pan, the scent of all the spices making my mouth water.

But that wasn't why I had a stupid smile on my face. Nope, that came from reliving the dream I'd been having before my alarm had interrupted me that morning—the one where Caleb hadn't interrupted me and Ryder, no one had, and he'd nudged me up against the counter, peeled me out of the sweatshirt I was never giving back, and—

"Why do you keep letting out dreamy sighs?" Vi asked from her station next to me, which wasn't organized chaos. Just chaos. I had no idea how she knew what she was even doing with the mess around her. "You must be dreaming of more sleep, chocolate, or about a man."

"More sleep," I said instantly. "And chocolate."

She turned to me, studying my face. "Lie." She pointed at me with a spatula. "Two lies. Explain."

Only if someone first explained it to me. Yes, the kiss had been...wow. But it was more than that. Last night, I'd gone through the email Ryder had sent me and Grandma. It'd been the list of things he recommended for our kitchen, including approximate materials costs, leaving it up to us to decide what we could and couldn't afford. He'd even included a price for replacing the roof, if we wanted to go that far. It'd been thorough and thoughtful, but more importantly, it had given Grandma and me all the power.

"Hello?" Vi had switched to a knife and waved it at me. "Earth to Penny. What's going on with you?"

"Um...it's a nice day?"

"Uh-huh." Vi gave me a *get on with it* gesture. "And...?"

"And..." Now that I'd taken away the pressure of going out with Ryder, I somehow wanted to be with him even more. "I just really like my assignments from Kiera for the week."

Renee came out of her office and beelined right for us. She snagged a mini quiche from Vi. "What are we talking about?"

"Penny's new lying to my face habit." Vi looked at me. "You can't possibly like your assignments, not when you handle more than anyone else. And not because you're one of the newer people here, but because you're willing to work harder than everyone else, so Kiera takes advantage of you. All of us know it."

Renee nodded confirmation of this. "She likes you best, for sure. People are jealous."

"Is that why everyone always tells me they'd be happy to take Colburn Restorations off my hands?" I asked.

Renee snorted.

Vi outright laughed. "Honey, that's no secret. Colburn Restorations is filled to the brim with smoking-hot men, led by the smoking hottest man of them all." She looked deep into my eyes. "But as my BFF, you do realize if you ever want to dump that account, you're obligated to offer it to me first."

I laughed. "You're ridiculous."

"That's a yes, right?"

When I ignored this, she stepped closer and lifted my chin, turning my head this way and that until I smacked her hand clear. "Do you see what I see, Renee?"

Renee eyed me. Smirked. "Yep, and now that I've seen it, I don't know how we missed it."

"Missed what?" I asked.

"You got some."

"Some what?"

Vi's brows jumped up and down exaggeratedly.

I gaped, then laughed. "I'm not even dating anyone."

"Since when do you have to be dating to get some?" Vi wanted to know.

"The smile says it all," Renee said. "I wish I was smiling like that right now. I've even been sitting outside at night trying to catch sight of the Legend, but so far nothing." She sighed dramatically. "I want a reason to smile all goofily like you are."

"I'm not smiling like anything." But I was. I could still feel it. It'd been there since that morning days ago now. I couldn't get it to go away. I'd tried. "And I didn't get any."

"Maybe not the main event, but we're missing something good," Vi said, not taking her eyes off me.

I tried even harder to lose the smile and utterly failed, and her mouth fell open. "Oh my God. I'm right. Who is it? It's Ryder Colburn himself, isn't it? You like him, right? Like, you *like him* like him."

I gave myself whiplash from craning my neck to make sure no one around us had heard her. "Ohmigod, shhh!"

Vi looked around too, then tugged us out the back door, where there was a small patio that no one ever used. The early morning spring sky was a canvas painted in soft shades of blue and streaky white clouds. A gentle breeze cooled my overheated face. The only sounds were some ridiculously happy birds in the massive birch tree behind us.

Vi stared into my eyes. "You know how much I love you, right?"

Oh boy. Where was a loud airplane that prohibited a conversation when you needed one? "The last time you started a sentence like that, it was to tell me that my Indian-style roasted chicken sucked."

"It did suck," Renee said. "But your Italian roasted chicken salad is the bomb. I made it for a date once and got lucky."

Vi took my hand in hers, eyes serious now. "You never talk about guys. The only one you've ever mentioned even in passing is Ryder. I'm going to ask you again—is there something going on between you two?"

I sighed. "Maybe you've forgotten I'm broken."

"Hate to break this to you, but you don't have the market cornered on that. We're all broken. But sleeping with The Ryder Colburn would definitely fix me."

Outwardly, I rolled my eyes. Inwardly, I agreed with her. "I don't think he actually uses a 'the' before his name."

"You like him," she said.

Vi and I had been friends for much longer than my latest stint in Star Falls. We'd first met in middle school, when her and Renee's dad had run off with our very married school principal, whose jilted husband had been our science teacher.

To say life hadn't been easy on Vi and Renee was the understatement of the year.

So we'd stuck together like glue, becoming our own family. I couldn't lie to her. I mean, I could try, but Vi was like a human lie-detector test.

She snorted at the look on my face. "I'm going to take your deer-in-the-headlights gaping silence as a resounding yes on something going on with you and Mr. Sexy Pants."

"Sexy pants?"

"Self-explanatory," Renee said.

Vi nodded, not taking her eyes off me. "Tell us what's going on."

"Maybe you should define 'going on.'"

"He touch you?"

"Well, *technically* I touched him first."

Renee clapped in delight. "Yay, there was touching!"

Vi's brows vanished into her long bangs. "Did this touching involve loss of clothing? *Technically?*"

"No, Mom. We just…kissed." *Only there was very little "just" about it…*

"Maybe we should vet him," Vi said. "No one gets a free pass with my ride or die, no matter how hot he is. I'll need all the contact info you've got on him, and I'll—"

"Slow down there, Thelma. I've got this."

Renee gently set a hand on my arm. "We just worry about you."

"You don't need to. I'm fine." I tossed up my hands for emphasis. "Why does no one ever believe me?"

"After the ex-who-shall-not-be-named," Vi said, "my hatred toward any man who even looks at you burns with the passion of a thousand suns."

I managed a little laugh. "Please don't waste your energy hating on someone who no longer matters to me."

"Oh, it's really no trouble at all," Vi said dryly. "Now, will you pretty please tell us something about Ryder?"

"Well..." I figured the fact that he kisses like heaven on earth didn't apply here. "He's upfront and honest."

"Rare," Renee noted with an approving nod.

"How is he at communication?" Vi asked. "Is he willing to discuss problems?"

I thought about how he'd handled my grandma, who people most found pushy and difficult. "Maybe even more than me."

Vi scoffed. "That's not saying much. You'd rather have a root canal than discuss a problem, or heaven forbid, face a feeling."

I sighed at that true fact.

Pulling me in, Vi hugged me tight. "You know I love you, right?"

"I do." I tried to extricate myself from her hug, but she didn't let go, so I settled for patting her gently on the back. "I love you too, okay? Look, this thing with Ryder isn't really a thing. I mean, is he very attractive? Yes. Have I noticed? Also yes, because I'm not dead. But you've nothing to worry about because he's a ten and on my best day I'm a six-ish."

She pulled back and glared at me. "You're off the scale, you lovable idiot."

"*Off* the scale," Renee agreed. "I'd totally do you."

Vi's eyes were fierce. "Did he say this stupid thing about you being a six?"

"No! *No*," I repeated more softly. "Of course not. Please don't worry—this isn't going anywhere."

"Just tell me you didn't sleep with him and then get the 'this isn't going anywhere' speech."

I gently squeezed Vi's fingers. "Honey, that's what happened to *you*. And I still feel murderous enough that Kyle should be happy he moved out of town. We've all been through it, but we're smarter now, and tougher. We don't give away our heart on a whim."

Vi sighed out her tension, then held out her pinkie. "Swear it. We don't give our hearts away on a whim. Not ever again."

"Amen to that." Renee stuck out her pinkie.

Since I could get behind that, I did the same.

Thirty minutes later, I was inside Colburn Restorations. Yesterday, Kiera told me that a request had come through for me to prep a conference room with food for a large production meeting. I headed there first and hadn't done more than set the brakes on my cart when Ryder poked his head in.

"Hey," he said, voice and smile warm.

It caused an answering warmth low in my belly, and just like that, the goofy smile was back on my face. "Hey."

We stared at each other for a beat. I could get lost in those hazel eyes, the way the golds mingled with the greens and browns. I had no idea what he was thinking, but I was thinking *yum*. Needing a distraction before I made a fool of myself, I looked around, settling on a picture on the back wall of a very old, beat-up work truck parked in front of a building even older than the vehicle. Ryder followed my line of sight. "When Auggie and I started this company, we had nothing more than that ancient Chevy full of second-hand tools and our hands. Our first job was the Devereux building on the commercial row of downtown."

"Really? I love that building. I don't remember much about what it looked like before, but now I marvel at it every time I pass by."

He came up to my side, hands in his pockets. "The property belonged to my grandfather," he said, gaze on the pic. "When he died, my siblings and I inherited it. It was basically falling off its axis."

"It had flooded, right?"

"Yeah. It was a mess when we got it. Not worth much, but I knew there was potential." His smile was rueful. "We borrowed on the equity up to the eyeballs. Then I renovated, hoping to give us a shot at selling high so we could each have a fresh start."

"You renovated by yourself?"

"At first, yes. I couldn't afford subcontractors or employees back then. Hell, at the time, I could barely afford food. Auggie came on board during that project to manage the paperwork and permits. And Colburn Restorations was born."

I could picture it—a younger Ryder, driven to bring a beloved building back to its former glory, working his ass off to make something of himself while he was at it.

"It couldn't have been easy."

"No," he said on a rough laugh. "Nothing about that job was easy. I lived there, working on it day and night, practically having to beg, borrow, and steal for materials. My siblings helped out as they could, but eventually, I hired Bill too. We stripped it down to the studs, put in new electrical and plumbing, new everything. Auggie's sister was a budding architect and had a roommate who was into interior design. The two of them were broke too, and pretty much worked for pizza and beer until I was able to sell and then pay them. Pay all of us."

"Not just a pretty face," I teased.

He snorted, then looked at me for a long, charged beat, in a way few others ever had. As if I were entirely unbreakable, a force in my own right, like maybe he found that extremely attractive.

Not quite knowing what to with all that sexy, male focus on me, the undiluted attention, I squirmed a little bit. His eyes lit with amusement, but he didn't actually smile. Stayed serious.

"I want to show you something," he finally said.

"Ha. For that, I'd need at least three dates, and one of them would have to include dessert—but it's all a moot point since I'm not dating."

The corner of his mouth twitched. "All good to know, but not what I meant."

He took me to his office, gesturing me in ahead of him, and damn, the man smelled so good I almost turned into him and pressed my entire face into the crook of his neck.

One wall of his office was entirely windows that showed off a stunning view of the Russian River, a ribbon of silver winding through the heart of the countryside, lush meadows either side of the riverbank. The office itself had been done in the same theme as the rest of the building, wood and metal accents, masculine while also warm and welcoming. Nothing on his desk except a closed laptop, two sets of rolled up blueprints, and…two sippy cups, the kind toddlers use, along with two tiny tool belts, complete with little tools in the compartments.

I smiled. "You've had some company."

"It was my morning with them before preschool," he said. "They love it here."

What's not to love?

Ryder took a photo album off the shelf and set it on the desk in front of me.

I smiled. "Okay, Grandpa."

"Just open it, smart-ass."

I began flipping through the incredible story of the Devereux Building's transformation and found myself transfixed.

"It was built in the late 1800s by a prominent winemaker," he said. "So the bones were amazing. It just needed some love."

It was fun to see the progress in pictures. The stone structure had been meticulously restored, blending its classic Victorian character with contemporary elegance, complete with large picture windows, fieldstone façade, and a massive wraparound porch adorned with intricate latticework.

"Auggie was a photographer at heart." Ryder stared at the photos, memories in his eyes. "He took these to record the progress. I've got it all saved on the cloud, but this book's my favorite thing of his that I have."

I let out a slow breath, understanding. Deeply. Flipping through the pages, I took in the incredible before and after shots. "This is amazing." *He* was amazing. "What did you do next?" I asked.

He gave a slow shake of his head. "Your turn."

"Oh, well, um..." Honestly, I never knew how to talk about myself. I didn't have a colorful story like he did. No *aha* moment defining my chosen path in life. I'd grown up, worked to support my family, and slept. The lack of a personal life felt...embarrassing. I looked around for another distraction but failed to find one.

So I pulled out my phone and gestured to it, like *oh look at that, I'm getting a call...* I even went so far as to put the phone to my ear. "Hello? Yes, absolutely," I said to no one. "I'll be right there—" I broke off as...

My phone rang. For real.

Stifling a grimace, I glanced at Ryder, expecting annoyance or even anger.

He was grinning.

As my phone kept ringing...

"You need to get that?" he asked, leaning back against his desk lazily, like he had all the time in the world to watch me embarrass myself.

Since it was my brother calling, I answered with, "The person who owns this phone has reached her people quota for the day, please hang up and try again tomorrow."

"Not funny," Wyatt said. "I need you to pick me up after school, my bike's got a flat."

I sighed. "I'll be there." I disconnected and eyed a still grinning Ryder. "This is your fault."

"Do tell."

"You're standing all close to me, smelling so good I can't think. You need to back up."

Looking quite pleased with himself, he lifted his hands in surrender and backed up. "Anything else?"

"Stop smiling."

"That might prove difficult."

It really should be illegal how sexy he was. "I'm going now."

He didn't stop smiling.

With a roll of my eyes, I managed to walk out of there calmly, but the minute I crossed his doorstep into the hallway,

I broke into a walk/run, fleeing like the hounds of hell were on my heels.

Or the biggest, hottest distraction I'd ever met.

CHAPTER 12

Penny

LOVED IT WHEN ONE of my clients at Hungry Bee needed to reschedule a delivery, especially if it was the first client of any given day. The luxury of a few extra hours of sleep always did wonders for my skin.

And for beating down murderous urges.

And yet, something had me on edge. I wasn't sure what would help. No, scratch that. I knew exactly what would help—a onetime thing with one sexy CEO Ryder Colburn.

No strings attached.

No emotions getting tangled.

No promises.

No looking back.

But even if just thinking of it revved my engine, I wasn't sure I had the nerve to go there. I'd never been able to sleep with someone and not attach a string or tangle my emotions.

Rolling over, I checked my phone. I had a text from Grandma

letting me know she was taking Wyatt to school, and then Hank to the library for story time.

Having the house to myself was so rare, I immediately slid out of bed, intent on scrounging up the ingredients for a big breakfast.

Then I remembered...renovation. Today after work, Ryder was going to help us demo, so we hadn't gone to the grocery store and stocked up this week. By tonight, the electrical, gas, and water to the kitchen would be disconnected, and the kitchen sealed off from the living room to try to minimize dust to the rest of the house. The appliances would be pulled, with the exception of the fridge, which would stay either in the laundry room or on the back porch until Ryder was ready to lay down the new flooring. Grandma and I had been poring over samples for that, along with paint colors, granite for the countertops, and new appliances.

A thrill went through me every time I thought about it. Okay, so I'd make do with instant coffee and a granola bar instead this morning. Breakfast of champions. Padding barefoot in my pj's, I walked through the quiet house. Another luxury.

"Boo!"

I jumped, then sagged, a hand to my heart as I eyeballed Pika-boo watching me from his perch. "That's just mean."

Pika-boo paused, then, as if he couldn't help himself, whispered, "Did you poop today?"

"Did you?"

He immediately starting bebopping his little head up and down, the parrot equivalent to a dog's poop zoomies. "Good for you."

"I'm a good boy! The goodest of good boys!"

"You are," I told him as I headed to the kitchen. There were tarps out and tools, and I realized the floor was a danger zone for my bare feet. Just inside the doorway, against a wall next to a broom and a massive pry bar and a ladder, was a tool belt and a pair of work boots.

Ryder had left them here along with the rest of his tools, so he didn't have to cart them back and forth while the job was ongoing. Hmm. Why not, right? So I stepped into the massive boots, then stared down at the tool belt. It seemed lonely down there by itself, so I buckled it around my waist. Everything that hung from the belt jingled—a hammer, putty knife, utility knife, screwdriver, and some other stuff, all of it weighing so much it nearly took me down to the floor. How did he do it?

Maybe that's what all the muscles were for.

In the big boots, I clomped and clinked across the kitchen to the box in the laundry room where we'd left our to-go cups and instant coffee, heading straight for the fridge in hopes of finding a miracle.

As expected, it was meager pickings, even in the freezer, but just in case, I bent low to see if there was, say, a chocolate cake mysteriously left in the veggie drawer.

At a sudden sharp inhale behind me, I jerked upright, smacking my head on the still-open freezer door. Stars danced in front of my eyes as I fell to my butt.

"Shit." Suddenly Ryder was there, hands in my hair, checking the top of my head with gentle fingers. "You okay?"

I opened my eyes to glare at him, but something about the sight of him on his knees, looking a little hot and sweaty in jeans and a long-sleeved tee covered in some construction dust made me forget what I wanted to say.

"Penny?" His hands were still in my hair, tipping my face up to see into my eyes. "Talk to me."

"It's not fair."

"What?"

I blew a strand of hair from my face. "I bet you didn't even brush your hair this morning and you still look edible."

He blinked, then gave a slow smile. "Just how hard did you hit your head?"

Not hard enough... I pushed him away, then rose with as much dignity as I could, given that I was in boots that could've belonged to a giant and wearing a tool belt that possibly weighed more than I did.

Still on his knees, he looked me over, from the tips of his own boots, to my...crap...itty-bitty Hello Kitty camisole and short shorts, to the tool belt slung around my waist.

His smug-ass smile was so full of himself, I wanted to kick him. Which was much better than wanting to kiss him.

"Are you wearing my tool belt?"

"I can explain," I said.

Grinning, he sank back on his heels and gestured for me to have at it.

"So...I woke up *starving*. I came down to grab some food before I remembered I live in a construction zone, and I wasn't wearing any shoes." I looked at his feet. "Why aren't you barefoot?"

"These are my demo boots. They get too dirty to use for anything else." He pointed to the ones I wore. "Those are my regular work boots. They look great on you, by the way."

I felt my face flush, and he laughed softly. "And the tool belt?"

"I can't explain that."

He nudged a chin at me. "New pajamas?"

"No." I looked down at the Hello Kitties all over my little shorts, and the singular Hello Kitty across my breasts. "But they're cute, right?"

"Not my first thought."

Lifting my head, I met his gaze. His dark, heated gaze. "Oh," I murmured brilliantly.

Amusement came into his eyes. "Yeah. *Oh*. And you should keep the tool belt, it looks better on you than me."

He was wrong about that, very wrong. Then he brushed calloused fingers along my hip, just above the leather of the belt, and my brain stopped working.

Tipping his head back, he looked into my face. "You seem dazed. You sure you're all right? What day is it?"

I had no idea, and the stupor had nothing to do with hitting my head. The cause for it was on his knees before me. "I'm good."

"Yeah? How many of me do you see?"

I took in his jeans, the ones that looked buttery and soft, cupping him in allllll the right places. "Just the one," I managed.

His eyes crinkled at the corners. "You're drooling."

I swiped my mouth before thinking, glowering at Ryder's rough and throaty laugh. "Hate you."

He gave me a very slow, very dirty smile. "Liar."

True. I was absolutely lying to myself, pretending I didn't have feelings for him. And though I had no idea why, I was pretty sure he had feelings for me too, even if he was being careful with me, not pushing. Somehow I knew he never would. I'd have to be the one to make the next move. Was I ready for that? Testing myself, I leaned in so that we were almost, but not quite, mouth to mouth.

His eyes softened, but he didn't so much as shift an inch. "Penny? Whatcha doing?"

I froze. "I thought that might be obvious."

His gaze dropped to my mouth. "I'm trying to respect your boundaries."

"I didn't stipulate any boundaries."

"Not out loud," he agreed. "But your body tells me everything I need to know."

I looked down at myself. Crap. I had my arms crossed. And in response, he'd leashed himself.

But I didn't want him leashed. I relaxed my arms and shifted closer. Testing. Still on his knees, his hands fisted on his thighs as though it was an effort to hold back.

"Penny." Almost an inaudible groan.

I wasn't trying to tease. I was trying to see how comfortable I felt, and apparently I was *very* comfortable testing my limits, and his too—and he was letting me. I couldn't stop staring at his mouth. Could I just take what I wanted? Was it that simple?

"Can I…"

"Anything," he said.

I met his gaze. "You too."

He never took his eyes from mine as one of his big, warm hands slid to my nape while the other cupped my jaw, the pad of his thumb gently running over my scar.

"Okay?" he whispered.

"Very." I slowly placed my hand on his chest. "Can I kiss you?"

"*Yes.*" His eyes turned liquid fire. "And for future reference, I'm checking the I-accept-the-terms box in perpetuity—"

I was laughing when I kissed him, but I melted at the first

touch of his tongue, letting him in, drawing a rough male sound of approval that reverberated into my chest and headed south. Within a single heartbeat, he'd pulled me into his lap and wrapped me up in him as if he was afraid I'd disappear. We kissed slow and long, rocking into each other, the feel of him against me softening every inch of my body.

It had the opposite effect on every inch of him. A little unnerved at how much I wanted to explore those inches, I reluctantly pulled back.

"Damn," I said softly. "It's still there."

"My tongue?"

I laughed. "The attraction."

"Did you expect it to stand up and walk away?"

"I didn't expect it to happen at all."

The front door opened, and a few seconds later, Grandma stuck her head into the kitchen. "Hey, kiddies, we're back—Oh," she said when she caught sight of us.

"Ah," Hank said, coming up behind Grandma, and pointed at us.

"What Hank's saying is we're going to go out to breakfast," Grandma said, grinning from ear to ear. "So you just go back to...whatever you're doing."

Hank nodded, like that was exactly what he wanted to say too.

"How do you feel about pancakes, Hank?"

"Ahhhhhhhhh."

"Hank feels real good about pancakes," Grandma said. "So no worries. I'll bring you some back."

And then Ms. Nosy was gone.

"You know what she thinks we're going to do, right?" I stared at Ryder, daring him to laugh.

He just smiled. "She loves you."

"Actually, she loves *you*."

He shrugged. "I'm extremely lovable."

"Says you."

"Says everyone."

"Wow," I said. "How do you get your big head through a doorway?"

A mischievous light came into his eyes, and he opened his mouth, but I covered it with my hand.

He nipped my finger.

With a laugh, I pulled my hand back, but he got a hold of me, his hands tightening on my hips so I couldn't go anywhere.

"What happened to my boundaries?" I asked.

"You dropped them and let me in."

True story. So I kissed him again. His lips were warm, and tasted like my forgotten hopes and dreams, and something more. Something I'd been missing.

Heart-stopping and heart-melting spontaneity.

Bliss.

His fingers tightened in my hair, gently tugging just enough to break the kiss so he could stare into my eyes, his own warm, curious. I wasn't sure what he was looking for exactly, but I did my best to look like a woman who knew what I wanted—an orgasm *not* of my own making, please and thank you.

A corner of his mouth tipped up in a sexy almost-smile, and I really hoped that meant good things were coming. Like maybe *me*.

"Penny."

"Ry," I said in a low register, mimicking his serious tone.

The whole smile appeared on his face and whatever bones hadn't already melted were complete liquid now. And all I could think was how long did we have before Grandma and Hank returned? For instance, did we have enough time for him to whisper in my ear exactly what he wanted to do to me while stripping off my clothes, those hazel eyes heated and hungry as he laid me out before him like his own personal platter of pancakes—

A laugh then, soft and throaty, brought me out of my erotic daydream.

"Yes to whatever you're thinking," he said, voice so deep as to be almost inaudible. "Tell me everything, slowly, in graphic detail."

Oh boy. "I'm better with show, not tell." I started to pull off my top, then hesitated. "But this isn't going to mean anything… right?"

"I'll let you wrestle with that one." He didn't hesitate, didn't pause as his mouth settled on mine. I don't know what I expected; short and sweet, or wild and frenzied…but it was neither.

And better.

With a nip of his teeth, he coaxed my lips apart. He didn't have to try very hard. I was so eager I pulled him as close as I could get him, and—

"Oh man, in the kitchen?" Wyatt stood in the doorway, looking disgusted as only a twelve-year-old could.

I jerked back. "What is happening?" I pointed at my brother. "Why aren't you at school?"

"Because it's some stupid in-service. Tommy messed up too. His mom came and got us." A smug, payback light came into his eyes as he looked at me. "Did you get verbal consent? Were you respectful of his personal boundaries?"

Ryder looked amused. *Better than horrified...* "She was very respectful," he said.

"Good." Wyatt gave me his most evil little brother smile. "Oh, and remember, don't be a fool, wrap your tool." He stepped over us to peer in the fridge. "So...what's for breakfast?"

CHAPTER 13

Ryder

ON FRIDAY MORNING, I stood in the parking garage of Colburn Restorations in front of one of our work trucks, staring at Bill and Grif, both of whom were grimacing.

"So you're telling me," I said, "that this truck, already loaded with what, thirty thousand dollars' worth of lumber…"

They both nodded.

"…is due on the Somerset job in one hour, where a framing crew will be waiting, only the truck won't start, probably the battery's dead, and there's no other truck available."

Two more nods.

"How?" I asked.

"Here." Grif turned his ever-present iPad around to show me the vehicle schedule for the week. "It's a hot mess."

He was right. We were overloaded and there was not a single other truck available, which meant that one very expensive framing crew was going to sit on their ass at the jobsite, every breath they took costing us a fortune.

Bill rubbed his bald head and sighed. "Eddie was supposed to show up here last night for a service. I don't know why that didn't happen."

Eddie was the mechanic who handled our entire fleet as needed. And it didn't matter why it didn't happen—what mattered was *not* wasting an entire team's salary for the day.

"It gets worse," Bill said.

Of course it did.

"Daniella called in sick. So I was going to run to the Phillips job for her, make sure the guys know what to do, then get back here in time to take this load to Somerset."

"Do we have a battery here?" I asked.

Grif's fingers flew over the iPad. "Yes. We do."

I began to shrug out of my suit jacket.

"I can call the crew," Bill said. "Push everything a day, but they'll still charge for—"

"No need. I've got this." I started rolling up my sleeves.

Bill blinked in surprise. "What are you doing?"

"We can't have a dime holding up a dollar."

Bill narrowed his eyes. "*You're* going to change the battery?"

"What, you don't think I can?"

"I think you could rebuild that entire truck without breaking a sweat, but you're dressed all fancy like for a bunch of meetings you've got on the books for today. The accountant, the lawyer…"

Yep, but suddenly I saw a way out of those boring meetings. "My problem, not yours. Go. The truck'll be ready when you get back."

Bill just shook his head. "You want to play hooky, boy, why not call in sick and go climb a mountain or something?"

I looked pointedly at the time on my phone and he sighed.

HE FALLS FIRST

"Right. Fuck. Fine, I'll hurry." He turned to go, then paused. "You know how I bitch about your generation being lazy dumbshits?"

I just looked at him.

"You're not one of them."

Then he was gone, just as my phone buzzed an incoming text on the Colburn sibling thread.

CALEB
> Need a ride to work.

TUCKER
> Call one of your leftover hockey bunnies.

KIERA
> Offensive.

CALEB
> VERY offensive.

TUCKER
> Translation—you can't call one of them. They're like cats. If you call, you can't get rid of them.

ME
> What's wrong with your truck?

CALEB
> ...

ME
> ??

CALEB

Fine. Some asshole slashed my tires.

TUCKER

Translation—you ghosted a woman and she retaliated.

CALEB

I didn't ghost anyone. I always make it clear I'm a bad bet. But some asshole posted online that I saw the stupid Legend the other night and women are coming out of the woodwork.

TUCKER

You're the asshole. You made that post.

CALEB

Is someone coming to get me or what?

TUCKER

Or what.

I bang my phone against my forehead.

ME

Go get the truck fixed.

CALEB

You need me at work. You can't live without me.

TUCKER

> The only thing he can't live without is his phone charger, which you are not.

CALEB

> Wow. You're just jealous because no one DM's you asking for a pic of your six-pack.

TUCKER

> Hate to break it to you, but the only six-pack women really want to see are empathy, authenticity, integrity, maturity, self-awareness, and communication.

CALEB

> You got stuck at the dentist office and had to read a touchy-feeling book again, didn't you?

TUCKER

Thirty minutes later, I'd just finished up replacing the battery and texting Bill and Grif that it was done and ready to go when I heard the sound of a cart and familiar light footsteps. I straightened from the engine compartment of the truck in time to catch Penny Rose staring at my ass.

"See anything you like?"

Her cheeks pinkened. "As if you don't know you've got a great ass."

I laughed, but as she shoved at the cart, fighting two bad wheels, my smile faded. "That thing's going to get you killed. Let me fix the wheels."

"Seems like you're already pretty busy."

"I just finished."

She used her forearm to swipe some hair from her face. Her ponytail holder had once again failed her. She wore her usual work uniform of a simple white blouse and black pants, which I'd seen a hundred times before, little makeup, and her usual morning scowl, and I thought she looked beautiful.

"Don't you usually park out front?" I asked.

"You were getting a big delivery and there wasn't room."

I really needed to assign her a parking spot.

She eyed my suit jacket hanging off the side-view mirror. "What are you doing back here getting all dirty?"

I flashed her a grin. "I keep telling you, I like getting dirty."

She rolled her eyes, and I laughed. "Our mechanic isn't available, but we need this truck today. It just needed a new battery." I shrugged. "Easy enough."

"For you, maybe."

"You already know I like working with my hands."

"You're trying to ruffle me," she said.

"Is it working?"

"Absolutely not. And you realize you're the boss, right? You could've called a mechanic."

"I have one—he's not available. Normally, it could wait, but we need the lumber on this truck at a jobsite ASAP."

"The buck stops with you." She nodded. "I understand that."

I knew she did. In her world, she was the same as me—the person who solved all the problems. I crouched before her cart and examined the wheels.

"Can I help?" she asked.

"Hand me the pliers from the toolbox?"

She shuffled through the box. "These?"

"Yep." I traded the wrench in my hand for it, which she dropped back into the toolbox, then stared at her hands.

Dirty. Shit. I straightened. "Sorry, just swipe your hand on my pants."

"What? Are you nuts?" She eyed my suit. "Your pants are probably worth more than my entire year's clothing budget."

"You're thinking like a girl."

"Hello, I *am* a girl!"

I started unbuttoning my shirt.

She squeaked but didn't take her eyes off me as I shrugged out of the shirt and hung it next to my suit jacket. I then tugged off the white t-shirt I'd worn beneath and held it out to her. "Here, use this."

She gaped at me like I'd asked her to jump off a cliff. "I'm not using your spotless t-shirt to wipe my grubby hands!"

Cute. Taking the shirt back, I used it to clean off my hands first. "There. No longer spotless." I tossed it to her, giving her two choices: catch it with her face or with her hands. She used her hands. Smart girl.

"Are you always this chivalrous?"

"No."

She laughed and rubbed her hands clean while running her eyes over my torso. I opened my mouth to tease her about it when she reached out and ran a finger over the healing gash on my side.

I nearly closed my eyes at the touch. It was a huge effort on my part to stand still instead of scooping her up and finding a more private place to let her touch me wherever she wanted.

"It's going to scar," she said unhappily. Her other hand went to her jaw. "Like mine."

Scratch wanting her to touch me. I wanted to wrap her up tight and assure her that she was safe here, with me. That, if she allowed it, I'd make sure nothing like that happened to her ever again.

There was a darkness to her gaze now, and I could see her closing ranks, pulling inward, and fuck, I needed to go hunt down the asshole who'd laid a hand on her. But that wasn't what *she* needed. What she needed was to feel in control, to feel strong and safe, on her own.

I slowly lifted a hand toward her. "Can I?" I asked quietly.

She nodded, trusting me. A fact that made my heart squeeze so hard it hurt. I gently cupped her face, letting my thumb glide over her scar. "Does it still hurt?"

Her eyes closed and she gave a small head shake, but whether that was *no, it doesn't hurt* or *I don't want to talk about it*, I had no idea. What I did know what was that she felt shame about the scar, and I hated that most of all.

"Does yours?" she whispered.

My heart gave a good, hard squeeze. And how had she even gotten to my heart? I had no idea, but I couldn't deny it, couldn't pretend she didn't mean something to me.

I shook my head. "I had a good medic." I smiled. "Good thing too. My flag football team's in the finals tonight and we intend to win."

"You're going to play injured?"

"Wouldn't be my first time."

She gave a snort and stepped back.

I cocked my head, seeing a flash of something in her eyes. "You okay?"

"Sure." She was looking anywhere but at me now. The other vehicle, the toolbox, the ceiling...

I snagged her hand, worried I'd missed something. "You know it's also okay not to be okay." Fact was, I lived in that state a lot of the time.

She lifted her head, staring at me.

"What?"

"No one's ever said that to me before."

I gave a wry smile. "I learned it the hard way."

Her features softened and she squeezed my hand back. "What do you do when you're…not okay?"

"Stupid shit." I gestured with a head tilt to the truck behind us. "Exhibit A: problem solve when I have a million other things to do."

That earned me a short laugh. Her hair had slipped almost entirely out of her ponytail now. With a sound of exasperation, she lifted her arms and redid it. And then frowned and redid it again.

"Hey." Gently, I caught her hands. "If you're having second thoughts about how we interact, it's okay."

"It's not that." Her eyes held mine, willing me to understand. "It's just…"

"You're not ready."

"But not because of you. It's me. I don't…gah." She drew a deep breath. "I don't trust myself. I mean, I'm working on it, but…"

My chest ached for her. I nodded. "I understand."

"I hope you do, because"—she stared at me for a long beat—"I'm having regrets."

Heart. Stopped. "It's okay—"

"No. My regrets are about deciding not to go out with you."

I blinked.

She gave me a small smile. "I realized that sitting at a table in a restaurant somewhere talking and laughing wouldn't be any different from standing here in front of a big truck…right?"

Her eyes were round, and I realized her worry was more about the possibility I'd lose interest than her being ready. As if I could ever lose interest.

"Penny." I brought our entwined hands to my chest. "I won't rush you on this. And I'm not going anywhere. Okay?"

She took a deep breath. "Okay."

"Baby steps?"

She nodded, giving me a relieved smile. "Baby steps. But we're still not going to stop, right?"

The question, asked with enough emotion that I felt another pinch to my heart now, telling me just how deep I was into her, made me want to sag with relief.

"Not until you want to."

"I don't." Her gaze dropped to my mouth and something much more than relief rolled through me.

"Whenever you're ready, Pen. No rush." I adjusted the wheels on her cart and steered it onto the elevator for her. Reaching in, I hit the button for the ground floor, then backed off.

She blinked at me. "You're not coming?"

"Not yet," I said, and smiled as she laughed while the doors slowly closed on her pretty face.

CHAPTER 14

Penny

ON SATURDAY MORNING, I awoke to the scent of coffee. Grandma was sitting on the edge of my bed, holding a steaming mug as she blew that steam towards my nose. When she saw my eyes open, she grinned. "So…isn't tonight the night? Whatcha going to wear to go out with Ryder?"

"Oh. Um…" I sat up and sipped the coffee. "Something came up."

Her face fell. "He canceled on you?"

"Actually…"

"*Penelope.* You bailed?"

"Not bailed…not exactly. I just…" I sighed. "Okay, yes. I bailed. But only temporarily."

Grandma nodded and stood, looking down at me, her eyes warm and kind despite her disappointment. "I know you don't want to talk about it, so I'll just say this one thing. If you let fear run your life, you'll never know what you missed out on."

I thought about that as I showered. Fear wasn't holding me

back. It was more about trust. But I trusted Ryder, more than I thought possible.

It was myself I didn't quite trust.

Twenty minutes later, I was in the kitchen going through some color samples Ryder had left for us when my phone chirped an incoming call from an unknown number. I'd long ago blocked Mitch's cell. It could be anyone calling, maybe one of Grandma's doctors, so I forced myself to connect the call.

"Hello?"

"Hey, Penny."

At the sound of Ryder's voice, I nearly sagged in relief. "Hey."

Long pause. "You okay? You sound...off."

I put a hand to my racing heart with a mirthless laugh. "You want the short or long answer?"

There was a beat of silence, like he was checking my pulse and mental health through the phone. "With you, I always want the long answer."

Had I ever met anyone like him? "When my phone buzzed, I didn't recognize this number and for a minute, I thought..." I took a gulp of air. Why was I telling him this?

"You thought it might be someone you didn't want to talk to," he said carefully.

I nodded, then realized he couldn't see me. "Yes."

"Has someone been...bothering you?"

"No." I touched my jaw. "Sometimes my mind just likes to rake me over the coals."

"Understandable," he said quietly. "Do you think you could do something for me? If you ever feel like you're in danger, I want you to call 911, and then me immediately after. I'll come to you, no matter what I'm doing, I promise you. Can you do that?"

My throat tightened. He *always* took me seriously. No "there, there" pats on the head, no empty platitudes. And it meant more to me than I could ever explain.

"Penny."

"Yes," I said softly. "I can do that."

"Thank you," he said, sounding relieved.

"Did you win your game last night?" I asked, desperately needing a subject change now.

"We did. Got a fancy trophy and everything."

I found a smile. "You going to carry it around to show it off?"

"No, but only because Tucker snatched it first. I plan to steal it back—if Caleb doesn't get to it before me, like last year. Almost got arrested too, when a neighbor mistook him for a cat burglar breaking into Tucker's place."

I was boggled. "You break into each other's places?"

"Sure. It's gotten trickier since the time Tucker set up sticky mouse traps in the closet where he'd hidden the trophy. Caleb still bitches about having to throw away his shoes."

"Your own brother set up traps for you."

"Yep, and he's damned sneaky about it too. So I'll probably wait until Caleb steals the trophy, then break into his house, because his traps are easy to beat."

"Unlike, I assume, yours."

"You got it."

I laughed. "Wow."

"Was that 'wow, I'm impressed' or 'wow, you dodged a bullet'?"

My face was beginning to hurt from smiling. "I mean... maybe both?"

He laughed then too, the sound making my day, but I didn't want to keep him from his. "Did you call just to make me laugh?"

"No, but it was a nice bonus. Just wanted to let you know I'll be over tonight to work on the kitchen, if that works for you."

Like I'd turn down the opportunity to see him in that tool belt again… "See you then."

Later that evening, I was out front watering grandma's flowers and making a mental list of what needed to be done outside now that spring was here. We needed to paint the trim, clean the bricks—and the biggie—replace the roof…

Ryder ambled up the walkway, stride loose-limbed, every lean hard muscle shifting with easy grace. He was in jeans and a t-shirt, hair still damp and curling around his ears like he'd just showered. I didn't realize I was staring until water soaked into my sneakers. I'd accidentally watered them.

"Dammit!"

He smirked, and it was only because I knew him now that I could see the exhaustion behind it. "Long day?"

"Felt like a month," he admitted.

"We don't have to do this tonight."

"I want to."

I nodded, biting my lip because I wanted to do a lot more than renovate the kitchen tonight. And when had this happened? When had I stopped being able to think about anything other than seeing him naked?

"You okay?" he asked.

"Yep. One hundred percent okay. In fact, I'm two hundred percent okay."

He raised a brow.

"You know what? I'm going out back to water. Let yourself in."

His smile was slow and sexy as hell. "Trying to avoid me?"

More like trying to avoid jumping him. Not that I could say so—it'd go right to his big, fat head.

"I just think it might be best if we're not alone." Ever…

His eyes lit like it was Christmas morning. "You don't think you can control yourself."

I grimaced, and he tipped his head back and laughed.

"I don't see how this is funny," I muttered.

His grin remained. "I'm going inside. To put on my tool belt. And get all dirty and sweaty. You know where to find me if you need anything." And then he sauntered into the house.

Ugh, he was so smug. And…and I couldn't stop smiling, so ridiculously comforted that this thing between us, whatever it was, wouldn't stop just because I was a chickenshit.

CHAPTER 15

Penny

OVER THE NEXT FEW weeks, Ryder came over almost every night, and all of us—me, Grandma, Wyatt, and Ryder—put in time on the renovation.

And as it turned out, I wasn't the only Rose family member who had a crush on our contractor. My brother and Grandma seemed to share my sentiment, though I doubted they wanted to press him up against the wall and have their merry way with him.

And I did. I wanted that. I wanted that badly. Do not ask me why I yearned and burned and fantasized about just that, and yet the idea of going out on a date paralyzed me.

It was dumb.

I was dumb.

Ryder had reminded me I was in the driver's seat. Which wasn't to say he'd stopped with the heated looks, the occasional touch that revved me up as we worked, as we talked about anything and everything…all of it telling me he was in when and if I got there. And if not, the friendship would remain on solid footing.

He was unlike any man I'd ever met.

It was late, just past midnight. After painting the kitchen, Grandma and Wyatt had gone to bed several hours ago now, and I'd finished cleaning paintbrushes and was sitting on the closed washing machine in the laundry room watching Ryder work on one of the four electrical panels scattered haphazardly around the house.

In a pair of faded, ripped jeans and a t-shirt advertising a local brewery, he had his eyes narrowed, concentrating on his task, his posture relaxed and easy, like what he was doing was second nature to him and even something he enjoyed.

And I did something *I* enjoyed—watching him, just your average successful, enigmatic CEO, a little rough and tumble, more than a little badass, who also happened to be far more confident than I was.

He squatted low, rifling through a toolbox, then stretched for a screwdriver, the leather of his tool belt crinkling, his shirt riding up... Did guys know how to move to purposely look jumpable? And why was his hind view just as good as the front? Why didn't he have a bad side?

"Something on your mind?" he asked.

Yep. Like what did he look like without those clothes. And what might he do with that body...to mine.

"You do realize," he said, hands still working, voice smoking hot, eyes flashing laughter, "that you're staring at my ass again."

Eep. Caught once more.

Ryder rose, and I couldn't look away from him—the breadth of his shoulders, the strong, capable, work-roughened hands that I wanted all over me.

"For what it's worth," he said, ambling closer, "I can't keep my eyes off you either." And then he was there, *right* there, bumping into my knees, ducking his head enough to see into my eyes. Mine drifted shut, thinking, hoping, he was going to kiss me... But when nothing happened, I opened up again.

Only a breath away, he slowly tilted his head. A silent question. Did I want this kind of attention from him?

And God help me, I did. "Is this a cliché?" I asked, staring at his mouth. "The hot contractor and the lonely homeowner making out in the laundry room?"

"Yes, but don't let it stop you." He held my gaze locked in his. "Are you lonely, Penny?"

"Not when you're around."

His gaze dipped to my mouth, and then slowly down the rest of me, making me shiver in the best of ways.

"Are there...other women?" I asked softly.

"No." His smile was self-deprecating. "It's been a while since I've...put myself out."

"Did you get hurt?" I asked.

Something came and went in his eyes. "Not like you."

Heat flooded my face, and I started to climb down from the washer, but he gently caught me.

"I'm okay, you know," I said quietly. "I'm stronger than I look."

"I know. I've seen you lift more than some men." His hands slid to my hips, squeezing gently. "You're one of the strongest women I know, Penny. Inside and out." He drew a deep breath. "I've had relationships. I was with someone when Auggie died. She stuck for a bit, but I was...overwhelmed, and it got to be too much for her. Since then..." He shrugged. "I've only wanted casual."

"And now?" I whispered.

"And now...." He ran a finger along my temple, then the rim of my ear as he tucked a loose strand back. "Now I'm...changing my mind on that."

He knew my stance there, and I could tell he wanted to hear more about my past but didn't want to push, which made it easier to talk about it. "I was with someone in college for a while, but life kinda got in the way. And then, my next relationship, I—" I drew a breath. "I left him."

His gaze slipped to the scar on my jaw and his own tightened. "Strongest woman I know," he repeated softly.

In that moment, I wished I'd gone through with our date. It'd been a hump I needed to get over, and I knew it. But now I'd made it a mountain. A part of me wished Ryder would make it easy for me, nudge and goad me into it.

But I knew he wouldn't. He wanted me to prove to myself just how okay I was. I just needed to find my brave.

"Can you do me a favor?" I asked softly.

"Anything."

"Move your ladder in front of the door?"

Without taking his eyes from mine, he reached out and first nudged the laundry door quietly closed, then slid the ladder in front of it so it couldn't be opened.

"Thanks." I laughed nervously. "I, um, realized that there's something I want to do."

"What's that, Penny?"

"I want to kiss you again. I mean, if you want—"

"Fuck, yes I want." His mouth was smiling, but his eyes filled with hunger and desire. Erotic desire. "Where do you want to kiss me?"

I laughed. "I'm trying to be serious here."

"I've never been more serious."

We were both breathing a little hard for two people who hadn't exerted ourselves in any way. Slowly, I spread my legs so he could step between them. When he didn't budge, I yanked him in.

Letting out a very sexy male sound of approval, he snuggled up against me, big hands on my thighs, mouth so close to mine that it was no effort at all to lean in and plant one on him.

It started out as a sort of "hello, so lovely to see you again" kiss...unhurried, leisurely, a slow exploration of mutual fascination. My hands glided up his chest to find his heart thumping steady as a rock, if not a little fast.

When I pulled back, he slowly opened his eyes, looking at me like I was the most beautiful woman in the world.

"More," I whispered, curling my legs around him, causing that thumping beneath my palm to pick up the pace.

He nodded, but for as turned on as he was—I mean, I had the extremely hard proof pressed quite insistently in the vee of my legs—he remained unhurried as he cupped my face.

"You have the sexiest mouth," he murmured. "Love the way you kiss me."

I rocked into him as he danced his mouth along my jaw, making me gasp when his stubble scraped against a sensitive area just beneath my ear.

"Love the way you taste," he said against my skin, his hands skimming my hips, my waist, up my arms, the pads of his thumbs grazing the sides of my breasts.

I shivered and he smiled against me. "When I kiss you here..." Again his lips brushed at that spot he'd found beneath my ear, the one that made me writhe into him. "I can tell you're feeling my mouth in other places." An indulgent lick had me arching into him.

A pleased rumble came from Ryder and another stroke of his tongue as goose bumps erupted over my entire body. "Do you, Penny? Feel my mouth in other places?"

Was he kidding? I'd melted so thoroughly he had to tighten his grip on me, an arm wrapped around my back to hold me to him. As for my "other places," they'd woken up and were doing the happy dance.

"You talk a lot," I managed.

His soft laugh had me clutching at him, grinding into him, and oh, he most definitely wanted me. Wanted me in a way that emptied my mind of any other thoughts as he moved with me into a rhythm that had me panting. By the time his mouth found mine again, his teeth tugging at my lower lip, I was nothing but a puddle of hunger and pulsing need, desperate to lose our clothes right here, right now—

"Penny?"

"Hmm?"

"Still okay?"

"I would be, if you'd stop stopping."

He'd been nibbling on my throat, working his way south, but he lifted his head, eyes twin pools of erotic invitation and a shockingly endearing hope, like he hadn't really believed this might happen.

"You said 'anything,'" I reminded him. "Anything I want. I want this."

"Here?" he asked, his voice so low as to be nearly inaudible. "Now?"

"Here. *Now*."

"Your family—"

"Grandma can sleep through a zombie apocalypse, and even if Wyatt were to wake up, he'd stay in bed playing a video game."

"You've thought this through."

"You have no idea."

He smiled, a very dirty, naughty smile that made me glad I wasn't standing because my legs were jelly.

"We'll have to be quiet." His hands moved with slow purpose over me. They had been this whole time, gliding, teasing, never staying in one spot for long, drawing my pleasure out in ways I didn't know what to do with.

"Can you be very quiet, Penny?"

Truth? I had no idea. But I was going to have an orgasm or die. "I can if you can." I was all talk, of course, and for a beat, he just looked down at me in that quiet, all-seeing way of his.

"Please," I whispered, rocking up into him for enticement, which I could feel that he didn't need, holy cow.

"No begging required," he murmured, nipping my lower lip. "Anything you want. What do you want, Penny?"

"More, faster."

He snorted. "Wonder Woman in a hurry, imagine that." He smiled a wickedly dirty smile. "Take off your clothes."

I eagerly went to tug my sweatshirt over my head, but it got bunched and caught in the clip I'd used to hold up my hair, leaving me all tangled up, arms included, so that I couldn't move.

"Help."

I heard a low laugh, then a pair of big, warm hands slid to my breasts, thumbs teasing my hard nipples before flicking open the front clasp of my bra.

With a heartfelt groan, he dipped his head and put his mouth on me. The heat and warmth, the caress of his lips against my skin, caused a decadent pleasure to skitter through me.

"I thought you didn't require begging," I managed breathlessly, squirming, struggling, still trapped.

"I don't." His voice was so low it was almost inaudible. "But I'm not opposed to having you at my mercy."

He swirled his tongue over a nipple, and when I cried out, unable to hold it back, he shifted and suddenly I was free of my sweatshirt, he was free of his shirt, and then his mouth was on mine. After a drugging kiss, he pulled back and took me in, sitting there topless on the washing machine, legs splayed to accommodate him.

His eyes darkened. "You take my breath away."

"I'm trying to take something else." I reached for the button fly on his Levi's, tugging them open, reaching inside like a kid on Christmas morning. I got him in hand—nope, correction. Hands. It took both, and I promptly lost a moment in time because while Ryder Colburn in clothes made me speechless, without them…well, there was a power outage in my brain.

He snorted. I'd said that out loud. "Live up to your expectations?"

"I mean…" I fumbled with words. "You'll do."

He rocked into my hands and I might have whimpered. With a rough laugh, he lowered his head, moving in for a hard, hot kiss while his hands went on a tour down my body, the calluses on his palms doing something to me I couldn't have imagined. When his fingers hooked into my jeans, he stared into my eyes as he popped the top button, the only sound in the room being my ridiculously labored breathing and the subsequent rasp of my zipper. Sliding an arm around my waist, he lifted me up to slowly pull the denim down my legs, taking his sweet-ass time. He smiled again when I yelped as my barely covered butt landed back on the cold metal of the washing machine.

Taking in the sight of me in nothing but a teeny tiny bit of lace, he stilled, giving a heartfelt groan.

"Oh, Penny. Look at you." His eyes zeroed in on the apex of my thighs. "I'm going to be the one begging…" Then he dropped to his knees. "I'm curious."

"About?"

My breath hitched as his fingers scraped the lace to the side, exposing me. "About everything. What turns you on. What you look like when you come unraveled. But right now…" He lowered his head to kiss first one inner thigh, and then the other.

And then in between.

"What you taste like." At the first stroke of his tongue, I cried out, then covered my mouth with my own hand. He let out what might've been a chuckle, then did that thing with his tongue again, and I'm pretty sure he whispered, "*Yum.*"

Then he added his fingers to the mix.

I gasped and fisted my hands in his hair.

"Don't worry, I've got you," he whispered, grinning up at me, the image so sexy I had to close my eyes as his clever tongue lapped at my center, his big hands wrapped possessively around my thighs. I bit my palm as I wriggled and writhed under his ministrations, touching whatever part of him I could reach, which wasn't nearly enough. When I let out a moan of frustration, he finally captured my hands in his and held them down on either side of my hips without missing a beat.

I came in shockingly little time, shaking, trembling, gasping his name, utterly outside my own body. When I stopped hearing colors and seeing sounds, he was still on his knees before me, pressing a chaste kiss to my inner thigh.

Looking like sin incarnate.

"I... You..." Nope, didn't have words back yet. Deciding to show not tell, I pressed my foot to his chest and nudged, wanting to reverse our positions so I could return the favor.

Instead, he rose and brushed a sweet kiss across my lips. A *we're done here* kiss. "But—"

His forehead pressed to mine. "I don't have anything with me."

And when I just stared at him, confused, his eyes softened. "A condom."

"Oh." Dear God, would I have even thought of it? "Guess you're not in the habit of seducing a woman on her washing machine."

"Believe it or not, this is a first." His mouth twisted in a wry smile. "Only with you, Wonder Woman."

I wasn't sure when the snarky nickname he'd given me had turned into a term of endearment, but it melted me. His hazel eyes, more gold than green at the moment, held affection, and a heated hunger and desire that gave me goose bumps.

"I'm on the pill," I said quietly. "And also, in case you couldn't tell by how fast I went off, it's been a while for me."

"It's been a while for me too," he said. "But..." He leaned into me with one hand at my side, the other lazily gliding down my still quivering body. "You deserve better than a laundry room, Penny."

"I love this laundry room."

His mouth twitched. "Yeah?"

This time when I gave him a shove, he backed up so I could hop down. He let me push him until he'd gracefully hoisted himself up, taking my spot on the washing machine. Leaning back on his hands, legs spread to give me room to stand between them, he watched me as I looked at him. He really was beautifully made, all hard muscle and sinew, and I wanted to taste. Everything.

So I let myself.

I kissed my way down his throat, his chest, then playfully bit a nipple, eliciting a sharp inhale and an arching of his hips beneath mine, his fingers tightening in my hair.

"Don't worry," I whispered, giving his words back to him. "I've got you." And then I wrapped my hand around the base of him, licking him up his length like a lollipop. Since he utterly stopped breathing, I did it again, relishing his rough groan of approval. With a smile, I slowly sucked him into my mouth.

"Fuck, Penny," he breathed, rocking his hips, which did beautiful things to the muscles in his torso.

I thrilled at the sight of him, head back, eyes closed, throat bared, a look of total abandonment and sheer pleasure on his face as low oaths and fervent praises and pleas tumbled from his lips. I pulled back only to sweetly murmur that I didn't require begging either. This had my name rumbling from his throat, and then again a few minutes later, a warning as his hands came up and tried to pull me from him. Knocking his hands away, I took as much of him as I could, smiling around him as I watched his triceps twitch with the need to fist his hands back in my hair.

He muttered something that sounded like "killing me," the words going straight to my head like a heady wine. I just hummed a wordless answer, unable to take my eyes off him. Reaching up, I ran my nails down the flat plane of his stomach, and he erupted, my name on his lips as he shuddered and shuddered, while I did what he'd done for me…stayed with him.

CHAPTER 16

Penny

THE NEXT MORNING, I pushed my cart into Colburn Restorations. It'd only been six hours since the Washing Machine Incident, and I had no idea what to expect. Would Ryder ignore what had happened? Did I want him to?

Grif was at the front desk and waved at me as I headed toward the kitchen. The man himself sat on the island, not unlike how he'd sat on the washing machine. Well, except he was fully clothed.

At the sight of me, he stopped thumbing through his phone and hopped down in one easy motion, crossed the room to me. "Glad to see you."

I managed a casual shrug. "Where else would I be at six a.m. on a Wednesday morning?"

"I thought..." He shook his head. "I don't know what I thought. That you might trade shifts or find a way to pretend last night didn't happen."

I sucked my lips into my mouth and he stilled. "You thought about doing both."

"No." I managed a laugh. "I thought *you* might."

With a slow shake of his head, he lifted a hand and rubbed his thumb lightly across my heated cheek. "How could I forget the best time I've ever had in a laundry room? For the rest of my life, I'm going to get hard just walking into one."

I snorted.

"I'm not kidding. You've ruined me for life."

I realized I probably had one of those goofy smiles on my face. Since I couldn't seem to control it, but didn't want to stand there like an idiot, or worse yet, ask if the kitchen door locked so we could have a repeat, I began unloading food.

"Let me help," he said.

"Not necessary."

He stayed anyway, pointing out his favorites as I unpacked and set up, which turned out to be everything. In fact, he loaded up a plate as I worked—some breakfast casserole, a muffin, a stack of bacon, fresh strawberries—feeding me a bite for every one he took himself.

"Thank you," he said when everything was set.

I raised my eyebrows. "For...last night?"

A filthy smile crossed his face. "I meant the food, although..."

"Don't you dare thank me for...*that*," I said on a laugh, and accepted one more bite before heading for the door.

He caught my hand as I went to pass him and reeled me in. Once upon a time, I'd have resisted, felt nerves bunch in my throat, but my body went so willingly, it practically jumped him.

"I hope you know how talented you are," he said, holding my gaze as his arms slid around me.

I playfully furrowed my brow. "We'd better be talking about the food."

He kissed the tip of my nose. "Your grandma's right, you know. You should be running your own business. A café, a restaurant, your own catering service, whatever you want."

What I wanted wasn't to be thinking about that right now, not when I was once again up against his warm, hard body. I curled my fingers into his collar and tugged his head to mine. He was smiling when his mouth collided with mine just as—

Caleb and Tucker strode into the kitchen, shit-talking and jostling each other, though they nearly swallowed their tongues when they caught us.

"*Again?*" Caleb asked with a smirk. "Maybe you two should get a room."

"Excuse me?" Ryder asked quietly in a tone that suggested he hadn't actually missed what Caleb had said at all.

Tucker had found the bacon and was halfway through his second piece already, so his mouth was full when he helpfully answered for Caleb. "He said maybe you two should get a room."

I was pretty sure the color on my face was tomato red. "I'm sorry," I said. "That was so unprofessional—"

"Please don't be sorry," Ryder said.

"*Absolutely* do not be sorry," Caleb agreed. "We like this guy smiling instead of chewing us out, so thank you for that."

I'd also been smiling lately, and God help me, but I wanted more.

So. Much. More.

Which, of course, I wasn't ready for and maybe never would be.

A sobering thought. I could feel the weight of Ryder's gaze on me, but I didn't meet it as Caleb headed toward the chafing dishes. "Tell me you made that breakfast casserole again," he said. "The one that's clearly got crack in it."

I smiled. "No crack, but yes, it's there."

He clapped a hand to his heart. "Can I marry you and have your babies?"

I laughed, but Ry made a sound that might've been a growl as his brother began pawing through the fridge.

"Ry, if you drank my chocolate milk again, I'm gonna kick your ass."

"*You* drank your own chocolate milk, dumbass. And what are you, twelve?"

Caleb sent a grin toward me. "You're probably wondering if we're really brothers since he's such an ass and I'm not. I'm also clearly the better looking one."

They were all ridiculously good-looking.

Ry put his hand on Caleb's face and, despite Caleb having two inches and a lot more bulk to his muscles, Ryder gave him a push. Right into the wall.

I sucked in air, a little worried about Caleb's pretty face since he was wearing his glasses as always. But he just laughed and shoved free, resettling his now crooked glasses on his face before retaliating by pulling some sort of hockey move that put Ry face-first into the wall.

Tucker snorted.

Ryder moved so fast I barely caught it when he kicked Tucker's leg out from beneath him, causing him to hit the floor like a 7.0 earthquake.

Caleb started laughing. He laughed so hard, he had to bend at the waist, hands on his knees. Ryder chuckled, watching Tucker give him an evil grin and rise to his feet.

"Are you guys going to fight like children?" I asked.

"Like children?" Caleb scoffed. "No."

"At least not right now," Tucker said. "Last time we ended up with a hole in the wall and Ry took the repair cost out of our paychecks."

"Translation." Caleb hitched a thumb in Tucker's direction. "As the baby brother, he's afraid to fight either of us."

I doubt that was true, seeing as Tucker seemed the most dangerously built of the three of them. And sure enough, he just snorted.

"I'd take you both on to prove otherwise, but I've got a meeting." He pointed at Ryder. "You too. The police finally assigned someone to the missing materials case. He's in the conference room."

"But first," Caleb said, "you've gotta little something right here…" He pointed to Ry's mouth. "Oh, my bad, it's just lip gloss. Nice color choice. Makes your eyes pop."

Biting my lip, I turned away to grab my cart, just barely catching Ryder smacking Caleb upside the back of his head.

Caleb then stuck his foot out and tripped Ryder.

Tucker rolled his eyes at me. "They were both dropped on their heads as babies."

Caleb flipped him off, then smiled at me. "Never did thank you for patching Ry up. He tried to tell us it was just a paper cut."

"We know he did something stupid," Tucker said. "Care to enlighten us?"

Ryder raised his brows at me. Not trying to stop me. Not trying to direct me. Just giving me carte blanch to do what I wanted.

"Those paper cuts can be brutal," I said.

He grinned.

Tucker sighed. "He's taken you to the dark side." He looked at Ry. "Two minutes in the conference room." And then he was gone.

"Paper cut, my ass," Caleb muttered to Ryder. "Remember that time you screw-gunned your hand to the ceiling? You claimed that was a paper cut too, in spite of needing like a hundred stitches."

I gasped in horror, and Ry grimaced. "*Thirty*," he corrected. "And I didn't start that bar fight, I just finished it. Which, if I remember correctly, saved"—he pointed at his brother—"*your* pretty face. You're welcome."

A laugh escaped me before I could stop it, but I turned it into a cough when Ry slid me a look before turning back to his brother. "You deal with the Anderson job yet? The holdup with the plans?"

"Yep, I sent you an email about it."

"How about the McQueen—"

"*Also* solved and in your email." Caleb found something that pleased him in the fridge, or so I assumed because he whooped with joy, then pulled out the last piece of chocolate birthday cake, which I'd made earlier in the week for Bill's birthday.

"*Score.*"

"Eat that and die," Ry said. "I have plans for that cake."

"I can make more," I said.

Caleb grinned at me as he hugged the cake to himself like a firedrake with a treasure. "Don't worry, he can't take me."

"I've taken you a thousand times," Ry said.

"In your dreams."

Ryder eyed the time. "Don't you have an early meeting with Caltrans?"

"Shit. Yes." Caleb pointed at me. "Don't listen to him. I'm the best of the brothers. Think about the marriage thing. I'm serious." And then he was gone as well.

Ryder sighed. "My brother's a time waster and a pain in my ass."

"Don't talk that way about my future husband."

He grimaced, and I laughed as my phone buzzed an incoming call from Kiera.

"Problem?" Ryder asked when I groaned.

"Nope, not at all." I gave him what I hoped was my most professional *I've got this* smile. "It's your sister. I need to take it."

"Of course." He moved to the coffee station on the other side of the room.

Drawing a deep breath, I answered my phone with a chipper "Good morning."

"You didn't check out when you left the kitchen, which as you know is required," Kiera said. "Where are you? Never mind, it doesn't matter as long as you get to the Yaeger Building in the next hour. They've got a breakfast meeting with a new, big client today, which is important to me because that client is looking for a catering service. Don't screw this up."

There was something about Kiera's tone that always insinuated the entire world was on her last nerve, but it was still uncomfortable to be the face of that world and take the brunt.

I eyed the clock. I had plenty of time. "I won't screw it up."

"Great, and when you get back, you can review our company policy on checking in and out here at Hungry Bee."

"Perfect." I disconnected. "*Perfect?*" I repeated and then

knocked my phone against my forehead a few times. "I'm going to get myself fired for being stupid."

"Take East River Street, less traffic this time of morning," Ry said.

Oh good, he'd heard everything. I grabbed my cart and headed to the door.

"Penny."

"Yeah?"

"Kiera won't fire you. I've tasted your cookies."

I turned back and our gazes met and locked. We both knew he'd tasted more than my cookies...

"You don't fire a woman like you. You keep her and hold on tight."

"I'm...not always someone people hold on to."

"Then those people don't deserve you."

Unable to go there, I moved to the door. "My job isn't like yours. Just about anyone can cook or bake cookies."

"Not me."

I looked back. "You'll have to excuse me if I don't believe you're actually bad at something."

He snorted. "I'm bad at plenty of things."

"Name one."

"I'll name two. Cooking and baking."

I took my phone from my pocket, scrolled through my recipes, found my favorite—and easiest—cookie recipe. Double chocolate chip.

"Air drop?"

He blinked, then pulled out his phone. A second later, his phone buzzed that he'd received my text. "My favorite and most simple cookie recipe," I said.

He paused. "You want me to bake you cookies?"

"I want *you* to bake you cookies. So you can see how not hard it is."

He stared down at the recipe I'd sent him, then back at me, his eyes crinkled in amusement. "What makes you think I'm capable of pulling this off?"

"You restore historical monuments to their former glory with incredible precision and loving care. What makes *you* think you can't make a few cookies?"

"I guess we'll see." He looked at me for a long beat, as if debating with himself over something. "Kiera's going through a really hard time right now," he finally said. "She isn't herself. I'm not excusing her behavior, because it's not okay how she talks to people. I just know deep, deep down past that thick skin of hers, she's got a really soft heart."

"You don't talk about her much."

There was a hesitation, then he said, "Auggie was her husband."

My stomach hit my toes. "Auggie, business partner Auggie?"

Mouth grim, he nodded.

"She lost her husband," I breathed. And he'd lost his best friend...

"And the father of her children."

I covered my mouth with my hand, sick for all of them, for Kiera, for Ryder, but especially for the kids, because I knew first-hand the pain of losing your dad young.

"I'm so sorry." Three words had never felt so inadequate. With Kiera, I'd mostly tried to stay off her radar, but now I wanted to give her a hug. The woman was just trying to keep her head above water while being tied to a cement block of fate, struggling to keep her family from drowning as well, *and* wanting to accomplish that all on her own.

We weren't so different after all.

CHAPTER 17

Ryder

I STOOD IN MY KITCHEN staring at the ingredients for the "simple" recipe Penny had challenged me to try a few days ago.

Behind me, Hank sat at the table with a big piece puppy puzzle for toddlers. I'd tried to put him to bed a bit ago, but he'd merely pointed at the bag of chocolate chips on the counter.

He was going nowhere until he had a cookie.

"You know this might be a disaster," I said.

He shrugged. He was willing to take that chance.

Great. I was going to have an audience of one.

Caleb walked in my back door. "Game night," he said, brandishing two pizza boxes.

Correction: an audience of two.

"What's wrong with *your* TV?" I asked.

"It's not as big as yours." He froze for a beat when he eyed Hank. As a rule, Caleb did his best to ignore the old man. I knew that was mostly self-preservation. But I also knew that out of all of us, Caleb held the most anger from our childhood. He hid it well, had buried it deep, but it was there. And I think it secretly shamed him somehow, but he wouldn't talk about it. Ever.

"I'll be in the living room watching the game," he said. "The pizza's to keep you from bitching."

"I never bitch," I muttered, even though he was already gone.

Hank started to get up from his chair to follow Caleb, but I handed him a piece of pizza and he forgot about the game. *You're welcome, Caleb.*

Fuck, I was tired. Exhausted, really. I'd been adulting as required on all fronts—at least on the outside. On the inside, I'd done little other than picture Penny on that washing machine, her long legs over my shoulders, hands fisted in my hair, holding my head in place like she was afraid I'd stop before I made her come. My brain had that recording on repeat, driving myself crazy with the need to do it again.

And again.

"Ah?"

Who needed a cold bucket of water over the head when you lived with your stroke-addled father? Once again he was pointing at the chocolate chips.

"Yeah, yeah. I'm working on it."

I'd read over the recipe like it was a set of blueprints. How hard could it be? "It's just another job, right?"

Hank made a sound that might've been a low chuckle, but when I whipped around to look at him, he was very carefully maneuvering the slice of pizza to his mouth. He'd already missed at least once, given the sauce on his cheek.

I brought him a napkin and gestured to his face. When he missed the spot, I took the napkin and cleaned him up myself.

There'd been a time I could never have imagined this—my once formidable father needing me to wipe his face.

Could be worse.

I measured everything out with the military precision Hank version 1.0 had drilled into me at a young age and was mixing it all together when Hazel let herself in the back door, a six-pack of beer under an arm. A cute, petite redhead with intelligent blue eyes, she wore her usual work jeans, snug tee, battered boots, and her favorite *I'll-slay-my-enemies* smile. Her armor against the world.

I pulled her in for a hello hug, and then she caught sight of Hank.

"Uh…" She gave the old man a brief head nod. "Hey."

He pointed to the beer.

"No," I said. "No drinking for you."

Hank flashed the smallest pout but went back to his puzzle.

Hazel turned to me. In school, she'd taken a lot of grief for being a tomboy, a term I'd never have applied to her. Yes, she favored worn jeans and tees, and yes, she could kick anyone's ass in just about any sport, but that didn't define her. She had a deep well of compassion and empathy, and she cared more than any friend I'd ever had. Whatever had happened to cool off her and Tucker's friendship, my brother was an idiot for not fixing it.

"Whatcha doing?" she asked, peering into the bowl.

"Making cookies." This from Caleb, who'd poked his head back in the kitchen, smiling wide at the sight of Hazel. Pulling her into a one-armed hug, he snatched a beer. "He's trying to impress this hot chick at work."

She laughed. "Makes sense."

"I am *not* making cookies to fucking impress someone." Much.

"Well, that's good," Hazel said sweetly, "since you burn water."

I ignored that. Mostly because it was true.

Tucker came in the back door, froze for a single beat at the sight of Hazel, then switched to an *I'm cool* stance that fooled no one. He flashed a small smile her way, which Hazel pretended not to see.

Huh.

"*Anyway*," Caleb said into the beat of awkward silence, giving me a *what the fuck is up with them?* look. "Penny dared him with a recipe and a sweet smile, and he walked right into her trap. I mean, shit, I dare him to do stuff all the time and he never bites."

Tucker snorted. "That's because he's not desperately in love with you."

I nearly dropped the bowl, barely catching it against my chest, spilling flour down the front of myself. "Good to know you're still The Department of Misinformation."

"Holy shit." Caleb's eyes were wide as he gaped at me. "You're in love with *Penny*."

I swiped at the flour on my shirt. "Do you like your nose where it is on your face?"

The son of a bitch just laughed. "Ah, man," he said when he got a hold of himself. "Been a long time since you resorted to stupid empty threats."

"Which means it's true," Tucker noted, helping himself to a piece of pizza while again trying to meet Hazel's eyes, something she skillfully avoided.

Hank nodded sagely. Fucking Hank.

"Maybe they're just friends," Hazel said.

I decided I loved Hazel more than anyone else in this room.

"Negative," Tucker said. "We caught him and Penny trying to swallow each other's tongues the other day. Pretty sure it's the Legend of Star Falls. He saw the stars, you know."

"We *all* saw them," I said.

"Not me," Caleb said. "I didn't see shit."

"Liar." I shoved them all out of the kitchen and into the living room, including Hank, so I could think. "In love, my ass." Did I like Penny a whole lot? Yes. Did I like her more than a whole lot? Also yes. But love? No. It was too soon.

Wasn't it?

Hell. I was so screwed.

A few minutes later, Caleb stuck his head back in just long enough to whisper, "Heads up, Hazel wants to talk to you about work. I don't know why, but she's feeling down, so don't get into it with her. It won't go well."

And sure enough, sixty seconds later, Hazel appeared in the doorway. Not smiling. Quiet. Pensive.

"What's up?" I asked.

"I heard you got that six-mil Henderson job in Sonoma County. Congrats."

I'd gotten word just this morning that we'd won the bid. We'd be renovating an 1886 historical homestead, the massive four-story mansion, barn, and surrounding property made infamous for its Prohibition-era bootlegging and basement speakeasy. I was thrilled, but also worried about the extra workload. I'd have to hire more employees or it'd spread us too thin.

"News travel fast. And thanks."

"I want in, Ry."

I had my gaze on the recipe—wait, what did it mean to "fold in the ingredients"—when her words sank in. I lifted my head. Sighed at her seriousness. "Haze—"

"Look, just think about it, okay?"

The problem wasn't me or her incredible skills. It was her and Bill's inability to see eye to eye on…well, anything. Their relationship was much different than, say, my relationship with Hank. Bill and Hazel loved each other. Deeply. They were just two very different people. Them working together on deciding the color of the sky would be a firestorm, much less a job with so much money on the line every single day.

A few weeks ago, Bill had been at the Cork and Barrel having a beer when Hazel had come in to pick up food. They had somehow devolved into such a huge fight that both were politely asked to leave and not come back.

If I gave the finish carpentry contract to Hazel's company, she and Bill would have to work closely together, with Bill in charge. There was no way in hell it would go well. No possible way. Off the clock…*maybe*, with a Colburn mediator. But on the clock, with my employees depending on their jobs and on me to make sure things ran smoothly, I just couldn't do it, no matter how much I would like to.

A long time ago, her mom had begged me to never hire both Bill and Hazel for the sake of their relationship.

"You know I can't hire you."

"Can't? Or won't," Hazel asked.

"Both." I put the recipe down on the counter and faced her. "Talk to me. Where's this coming from? You said your business is thriving, so much you've had to turn down jobs because you're too busy. So why—"

"I lied." She looked away, brows furrowed. "I lost big on a contract last month."

"The Quincy job?" My heart sank. "The one I told you not to take because Dennis Straton is an asshole and a crook—"

"He was overpaying, and I got greedy." Hazel swiped a hand down her face. "The profit was too good. Just before we were to start, I delivered all the materials for the job, agreeing to wait thirty days for payment because he was in a jam."

I sucked in a breath because I knew those materials had to have been worth 25K at least, and also that Straton had vanished from the face of the earth.

"Let me guess. Everything vanished when Straton did."

Hazel looked away. "Look," she said. "All I need is one really big job to recoup, something where I can get paid up front." She paused, then quietly said, "You know I'd never ask if I wasn't desperate."

Fuck.

"You know I can't," I said. "I'll recommend you for any outside job though. And I'll give you a loan to hold you over until you get something—"

Those blue eyes snapped. "Keep your pity money, thanks but no thanks."

"Haze—"

She waved me off. "I'm fine. I shouldn't have asked." And without another word, she left out the back door.

I blew out a breath.

"I feel the need to note the accuracy of my prediction," Caleb said.

I turned to find him leaning in the doorway, arms crossed, a pensive look on his face.

"I feel like an asshole," I admitted.

"Don't." He shook his head. "You weren't wrong. And it's not your job to solve everyone's problems, Ry. You warned her about that job. Hell, we all warned her. She's a big girl. It's not your fault she didn't listen and overextended her company. She's mad at herself, not you."

"Pretty sure it's both." Hazel didn't have family other than Bill and us, and while we'd always included her as if she were blood, she'd see this as a banding together against her, even though we'd never do that. "I'm worried about her. Something's up. And Tucker…"

Caleb shrugged. "If there's something we don't know, he's got it buried deep. You know how he is."

I did. He'd rather cut off a limb than let loose any real feelings. We were all like that, but Tucker was the master at hiding in plain sight.

"How are the cookies coming?"

"Guess."

He grinned. "You're so far gone."

Shit. "I know."

"We could make a store run and buy some."

"You think Penny wouldn't notice?"

Caleb snorted. "You're going to actually show them to her?"

"That's the idea."

"Then good luck." He cocked his head. "What else is wrong? You know, besides Hazel. And stupidly promising to bake cookies for a woman. It's something." This was why he was so good on the job. Instinct and intuition were his strongest traits. Right behind smart-assery.

"Tell me what to do to help," Caleb said.

"Handle the stacks upon stacks of things on my to-do list?" I quipped.

"Sure. Where should I start?"

I shook my head. "I'm kidding."

"I'm not."

It was true. His eyes were completely serious. "You want to drown in the daily and mind-bogglingly tedious paperwork required to keep us running?" I asked in disbelief.

"I've always enjoyed the behind the scenes stuff Auggie used to do. Look, everyone knows you're going insane in the office. Why not let me take some of it off your plate?"

"We tried this once before, remember? Three years ago, when you first offered to take on client relations because I was losing my ever-loving shit trying to keep up with everything."

Caleb groaned.

"I had you meet up with one of our biggest potential clients for drinks when I couldn't get there in time. Turned out he couldn't either, and he sent in his CFO instead—his daughter."

"Okay, to be fair," Caleb said. "I was still in my dumbass era. When she hit on me, I was flattered. How was I supposed to know she was also very angry at her dad and looking to get back at him by sleeping with his business associates?"

"It shouldn't have mattered—you don't mix business and pleasure. It never works out. And sure enough, we lost that client."

"I swear to you, I learned my lesson. Dumbass era long over."

I looked at him. He looked at me right back. Honest. Open. Genuine.

"I'm here to stay, so give me more to do," he said earnestly.

"Lean into my strengths. I got you, Ry. And I won't disappoint you again, I swear it."

"You're here to stay? Since when? I thought this job was just a placeholder for you, that you'd be champing at the bit to move on to something more exciting."

"Hey, I love this field as much as you. You think I killed myself to major in architectural history with a minor in business —while also playing D1 hockey—for fun?"

"Truthfully? I thought you majored in architectural history because it was easy enough that you could play hockey at the same time."

"Fuck you." He added a shove, and it was only two decades of experience with his power that kept me on my feet. "You really want to stick," I said, trying and failing to keep the hope dialed down. "With me?"

"I want to stick with Colburn Restorations. I'll put up with you to do it."

I couldn't even joke about this. I'd had no idea how much it would mean, that he wanted to stay.

"Yes, I'm sticking," he said, completely serious. "For as long as you'll have me. But I can do more, Ry. Let me do more."

Relief and gratitude hit me like a one-two punch. "You're going to be sorry you said that."

"No, I won't. Because I'm expecting a big, fat raise." He tried to peer into the bowl. I grabbed it so he couldn't see in.

"I just want a peek," he said, reaching his long-ass arm for the bowl.

I whacked his hand with the wooden spoon. "Back off."

His gaze flicked up to something over my shoulder and he gasped dramatically.

I whipped around to find...nothing.

With a pleased chortle, the asshole known as my brother snagged the bowl and stared into it. "This looks like spackle. I mean, I'm no expert, but it looks too...lumpy."

"Are you doubting my ability to make good cookies?"

"I'm doubting your ability to make even shitty cookies."

I snagged the bowl back. "These are going to be the best cookies you've ever tasted."

He slid me a look. "You hit your head today?"

"Shut up." I checked the oven. Preheated, just as the recipe said. I read the next line on the recipe.

Drop one inch balls onto a cookie sheet.

Shit. I didn't have a cookie sheet. Last week, I'd let Alex and Abi use it in the sandbox in my backyard and it was still there. I looked around, but the best thing I could come up with was a pot. Turning it upside down, I began to drop one inch balls onto the bottom of the pot.

"What the hell are you doing?" Caleb asked.

"I told you. Making cookies."

With a grin, he hopped up onto the counter and opened another beer. "Forget the ball game. This is going to be much more fun."

CHAPTER 18

Penny

A CHIRP FROM MY CELLPHONE startled me awake and very nearly out of my own skin. I lifted my head from…my steering wheel?

It'd been a long week, and I'd driven home on autopilot. Parked in the driveway, I'd set my head down for one second.

And thirty minutes had gone by. The sun had dipped behind the green rolling hills, its rays still spilling across the sky in a brilliance of reds, magentas, purples and blues above a line of churning, moody clouds.

I'd seen Kiera at work today. I didn't always. Hardly ever, actually. But today, I'd been cleaning up my station, which had taken longer than usual thanks to the new specs Kiera had put out. I'd been only half paying attention to the complaining about the changes, when someone said, "She's already a complete control freak, but now we're going to have inspections? What kind of bullshit is that? Doesn't she have anything better to do? Say, like hire more people, or better yet, pitch in herself? What the hell?"

I'd spoken without thinking. "She's been a fair boss, and we get slightly more money than the industry standard."

Everyone's eyes had gone wide, and I turned around and had come face to face with Kiera herself. *Great, we're all about to be fired...*

But our boss had simply said, "Back to work, please, everyone."

They'd all scattered like mice. Kiera had given me a brief nod, and for the first time, I saw the Colburn family resemblance, especially in her hazel eyes. I'd still been discombobulated when she walked away.

Now, in my car, an incoming text vibrated my phone.

WYATT

> I'm bored and hungry and there's nothing to do and why r u just sitting in your car?

Wyatt, of course. God forbid he come out and check me for a pulse. With a sigh, I gathered the leftover food I always brought home from work and headed inside.

"Can you smell what The Rock's cooking?" Pika-boo asked me.

I snorted. "Hello, smarty-pants, did you choose to use your powers for good or evil today?" It was a real question. Last month we'd had to lock down Alexa after the parrot had figured out how to order snacks from my Amazon account.

Pika-boo sighed dramatically.

I'd always assumed he'd gotten that from Wyatt, but I suddenly realized it was me. "Where's everyone?"

"Pooping!"

Shaking my head, I looked through the glass slider and saw Grandma and Hank at the patio table, doing a puzzle and chatting. Well, Grandma was chatting. Hank was just nodding his head, occasionally pointing to where he thought a puzzle piece might go.

I could go say hi, but I needed a moment. And a snack. And possibly a new life. I headed into the kitchen and stopped short.

A man lay on his back on the floor, head under the kitchen sink. Arms too. All I could see was torso and long legs, one bent, one straight out in front of him, feet in battered work boots. But I'd recognize that body anywhere.

"Jeez, take a picture," Wyatt said, and I jumped guiltily.

I hadn't even noticed him crouched at Ryder's side, manning a toolbox.

Ryder's arms appeared from beneath the sink, reaching up to grab the edge of the counter, biceps and triceps bunching as he pulled himself out and sat up in one easy, graceful motion. He was dusty and a little sweaty, and…

Wyatt was right. I should've taken a picture. I'd seen a lot of sides of Ryder. Just the other morning, I'd had to park in the back of his building again. He had an outdoor patio and grassy area for employees to take breaks and eat outside if they wanted, complete with picnic tables, a fire pit, even a basketball court. I'd found him and Tucker playing one-on-one with a fierce competitiveness that had been hot as hell. Sporty Ryder had really done it for me. I also enjoyed Corporate Ryder very much, but Builder Ryder…holy cow.

Of course even Builder Ryder had *nothing* on Naked Ryder.

He swiped a forearm across his forehead. "Hey," he said, and maybe it was my imagination, but the tone felt…affectionate. Even intimate.

"Hey back." That was me, master of awkward conversation. I turned to Wyatt, who was watching us. "Homework?"

"Done."

That was maybe a lie. "Did you get your clothes off your bedroom floor and either into the hamper or put away?"

"Yep."

For *sure* a lie. "How about—"

"Trying to get rid of me?" he asked with a lot of attitude for someone who still texted me when he was hungry. Or inconvenienced by life in any way, shape, or form. "Because I fixed the leaky roof."

I blinked. "What?"

My brother laughed. For whatever reason, he laughed, and the sound sent my heart pitter-pattering with joy. It'd been a long time, way too long, and I couldn't help myself. I wrapped my arms around him and squished him in a big hug.

"Ugh," he said, his arms trapped at his sides. "*Why?*"

I kissed the top of his head. "To torture you."

"This is child abuse. Call the authorities."

I tightened my grip. "Tell me you love me."

He was squirming, but also still laughing. "You need help, you know that?"

"Tell me, or I'll kiss your face all over." I made kissy-face noises and he caved like a cheap suitcase.

"Fine! I love you!" When I let him go, he jabbed a finger at me. "That was under duress, so it doesn't count."

"Totally counts," I said.

"Even if I admit I didn't fix the roof, Ryder did?"

"I'd say duh."

Ryder grinned at me. At least someone thought I was funny.

"But he showed me how," Wyatt said, looking so twelve that I wanted to hug him again. "So I can do it next time."

Ryder nodded, and now my heart pitter-pattered for another reason entirely.

"He let me go up on the ladder and everything," Wyatt said.

"Happy to have an extra set of hands," Ryder said.

I knew my brother was starved for a male role model, I'd just never been able to figure out what to do about it. That Ryder had included him, taught him something new, made him feel important... I was so grateful. But I knew Wyatt would rather die than have me say any of that, so I looked at Ryder and changed the subject.

"So...did you make cookies?"

He grimaced.

"You didn't have time," I guessed. "That's okay." I understood. He was a busy guy. It'd been silly for me to even think he'd try—

"Oh, he made them," Wyatt said.

Ryder shifted on his feet, a rare tell. "They're...subpar."

"How subpar?" I asked.

Ryder rubbed a hand over his stubbled jaw. "Let's put it this way. If the cookies were a restoration job, the building would have collapsed in on itself."

I fought a smile. "Are you telling me that *The* Ryder Colburn is bad at something?"

"I didn't say they're bad. I said they're subpar."

Wyatt snorted, then turned it into a cough when Ryder swiveled to give him a look.

"I wanna see," I said with gimme hands.

Ryder put his hands on his hips. "Hard pass."

"I got to see," Wyatt said, looking quite pleased at being trusted more than me.

"No fair."

Ryder rolled his eyes but pointed to the container on the counter behind him.

I just about danced over there and opened it up. Then bit my lower at the small, flat disks masquerading as cookies. Gamely, I reached for one, but they were stuck together. Still, I was no quitter, especially when it came to cookie tasting, so I broke off a piece and popped it into my mouth.

Wyatt watched me with a grimace, foretelling that I wasn't in for anything good.

Ryder watched me too, but his gaze was glued to my mouth, darkening as I sucked a bit of chocolate from my thumb. The cookie crunched in my mouth, and not in a good way, but I tried to keep a straight face. And failed.

He put a hand to his chest like I'd stabbed him, watching as my smile grew bigger and bigger. "My cookie failure makes you happy?"

"*Very.*"

"She does that," Wyatt said. "Next she's going to tell you what you did wrong."

"I'm not. I wouldn't do that." Much. "But...since you asked—"

"He didn't," Wyatt said.

I poked at the cookies. "You didn't use enough flour, so they didn't rise. And they spread out too much because you used too much sugar."

"Told ya," Wyatt said.

Ryder eyed his cookies with annoyance, then lifted his gaze to mine, shaking his head at my expression.

I playfully poked him in the gut. My finger bounced off his abs. "At least you're for sure human."

"What were the options?"

"When I first met you, I thought you might be perfect."

He blinked. "I'm nowhere near perfect."

I patted his arm. "Don't worry, I know that *now*."

CHAPTER 19

Ryder

'D JUST GOTTEN HANK to bed and was flipping through Reels instead of catching up on paperwork when someone knocked on my front door. Since people usually just let themselves in, I figured it was a late delivery of some sort.

Turned out to be something better.

Penny. "You live in a farmhouse on acreage?" she asked, gesturing to the land all around them.

"Hello to you too."

She held two groceries bags and wore a sundress, sandals, and an irresistible smile that most would probably label sweet, but I labeled *Trouble with a capital T*. The very best kind of trouble.

"Busy?" she asked.

For her? Never. "Why? Are you ready to let me take you out for 'just dinner'?" Something I anticipated far more than I'd let on, not wanting to rush her.

To my surprise, she said, "I'm leaning towards a solid maybe. But not tonight."

"Still feeling me out?" I teased.

"Can't be too careful."

"You're going to come inside though, right?"

She smiled. "Right."

I took the bags from her and she walked through my mudroom and into the living room, looking around with interest. "Tell me about this place," she said. "It's beautiful."

"It was built in 1902. I bought it eight years ago, with every inch in disrepair."

"You renovated."

"In bits and pieces in my spare time, so it took me five years. There's still stuff to be done."

"Did I see a barn?"

"Yes, which is now my woodshop." I peered inside the bags she'd brought. Flour, salt, butter, chocolate chips... "Round two?"

"If you're up for it." She flashed me a grin as she headed toward my kitchen, and I followed after her like a lovestruck puppy. "Figured we could try it the right way this time," she said, a laugh floating back to me.

"Ha ha." Her sundress had little straps crisscrossing her back and the lightweight material flowed around her thighs, showing off her toned legs as she moved. I liked the dress, a lot. I'd like it even more on the floor.

"How did you find me?"

"Grandma." She glanced back. "Wyatt told her about the cookies and how we laughed at your attempt, and she shamed me into coming over here and making it up to you."

Note to self: Nell deserved a gift basket with her favorite whiskey.

"I'm sorry if I overstepped," Penny said quietly. "I didn't even think about what an invasion of your privacy this was."

I realized she'd stopped, a worried look on her face. "Pen." Catching her with my free hand, I shook my head. "Don't be sorry. I'm glad you're here. I was just about to go dig up some store-bought cookies."

"The horror." She smiled with relief, and something else that called to a spot deep inside my chest. Lust, yes, but also…more. "It's nice in here," she said. "It's masculine, but cozy. Like a real home."

"Thanks." I tried to see it as she might. Old, dark gleaming wood floors, high beamed ceiling. Tall windows. Massive fireplace. A wall lined with shelves and bookcases with a hodgepodge assortment of books and family photos. My couch was a huge, overstuffed U-shape sofa, big enough for everyone who showed up for game nights.

"I like it too."

Penny took in the kitchen and sighed in pleasure. I'd heard that sound from her before, when my mouth had been on her sweet body, but this time, she was melting over the large, open room in front of her. She ran a hand over the rustic wooden countertops, taking in the handcrafted cupboards, the island with cushioned bar stools. Last, she looked out the large picture window, past the yard to the creek beyond, lined by weeping willows dipping their long tendrils into the water.

"I've got some *serious* kitchen envy," she breathed. "Gorgeous."

I agreed, but I wasn't looking at the kitchen or the view. Just the amazing woman who was now unpacking everything she'd brought, before hopping up onto my counter to sit, making herself at home. There she brandished a hand, like go ahead.

I laughed. "You're not going to help?"

"Of course I'm going to help. Think of me as your director. Get out your pan."

So bossy. It both turned me on and did something to my heart again. I could hear Caleb's shocked voice saying *you're in love with Penny?* I'd denied it then. I still wanted to deny it, but it was getting more difficult by the day.

"Ryder?" she asked while I stood there trying to catch my breath over my shocking epiphany.

Right, she wanted a pan. Which I didn't have... When I grimaced, she laughed. "I *knew* it," she said. "What did you use?"

"An upside-down pot."

She shrugged. "Nice improv. There's a new pan in the bag. Where's Hank?"

"Sleeping." And hopefully his nosy ass stayed that way.

She walked me through each step, jumping in to help here and there, and before I knew it, the dough sat in a bowl looking... most definitely not like spackle. I followed her lead on forming the dough into little circles and finally slid the pan into the oven.

"I'm setting a timer on my phone," she said. "Eight minutes."

I straightened to look at her and laughed. Somehow, she'd gotten dusted in flour.

She looked down at herself, taking in the two distinct handprints low on her hips.

Mine.

And I wasn't sorry.

She patted her hands in the flour still dusting the countertop, then turned to me, hands out like she was brandishing a weapon, an evil glint in her eye.

"Don't even think about it," I warned.

"You're not going to deny my revenge, are you?"

I probably couldn't deny her a damn thing. But I wasn't about to give intel to the enemy.

Hopping down from the counter, she slowly sauntered toward me, the material of that sundress playing around her thighs and with my head. When she stood in front of me, she set her hands on my stomach and gave a little push, backing me into a corner.

Loving the aggression, I held up my hands in surrender.

She smirked. "Giving up already? Chicken—"

The word squealed out of her as I hauled her into me, hoisting her up, wrapping those dreamy legs around my waist, my fingers digging into the sweetest ass on the planet.

Cupping my face, she stared down at me with hungry eyes. "Five minutes until the cookies are ruined. That's all you've got."

I gave her a wicked smile. "Plenty of time."

This had her biting her lower lip as if greatly tempted. I promptly forgot to breathe at how heart-stoppingly gorgeous she was with flour all over her face and in her hair, smiling at me like I made her world go around.

"Do you know how hungry I am?" I asked, voice sounding husky to my own ears.

"Don't worry. The cookies'll be great."

"I'm not talking about the cookies."

Her cheeks went a little pink as we stared at each other. Yearning. Aching... I felt bowled over with want, could've happily drowned in the sensation of all her soft curves in my hands. Unable to stop myself, I lowered my head and kissed her. With a sexy little hungry sound, she kissed me back, her floury hands gliding up my chest, my neck and into my hair, gently tightening her fingers, then not so gently, and I groaned, hungry for more of her little moans and shivers, for—

The timer went off.

Damn.

I let her slowly slide down my body, enjoying the way her breath caught at the full body contact, and the fact we were now both covered in flour.

"Told you," she said on a wry, regretful laugh as I pulled the cookie sheet from the oven.

Wielding a spatula with expertise, she scooped the cookies off the hot pan and onto a plate.

"Fancy," I said. "I'd probably have eaten them right off the pan."

"You'd burn your tongue." She was looking at my mouth again. "Which would have been a shame."

I laughed, and then she was sitting on the countertop again, eating a cookie and smiling at me, looking so at home in my kitchen that my heart stuttered. I stole a bite of her cookie, put the rest of it back onto the plate, then made myself at home as well. Between her thighs. Heaven. Planting a hand on either side of her hips, I leaned in and—

"Do you think your dad's still asleep?" she asked casually.

If there was a God. "Yes." I started to lean in again, and—

"The way you have him here with you, taking care of him the way you do…" She smiled up at me sweetly. "Not many would do that. Did you two become closer as you got older?"

I dropped my forehead to her shoulder and let out a rough laugh. I had the woman I couldn't stop thinking about in hand's reach and she wanted to talk about good ol' Hank. "Don't give me too much credit. My siblings and I drew straws. I got the short one."

Her pretty eyes were trying to read mine. "You could've put him in an assisted living home, but you chose not to."

"It wasn't a choice...exactly." I shook my head. "It's complicated."

"Family always is."

I'd heard Nell discuss her daughter—Penny's mom—enough to know that the woman had pretty much abandoned her kids. Penny had stepped up in a big way. She'd chosen to. I couldn't let her think I'd done the same.

"He's...not good with people. Especially people trying to take care of him."

She blinked. "Hank? He's such a quiet, calm guy."

"Now, yes. But..." I shook my head. "He was military born and bred. He lived and breathed an extremely disciplined lifestyle and expected the same of us. And when his young wife died, leaving with him four half wild, trouble-seeking hooligans, he ruled with an iron fist. Nothing about it was good, nothing. We hated him, Penny."

"I'm so sorry," she breathed softly. "What happened?"

"Each of us—me, Caleb, Tucker, Kiera—we all left home the second we could get out of Dodge. I'm still not sure he ever noticed. When he had his first stroke, he landed in rehab and then assisted living. He then proceeded to get himself kicked out of every single facility around over the next few years. None of us wanted him, but we had no choice. Then, before we could make a plan, he had his second stroke and everything changed."

I took a breath. "*He* changed, but we didn't. So it's been an adjustment, and not an easy one. Like I said, we drew straws, and I got the first shift."

Her smile had faded and I waited for her to nudge me away,

hop down, and walk right out the door. To brace myself, I picked up a cookie, but then couldn't manage to take a bite past a tight throat.

But she didn't walk out the door. Instead, she slid her hands up and down my arms, gentle now, tender. "All that. He put you through all that for your formative years and beyond, and you still took him in."

I stared at her, and then exhaled in an odd sense of relief. "I'm no hero, Penny. Yes, I take care of him, and I try like hell to be the buffer between him and my siblings, even though he's not that same man anymore, even though at this point none of us has anything to fear from him, but old habits are hard to break."

"You protect them."

I shrugged. "You do the same thing for your family."

She smiled. "So we're two of a kind then."

I found a low laugh. "We are."

Her fingers tightened in my hair as she slid her lips lightly over mine. "You thought telling me all that was going to send me running into the night."

"I can't live up to Wonder Woman."

"Neither can I..." She gave me a sweet kiss, then smiled. "Let's just be you. And me." Leaning forward, she took a bite of the cookie still in my hand, getting chocolate on the side of her mouth. She caught it on her tongue, smiled innocently at me, and then did it again.

I groaned. "You're teasing me."

"Little bit." She slowly tightened her thighs around me. "Ryder? I want—"

"*Anything*," I breathed, only dimly realizing how reckless I felt. It was madness, really, giving in to this when I was feeling way too much. But then she tightened her legs again, until all I could feel was her, so warm and sweet. When she captured my lips in a kiss that swept through my soul, I groaned again.

"Tell me what you want, Penny."

"You. I want *you*," she breathed, sinking her teeth into my earlobe and giving a little tug.

I whipped us around so fast that she laughed breathlessly as I strode back through the living room, bypassing the hall that led to the room Hank was in for the stairs. My bedroom was at the back of the house.

The room was illuminated only by the glow of the full moon slanting in through my shades, casting my bed in a pale blue light.

Penny inhaled deeply. "Smells like you." Pressing her face to the crook of my neck, she took another deep breath. "I can't see much, but I love this room already. Why do you always smell so good?"

I had no idea but was glad she thought so. With my arms full of warm, sexy, hungry woman, I turned back to the door and gestured with my chin. "Lock it."

She reached down and turned the lock. "What if we make too much noise?"

"We?" I murmured, making her blush because we both knew who'd had trouble keeping quiet the other night in Nell's laundry room.

She nipped my ear again, then laughed when I tossed her to the bed. Planning my retribution, I crawled up her body. "I bite back, you know."

"Wait!" she gasped, still laughing as she tried to escape. "I didn't bite you that hard, you big baby!"

"Then you won't mind when I return the favor." I had her hands in mine now, our fingers entwined above her head as I stared into her face with wonder, taking in the desire on her face, her breathless anticipation, and something new—*affection.*

Undone, I lowered my forehead to hers. "Penny."

"If this is going to be a speech about how you've changed your mind, I swear, I'll—"

"Not changing my mind." Hell, I was beginning to think I never would. "But now I'm curious. You'll what?"

She blew a strand of hair out of her face, giving up the struggle to free herself. "Beg. Kill you. Beg some more."

At the smile in her eyes and her voice, I lowered my head and took a very, very gentle nibble at her throat, then kissed the spot. Repeated the gesture at her collarbone. Her shoulder—

"Ryder," she whispered, writhing beneath me. "Let go."

I immediately released her hands, which she then used to pop open my jeans, slipping warm fingers inside, touching me exactly where and how I wanted. I decided I lived here now, right between her thighs.

"*Ry…*"

I smiled down at her, loving the erotic hunger and desperate need on her face, wanting never to close my eyes again if she kept looking at me just like that.

"Here's what I'm going to do." I kissed my way to the hollow of her throat, where her pulse fluttered wildly, and gave a slow exhale, smiling when she shivered and clutched at me. "I'm going to show you what I can really do with five minutes…"

"I don't want to discourage you," she murmured throatily, "but you should know, five minutes has never been enough time for me."

Challenge accepted. I made a show of setting my watch for five minutes. "Hold this," I murmured, rucking the hem of her dress to her waist.

She fisted her hands in the material.

I smiled down at the scrap of black lace masquerading as panties. "Pretty…" Sliding my hands up her arms, I tugged on her spaghetti straps until they fell to her elbows, exposing her perfect bare breasts.

"Oh, Penny…" I breathed, watching her nipples pebble. "You're gorgeous."

"I—"

The rest of her sentence never made it out of her mouth as I lowered my head, kissing, nibbling, teasing until she was clutching me to her, writhing beneath me in a rhythm that had me losing my mind.

"You're…on…the…clock," she reminded me, breathing heavily.

Chuckling against her skin, I worked my way south, planting hot, wet kisses along her ribs, her quivering belly. Thwarted by that sheer black lace, I hooked my thumbs in the sides and slowly slid them down, groaning at what I uncovered for myself.

"Don't worry." My voice was low, rough. I could barely think, much less find words. "I keep my promises."

"I think you're all talk—" She gasped, then slapped her own hands over her mouth when I got to the spot that I now knew drove her wild.

"Don't stop, please don't stop…" she chanted.

I didn't.

She was still shuddering and making the sexiest little panting whimpers on the planet when her timer went off. I lifted my head to find her hair wild, cheeks flushed, body language set to *I don't know where my bones went*, and I smiled.

Penny

"Show off," I managed, trying to suck air into my lungs.

He laughed, dark and quiet, and lowered his head again, knowing now exactly what to do to make me fall apart.

"Ryder—"

"One more, Pen." His hair brushed against my inner thigh and I moaned as he unraveled me again. I was still trembling with aftershocks when one hundred and eighty pounds of motivated, aroused male crawled up my body, forearms braced on either side of my head, his hard, muscular form blocking out the world.

I slid my hands up and down his sinewy back, managing to meet his eyes. "Hi."

"Hi." He kissed me, short but not sweet, then smiled at me.

I returned it, tracing his bottom lip with a fingertip.

Sucking it into his mouth, he made himself at home between my thighs, grinding his hard length against me. "And now, Penny? What do you need now?"

"You."

With a heartfelt groan of pleasure, he pressed into me. It was a tight fit, but he took his time, leaving me a panting, desperate wreck. His breath shuddered out as he held himself still, letting me adjust.

"More," I demanded with my last working brain cell, then

gasped in stunned pleasure as he began to move, kissing me deeper, demanding more, demanding everything as I moved with him, trembling as we rocked together in sync, hovering on the edge, panting his name in a plea, in praise, in utter desperation.

"I've got you, Penny." His voice alone could've sent me spiraling, but the hand at my hip stretched, reaching between us. And then the rough pad of his thumb stroked a slow circle against my center.

And then again.

I loved the feel of him around me, how he smelled, the way he touched me so hungrily, so demanding, and I let it all unwind me until I felt it barreling down on me with an intensity I couldn't control as he finally, *finally* unleashed himself, wild and untamed, finding a rhythm that drove us both mad, and this time when I convulsed around him, he followed me right over the edge.

I had no idea how much time passed when he lowered his mouth to mine, sweet now, a thorough exploration of my lips, over and over, until there was nobody and nothing in the world except this, us, until I melted boneless against the sheets. When he shifted off me, he ran a finger along my temple, smiling, all sated, lazy posture and decadently tousled hair. Dropping low for a light, sweet kiss, he stood from the bed and walked into the bathroom…giving me a view of the ten nail indentions across that world-class ass.

He was back in seconds, gallantly cleaning me up with a hand towel, then pulling me into him, wrapping me up in him. I couldn't remember the last time I'd been held like this, cuddled close enough to sync up heartbeats, and I knew I'd lost another little piece of myself to him.

"You okay?" he murmured, face pressed against my hair.

I felt my mouth curve. "I think you know just how very okay I am."

He chuckled as he ran his hands over me. Not with intent, just a calming touch to connect us.

Although, I already felt pretty damn connected. So much so that I had to force myself to disentangle. "It's pretty late. I should go."

"Or you could stay."

I could, and then I'd lose the rest of me. Because I knew myself, knew that too much of this with him and I'd fall. Hard.

We dressed in silence. I stood in the center of his bedroom awkwardly, trying to figure out the process for escaping without discussing what we'd just done.

He took one look at my face and came close, nudging my chin up to meet his eyes, his other hand at my waist, his touch gentle. "Feeling skittish?"

"No." *Yes*. My inner smart-ass was thrilled about the orgasms. But my inner chickenshit was shaking in my boots because I'd promised myself no more men for a really good reason.

Hell if I could remember it at the moment.

As if I'd telegraphed my loss of focus, he released me, his darkened eyes studying me with a gentle thoughtfulness and care that made me want to throw all caution to the wind. *Again.*

Gah. My emotions were giving me serious whiplash. "Well, that was..." I waved my hand vaguely, not having the words.

He smiled. "Yeah. It was."

I smiled back. And that smile remained on my face when, twenty minutes later, I slid into my own bed, still smelling like him.

CHAPTER 20

Ryder

WAS IN HEAVEN WITH Penny in my bed, her hair in my face, breathing slow and even against my chest, an arm and leg thrown possessively over me.

And then I woke up.

Alone.

I ran a hand down my face, wishing she'd stayed last night, when my phone vibrated with an incoming text.

HAZEL

> I just won the bid for a big job out in Healdsburg. You know anything about that?

I did, and I'd given Hazel's company a glowing review. And because I never recommended a subcontractor I didn't personally know, he'd taken the recommendation seriously. Not that I could tell Hazel that. She'd kill me. Well, first she'd beat me up for the pity—which it wasn't—and then she'd kill me. She was tiny, and cute as hell, but she had a mean right hook. I knew, because I'd taught it to her myself.

I looked out the window and caught the unhindered streaks of color painted across the sky that signaled the sun was ready to start the day. Which meant I was already behind.

"Ah…"

Hank appeared in my bedroom doorway, wearing nothing but his birthday suit. Old man junk was not my favorite thing to wake up to, but unfortunately, I was getting used to it.

"What happened to your pajamas?" I asked, rolling out of bed.

Hank shook his head. Code for I didn't like the color.

I didn't bother to argue, since doing so would be the same thing as bashing my head into a wall, repeatedly. I started to walk past him to go to his room, but he took my hand in his. The hand that once upon a time had seemed so massive to me. Now, it felt small and fragile in mine.

"What's wrong?" I asked. "You okay?"

"Ah." With his free hand, he reached out and patted me on top of my head.

Affection. From the man who'd never known the meaning of the word. I sighed and patted the top of *his* head.

He beamed at me.

Thirty minutes later, I dropped him off with Nell—fully dressed—and had just walked into my office when my phone buzzed an incoming call from Hazel.

"You recommended me for the job, didn't you?"

A statement, not a question, and I wasn't sure if she was pissed or not.

"Either you just had a stroke, or the answer is yes, you recommended me."

I opened my mouth to reply, but she beat me to it. "Thank you," she said quietly. "I shouldn't have come to you like I did."

"You can always come to me."

"I know, but it was wrong of me to ask when I know why you can't. I owe you a beer."

I was glad we were okay, but I really wanted to ask why she and Tucker weren't. But my brother, infamously private, wouldn't thank me for butting my nose in.

"A beer sounds good."

We disconnected and I eyed the iPad in the center of my desk, the one with a long-ass list of shit I needed to get done today. I started to dig in, remembered my convo with Caleb, and smiled as I forwarded a whole bunch of it to his email. I might've even cackled as I hit *Send*.

I eyed the clock and headed to the kitchen, telling myself I was starving.

Myself was a liar.

Every time I closed my eyes, a video replayed across my eyelids from last night. Penny breathing my name like it was the only word in her head. The feeling of her soft, warm skin up against mine. The look on her face when mine was between her sweet thighs, her fingers fisting in my hair.

Don't stop, please don't stop...

The words she'd whispered as I'd pleasured her with my mouth. As if I could ever stop when she asked me anything, especially like that, her voice needy, breathless. Stop? I wanted *never* to stop. At that thought, I froze in my tracks right there in the hallway, brought back to reality like I'd been dropped on my head.

Never? I wanted *never* to stop? I ran a shaky hand down my face. *You're in love with her...*

"You look like you just saw a ghost." Caleb, of course.

I looked up as he stepped into my space, his hulking height and build filling the hallway. I was the oldest Colburn brother, but at six foot, I was also the shortest.

"I'm fine," I said. "What's up?"

He slid his hands into his pockets. "Have you heard the local news?"

"No, what happened?"

"The hardware store sold out of binoculars. Everyone's going to Harvest Peak tonight to look for the Star Falls Legend."

I blinked. "And?"

"Daniella asked to borrow some binoculars, but I don't have any. Do you?"

"Why would I have binoculars?"

"I don't know, man. Why do you have more tools and stuff than anyone I know?"

I pinched the bridge of my nose. "I'm sure there are some in the stock room somewhere. She's welcome to them. Or you can tell her she can take the sighting we already had. Let's hereby officially pass it on."

"I don't know what you're talking about. I didn't see shit."

I snorted, but Caleb began fiddling with his glasses like he only did when he felt unsettled.

"Spit it out."

He looked around, then lowered his voice like someone might overhear. "You still think the Legend's bonkers, right?"

"Uh, *yeah*." I paused. "Don't you?"

"The news reported a confirmed ten new romances in the past two days. All people who'd seen three stars arching across the sky."

"Is that 'news' TMZ?"

He let out a breath. "You think it's all BS."

I saw an opportunity to fuck with him, and sue me, I took it. "I think…" I also looked around, then lowered my voice. "We should be really careful until the news says it's safe."

He nodded grimly, then walked off. Hopefully to do his job.

My peace lasted twenty seconds before Bill found me.

"Got to the bottom of the missing materials," he said with his usual scowl.

"And?"

"It was an internal mistake, made on the inventory side. Remember that day the power went out here for a couple of hours?"

"The scheduled outage," I said. "For the PUD to do some street work. What about it?"

"The materials had been scheduled to be moved to the job that day. Only they weren't because Daniella had called in sick at the last minute. The materials never left our warehouse."

"So they were never missing off the job because they never got to the job?"

"Bingo," Bill said.

"Why were they marked as gone from our inventory?"

Bill did a palms up. "Dunno. But bright side, no theft."

I nodded, still not liking it. Our system had failed us. "I'm giving Caleb a bigger role at the company."

Bill chewed on that for a beat. "Because you think we have a bigger problem, and you trust him because he's blood?"

"Because I need help on the business side of things."

"He's our fixer. We need him in the field."

"He's going to do both." We were both going to do both, and I couldn't wait. I watched Bill thinking too hard and waited him out.

"It's a good call." He nodded. "Caleb's got a way with the clients, so things are smoother in the field now. He's charming and it lulls people. Truth is, he's sharp as a tack and doesn't miss much. Too bad you can't also get Tucker full time. He's good too. He's nosy, and nothing gets by him, which means no one gets away with shit, and that's always a good thing."

I nodded. A very good thing.

Bill drew a deep breath, then hemmed and hawed a moment. Code for: *I don't want to talk about this but I have to.* "I, uh, talked to Hazel. She shouldn't have come to you like that and put you in a position of having to choose between us."

"We're square."

He nodded and shifted on his feet some more. "We're working at being square too. I actually think we could probably make something work, she and I. On the job. Together. If we had to."

I met his gaze. "You once told me you and she would probably kill each other if you had to decide something as simple as what to eat for dinner together."

Bill grimaced. "That was a long time ago."

"Two weeks ago you had a blow-out fight at the bar."

"Okay, so it's a work in progress. But fuck, Ry…" Bill put his hands on his hips and stared down at his boots. "She's…in trouble."

And as her dad, he wanted to help. I got that. As her friend, I wanted to as well. "She just picked up a big job this morning. She's going to be okay." I'd make sure of it.

He stared at me for a long beat. "You helped her somehow."

"Her work speaks for itself."

A glimmer of pride in his eyes, Bill nodded and walked off.

I continued into the kitchen. Penny was there, and I could feel my blood pressure lower by just taking her in. Her back to me as she unloaded food, moving with easy, effortless grace, softly singing something I couldn't quite catch, wriggling her hips a little to the beat only she could hear.

I could've watched her all day. "Morning."

She jumped, then turned and pointed at me with a spatula. "You, sir, need a bell."

I smiled, and she returned it. "Looking for breakfast?"

"For starters."

She bit her lower lip, and all I wanted to do was bite it for her. Instead, I took the plate she handed me.

"Load up," she said.

I did, and then handed it to her. "You first."

"I'm fine."

The words weren't even out of her mouth when her stomach growled, loudly. I raised a brow.

She clapped a hand over her belly. "Ignore that." It rumbled again. "And that too."

I handed her a fork.

"It's supposed to be for you."

"I know. But that's not what I'm hungry for."

"Oh," she breathed shakily.

"Yeah. *Oh.*" I shifted close enough to lightly brush my mouth over that sweet spot I'd discovered just beneath her ear. "I want to taste every inch of you, Penny."

"Y-you already did that."

"I want to do it again. I want to hear those little sounds you make. I want…" Pausing, I realized the truth. I wanted to be hers.

Just as I wanted her to be mine.

Knowing she'd run for the hills if I alluded to that, I kept my mouth shut and instead took the plate back and the fork. I stabbed a big bite and brought it to her mouth. Then, as she finished unloading the food, I alternated, one bite for her, one for me, while getting a closer look at her, and the dark smudges beneath her eyes.

"You okay?"

She gave a vague shrug and chewed on a bite of her cheesy, vegetable-ladened eggs. When she swallowed again, she caught me waiting on a real answer and seemed surprised. *Did no one ever look after her?*

"It's just life," she finally said. "Sometimes it makes me tired."

"Your hours would make anyone tired. It's hard to get up so early, and by now you've been up for hours. And…" *Tread carefully.* "Your boss can be…difficult."

She choked on the bite she'd just taken.

I clapped her gently on the back until she waved me off.

"I get the feeling you're used to dealing with difficult people," I said.

Her gaze flew to mine for a single beat before she mastered herself. "Isn't everyone?"

"Some more than others."

She looked away and shrugged again, smaller this time.

The gesture broke my heart. I could still see her scar, about an inch long, less pink now than it had been a month and a half ago.

As if she felt where my focus had gone, she put a hand to her jaw.

"Must've hurt," I said quietly.

Another slight lift of one of her shoulders.

"I'm a good listener, if you ever want to talk about it."

She busied herself, fussing with her display. Finally, she took a peek at me and found me still watching her. She sighed. "You ever do anything…stupid?"

"Only a million times."

"Name one," she challenged. "Other than having an"—she used air quotes—"*incident* with a ladder."

I laughed. "Rode a shopping cart in a half pipe with Caleb, went snowboarding with Tucker in our birthday suits, attempted wakeboarding behind a truck in a canal on the side of a road with Auggie driving—and he was a shitty driver. Oh, and one time all of us attached skis to a couch and rode it down a sand dune. I could go on…"

She gaped at me, looking caught between horror and amusement. "You went snowboarding naked?"

"Trust me, it was a one and done." I winced at the memory. "Snow burn."

She blinked and then laughed. "Ouch."

"You have no idea."

"You ever land in the ER?"

"Many, many injuries." I shrugged. "Stupid is a one-word definition of a teenage boy."

Her smile slowly faded. "Well, I wasn't a teenage boy, but I made far worse mistakes, trust me."

My gut tightened. "We're talking about your last relationship."

She hesitated, then nodded. "I've never been very good at relationships. I'm too busy and...well, I'm not that great at letting people in."

I smiled gently. "Hello, Pot. Meet Kettle." I pointed to myself.

She smiled, then drew a deep breath. "But bad as I am at relationships, I sort of fell into one more than a year ago now. It was lovely at first. He was charming and smart and successful."

She went quiet a moment, and I held my breath, knowing I was going to hate what came next.

"But with those things," she said quietly, "came a negative side."

Yep. Hated it already. "He hurt you."

She looked away. "It's why I don't date anymore."

Anger was the wrong word for what coursed through my veins. Rage was better. Rage for her, at what she'd been through, at *anyone* who hurt others.

"I'm so sorry you had to go through that. I hope you know it wasn't your fault and that you're safe here." I'd make sure of it.

Her cheeks heated. "I know that being silent about this kind of thing gives it power, and I definitely don't want to do that, but talking about it is hard."

"I know."

Her gaze came back to mine. I gave her a small smile. "I can't tell you that the memories go away, but with some distance, they get a little easier to face. I know this because my mom stayed with my dad, for us kids, when she would've been safer running. But she never did."

"She loved you too much."

I nodded, and her eyes softened with the understanding that this terrible thing we had in common sometimes still haunted me too. Lifting a hand, she placed hers over mine, still on my chest.

"Are you safe?" I asked quietly, wanting to hear he was locked up, but knowing he probably wasn't.

"I've got a restraining order."

"Good." I still hadn't forgotten how she'd flinched from me over a month ago now, and what Nell had told me, how Penny had grown up watching the women in her life choose poorly in love. Or how whenever we danced around this, she wouldn't hold eye contact, as if she was mortified.

But it was satisfaction shimmering in her gaze now, not regret or shame, and I wanted to tell her how proud I was of her. I wanted to tell her how beautiful she looked standing there with her head held high, speaking her truths that pained her to her very core but were necessary in order to feel again.

"What you did, leaving, getting out, was incredibly brave."

"I ran away and came back to Star Falls."

"To take care of Nell and Wyatt." I paused. "Do you want to go back?"

"No." Her voice didn't waver in its resolution. "Not even a little bit." Her eyes searched mine. "I *like* what we have, Ryder. So much. Undefined and all."

"And you think going out with me would define things in a way that scares you," I said carefully. "In spite of the fact that we've gotten close, been intimate."

"It's not you I'm scared of." Her hand slipped into mine. "I'm not," she insisted, holding my gaze. "I'm scared of me, of my feelings, of trusting myself."

I knew all this, and I could hardly fault her for feeling that way, but it left a little hole in my chest just the same.

CHAPTER 21

Penny

A LITANY OF SWEARING HAD me glancing over at Vi. She stood at her workstation, a plume of smoke rising from her saucepan, looking so egregiously insulted that I laughed.

"Not funny." She pointed at me with a wooden spoon. "I've burned my cheese sauce, and I'm getting a stupid hot flash. Can you hot flash at twenty-eight? No? Maybe I'm dying. Today would be a good day for that. *Right now* would be a good day for that, before I have to start over on this sauce."

"No one's dying today," I said. "*Love Island*'s dropping new episodes tomorrow night."

"Ugh, you're right." With a low growl, Vi yanked off her apron and then her mandatory white blouse, trying to cool down. The thin white tank she wore beneath said, *The tits are real, the smile is fake.* "I can't believe I screwed up the sauce and have to remake it."

"Be quick…" I checked my maps app. "There's traffic on the 101. I'm heading out. Try and have a good one."

"Hey!" she called after me. "Don't forget, it's girls' night! I'll see you at the Cork and Barrel."

Which was why, ten hours later, tired but starving, I took an Uber and met up with Vi and Renee at our favorite local bar and grill. *Very* local. The place was actually more of a dive bar, complete with terrible lighting, worn tables and chairs, a back room for pool and darts, and a grumpy bartender named Mack. I'd gone to school with Mack, who under his "fuck-that" attitude was a good guy, so I felt very safe, and comfortable—even if he refused to play any music outside of eighties rock. Locals loved it because the prices were good, and surprisingly, the food even better. But the biggest bonus was that tourists tended to drive right on by the dingy building, so it was never overcrowded.

We ordered burgers and fries. Correction: Renee and I ordered burgers and fries. Vi abstained.

"My body's a temple," Vi said. "At least until I lose five pounds."

"My body isn't a temple," Renee said. "It's a Catholic church. Filled with wine, bread, and guilt. Oh, and cookies."

Vi ordered us a pitcher of margaritas. Mack delivered with his usual irreverence. "Ladies," he said, pouring each of us a glass. "Looking good." He switched on the sarcasm when he met Vi's gaze. "Ready to admit you're dying to go out with me yet?"

"Am I dead?" Vi asked sweetly, returning his easy smile. "No? Then not yet."

Mack grinned. This had been going on for years. "One of these days, you're going to get tired of the assholes and realize I've been standing here all along."

"Maybe," Vi said. "But today is not that day."

Mack shrugged good-naturedly. "I'll wear you down eventually." With a wink at all of us, he headed back to the bar.

"You could do worse," Renee said. "And you have."

Vi sighed and slumped in her seat. "I know."

"He's a really good guy."

"I know that too. It's just that...he's a keeper, and...I'm not ready."

Renee bumped her shoulder to her sister's. "Take your time. I'm certainly doing the same."

"Apparently, we all are," I said, and we lifted our glasses and clinked them together.

"When life gives you lemons," Vi said, "grab the salt and the tequila."

"Hear, hear," Renee said, and we all drank.

"What a week," Vi gasped as her margarita went down. "If by any chance, I work myself into a coma, I need one of you to promise you'll make sure all my fanfic tabs are closed and history deleted."

Renee snorted her drink out her nose.

"I got you," I wheezed.

When our food came, Vi stole a French fry from my plate. "You look like you've got news."

I shook my head. "No news."

Renee studied me. "Oh, there's definitely news."

Knowing it was fruitless to hold back, I leaned in. They dramatically mirrored the move. "Okay, maybe I have one problem," I said.

"Is it about a guy?" Renee asked, then clapped her hands. "Oh, please let it be about a guy."

"Fine. It's about a guy." A guy I'd spent a week avoiding now in favor of overthinking everything...

Vi's brows went up. "As in his body won't fit in the bag kind of problems or…you *like* him problems?"

I promptly choked on a sip.

Renee smiled. "Door number two. Nice."

But Vi wasn't smiling. She knew about Mitch, and what I'd left behind in the dust—that being my self-worth and confidence.

"Does it have anything to do with the new glow you're wearing?" Renee asked.

Vi's head spun my way so fast I got dizzy. "How did I miss the glow?"

"I'm not glowing."

Violet pointed at me. "You bumped uglies with Ryder Colburn."

"Ohmigod, shh!" I looked around, but thankfully, no one was paying us any attention. Just Vi and Renee, staring at me, waiting. "Fine!" I tossed up my hands. "We did it, and now I'm low-key freaking out about it, okay?"

"Seems kinda high key," Renee said into her glass.

Vi looked worried. "We don't need details, but…was it that bad?"

I sighed. "It was that *good*."

"What's he like?" Renee asked. "Does he look good naked? How many times did you do it?"

"Those are details," I pointed out.

Vi was looking at me. Solemn. "Have you given him the bad temper test?"

"What's the bad temper test?" Renee wanted to know.

Vi didn't take her eyes off me. We both knew I couldn't really trust someone until I'd seen him lose his temper. But I'd seen Ryder mad, several times now, and while I'd definitely caught a wisp of steam coming out of his ears when I'd nearly been run over, for example, and also when his brother had been yanking his chain, he'd remained cool, calm, and collected. In fact, the only time he hadn't been cool, calm, and collected had been in bed, where he'd been all unleashed passion and zero inhibitions.

It'd been contagious.

And the most erotic evening of my life.

"The temper test is simple," Vi told her sister. "You get into a long line or disconnect the internet, and then see how he reacts. That's when you'll see the real guy beneath the façade."

"I've seen the real guy beneath the façade," I said.

Vi lifted a brow. "And?"

I drew a deep breath. "Mitch presented himself as a kind, caring guy. But he wasn't, not on the inside. Not where it counted."

"And Ryder?" my best friend asked.

"For months and months, I only saw Work Ryder, but even then, he was kind and caring all the way through. No front. No pretense. But now we've gotten…closer, and it's still all true."

Vi looked at me. "If it's Kiera you're worried about, you could ask to dump the Colburn Restorations account. It wouldn't be hard to pawn off, you already know just about everyone on Kiera's payroll would take it in a heartbeat."

"I mean, I mostly bat for the other team," Renee said, "but even I wouldn't kick him out of my bed for eating crackers."

Vi looked at her. "How old are you, eighty? Who eats crackers in bed?"

Renee raised her hand.

"Wow." Vi turned back to me.

"I don't want to give up Ryder's account," I admitted.

Vi smiled as she squeezed my hand. "Do you have any idea how good some happy looks on you?"

All I knew was that it felt good.

But could it last?

When I finally got home—a full pitcher later—it was somewhere around midnight. The night was cool, the air scented like sea salt and cedar, and the sky was lit with a myriad of stars and a glowing moon as I walked through our front yard and in the front door.

Where I promptly collapsed on the couch. "Just resting my eyes for a sec," I announced. "No one let me sit here for more than five minutes!"

Pika-boo squawked, then said in Grandma's voice, "Honey, take your time!"

"Haha," I muttered drowsily. "But I mean it. Don't let me fall asleep."

A minute later, I realized the house felt incredibly still and quiet. I opened my eyes and gasped. Early morning sun was just barely slanting in the living room window—and stabbing my eyeballs.

In shock, I sat up, arms flailing in confusion, nearly taking out the mug of coffee someone had been wafting beneath my nose. I wanted that coffee, wanted it bad too, but...please, please, *please* let it be Grandma or Wyatt and not—

"Wonder Woman awakens." The voice was unbearably familiar, low and husky, and...highly *amused*.

I sighed because I knew what my hair looked like—an explosion in a mattress factory. I drew a deep breath of the coffee and got sexy Ryder Colburn-scented air as a bonus.

I'd indeed fallen asleep on the couch and had slept the night through. Slowly, very slowly, I sat up, hands on my head, holding it onto my body.

Ryder, the ass, had the nerve to stand there, freshly showered, dressed for his day, eyes clear and alert, looking good enough to eat.

The sheer injustice of it...

Crouching in front of me, balanced on the balls of his feet, he took me in, the way I held my head. Then he studied my face, and finally, dipped his gaze to take in the rest of me, still wearing yesterday's clothes, then back to my face, and...that was *definitely* a smile on his.

"Don't even try to tell me you haven't seen a woman wake up in her natural state before," I said.

He laughed. "You don't scare me, if that's what you're worried about."

I was more worried I was going to throw myself at him for looking so damn good, not to mention smelling even better, making me want things I had no business wanting. I snatched the coffee from his hands, and in tune to his soft laugh, I drank deeply and gratefully before handing the mug back to him, empty.

We rose at the same moment, and I found myself standing so close that if he leaned in an inch, he could put his mouth on mine. My eager nipples peaked, which, given the flare in his eyes, didn't escape his attention as he slowly lifted his gaze to mine.

All along, he'd seemed okay with my no-relationship stance, but right now, in this intimate, sensual bordering on erotic position, his eyes said something else entirely.

And I trembled with the need to give in.

Good thing then that I could hear Grandma talking to Hank in the kitchen and my brother stumbling around upstairs. I couldn't say something stupid, not with a possible audience. Whew.

Ryder's hands gently ran up and down my arms before catching and entwining our fingers. "One thing at a time," he repeated softly and brushed a kiss over my lips—

Just as my alarm went off.

With a groan, he pulled me in like he didn't want to let me go. And maybe I also took a beat to burrow in like I didn't want him to. Pika-boo made a bunch of kissy sounds and we broke apart with a laugh. I headed up the stairs to shower, and when I came down twenty minutes later, Ryder was gone.

And so were the appliances and countertops.

Wyatt stood in the center of the kitchen, filthy from head to toe, and...*grinning* from ear to ear.

I could have burst with love at the sight.

"This stuff's fun," he said with pride, practically bouncing with joyous energy, which I hadn't seen in far too long. "He said he'd show me how to do all of the trades if I wanted. Said he'd pay me by the hour if that was okay with you."

"That's great, Wy." I ruffled his hair, realizing I had to reach up farther than usual. Every day we fed and watered him, and he woke up taller, like a weed.

"You're okay with it?" he asked.

"Of course." Even if I suspected that Ryder would pay Wyatt out of his own pocket, "forgetting" to mention the expense to me. I took one last look around before heading out for work. The kitchen was now officially an empty shell. And only a few months ago, I'd have said the same thing about myself. But somehow, when I hadn't been looking, this place, this town, these people...they were bringing me back to life.

Including one steadfast, calm, enigmatic Ryder Colburn.

A few days later, I entered Colburn Restorations at a dead run like my tail was on fire. Somehow my alarm had gotten turned off, then the kitchens at Hungry Bee had been all aflutter because Kiera had done a surprise spot check that morning, meaning she walked around sampling all the food we were cooking, making changes on the fly. When she got to my station, I held my breath as she began tasting things at random.

"Nice," she said.

I blinked. "Thank you."

"Don't change anything." She eyed her watch. "Except for your propensity to be right on time. Right on time is the new late. Change that."

"Got it," I said.

So of course traffic had been a bitch. By the time I parked and pushed my cart—with the now perfect wheels—into Colburn Restorations, it was five minutes after six. I came to an abrupt halt in the kitchen doorway, finding Ry leaned against the island, working on his phone. He lifted his head and took me in from head to toe, not missing anything.

"You're tired."

"Aw, thanks. You look great too."

He came close, ducking his face to see into mine. "You're beautiful—"

"Stop—"

"—inside and out, *always*. But you're still tired."

I shrugged. "It's a way of life."

"You work too hard."

I busied myself with the food until two warm hands turned me. Two equally warm hazel eyes met mine. Slowly, he cupped my face, his thumbs lightly tracing what I knew were purple exhaustion smudges beneath my eyes.

"I'm okay, I promise. Were you waiting here for me?"

"Yes." He cocked his head. "You've been avoiding me."

"Yes."

He smiled at my honesty. The kind of smile the big bad wolf probably had given Little Red Riding Hood.

"How is that funny?" I asked, because he should've been insulted. I'd needed some time to hopefully move on from this ridiculous crushing need to see him constantly. See him, think of him, *ride him like Zorro...*

It'd been days and not an ounce of that need and hunger and desire had dissipated, not in the least.

In fact, just standing there, my attention wandered to his mouth, wanting to hear his gravelly rough morning voice again. Wanting also to feel that stubble on my skin as he kissed his way down my body, making himself comfy between my thighs and—

"You have no idea how much money I'd pay to know what you're thinking about right now," he murmured.

I could feel the blush crawl across my face. Damn, he was potent. "I'm *not* thinking about anything. Nothing at all. Like, not a single thought going on up here." I tapped my temple. "Completely empty, and..." *Why was my mouth still moving?*

He smiled. "Liar."

His face was close to mine and he let the very tip of his nose ghost over my jaw, making me shiver. "You really want to know what I was thinking?" I asked.

"More than my next breath," he said fervently, so close I could almost feel the several-day-old stubble on my skin as he inhaled deeply, like he adored my scent and couldn't get enough.

"I was thinking about everything *I'd* do to *you* if we had five minutes alone."

A groan rumbled from his chest to mine. Shifting a little closer, he slid his arms around me. "Evil, woman. Now that's all I'll be thinking about in my meeting."

"Good."

He stared into my eyes, his heated. "You have no idea how badly I want to drag you to my office and forget the world."

"Maybe we put that on the schedule."

He smiled. "Now you're just teasing me."

"Am I?"

"I gotta go. Being early is the new on time. Have a good day," I said sweetly. "Oh, but maybe stay off ladders. Leave the crazy stunts to the youngsters."

He raised a brow. "So I'm old man now?"

Why did I so love yanking his chain? "I mean, aren't you?"

His hands settled on the edge of the wall behind me, on either side of my hips, caging me in. "Just how old do you think I am?"

"Not a day less than sixty," I quipped.

"Wow."

"Okay, fifty, tops." I sounded annoyingly breathless, damn his sexy, smug ass.

He shifted a little closer. "I'm thirty-two. In my prime, I can assure you."

My heart kicked, but I just playfully slid my gaze over him, up, down, then back again, slowing in all the good spots. I knew

I was playing cat and mouse, just as I knew I was the mouse, but I couldn't seem to help myself.

"I'm pretty sure a man's *way* past his prime at thirty-one. Don't you all peak at nineteen?"

That grin went a little wicked. "Give me five more minutes, and I'll be happy to prove you very wrong. Again."

"I wouldn't want you to tax yourself when you have work," I said demurely.

He laughed and stepped back. "You know how to get a hold of me, Wonder Woman."

The way he let me be in control and determine the pace meant…everything. Yes, I needed to think, and no, I couldn't do that with my lips attached to his, but I couldn't resist fisting my hands in his shirt, yanking him closer, and giving him a helluva goodbye kiss.

CHAPTER 22

Ryder

THE FEEL OF PENNY'S mouth on mine detonated all common sense, and my body reacted without permission, hauling her into me, making us both let out a soft moan just as someone cleared their throat behind us.

Caleb stood in the doorway, juggling a laptop under his arm, two coffees, and an eye roll.

Penny slid out of my arms and hugged herself. "Sorry."

"Nothing to be sorry for," he assured her. "You good? 'Cause I can kick his ass if needed. Anything for my future wife."

"No," she said on a startled laugh. "I was…we were just, um, saying goodbye."

Caleb smiled gently at her, then turned to me. "You never kiss any of us goodbye like that."

My brother, the family comedian. I pointed to the door.

But it was Penny who headed toward it. "Don't let him work too hard," she said to Caleb. "Also, don't let him do dangerous shit alone. Watch his back, you got me?"

He saluted her with a smart-ass, "Yes, ma'am."

And then she was gone. A ray of sunshine loose in the world.

He grinned my way. "Your girl's hot as hell."

True story. If she was really mine, that is.

"We've got a bunch of stuff to go over before the Tuscany site meeting this afternoon," Caleb said. "Your office?"

"Yeah. Give me ten minutes, though."

"After that kiss, I'd need at least ten."

I flipped him off and had just entered my office when my cell rang. If it'd been anyone other than my sister, I'd have ignored the call, but Kiera rarely contacted me first. Three days a week, I picked up her and Auggie's wild wolf cub rug rats, took them to breakfast, and then dropped them off at preschool. This gave me time with two of my very favorite people, but also gave Kiera a break because mornings at her house were like being at the circus.

Unfortunately, one of my *other* favorite people, Kiera herself, did her best to keep interactions with me at a minimum. With all of us actually. She was doing better, but it was a slow process. She still got overwhelmed easily, so we'd done our best to protect her from things she didn't need to worry about.

Things like Hank not being in assisted living. It hadn't been easy. More than once, Kiera had caught a sighting of one of us with Hank out and about. Doctor appointments, I'd told her, and the fact that she'd readily accepted the simple explanation without any follow-up questions told me we'd done the right thing in not telling her more.

But...the longer we waited, the harder it would be. We had no idea how she'd react. Would she hate us for keeping her out of the loop or thank us? It could go either way.

I connected the call with, "You okay?"

"Define okay."

Fuck. "Alive," I said tightly.

She snorted. "Then yeah, I'm okay. I mean, one toddler's refusing to eat, and another's sobbing because I won't give him a second cookie, and I'm staring at Laundry Mountain, plus I've run out of peanut M&Ms, but hey, we can't have everything."

I took a deep breath. This was good, right? She didn't have an emergency, and yet she'd still called to talk to me. Progress. "I can have M&Ms delivered by end of day. What else can I do? You know I'm shit at laundry."

She snorted. "I need to go to Costco, but I can't bring the kids."

"Why not? They love Costco and their 'examples.'"

"Yeah, well, apparently, toddlers can scream when they're tired, but if I do it, I'm 'being difficult.' I need a *kid-less* trip to Costco—"

"Sure."

"—in Hawaii. I want to go to the Costco that's in Hawaii. For like a week."

A week with the cutest, most adorable heathens I'd ever met. I'd need reinforcements. Two of them, named Tucker and Caleb.

"Consider it done. I'll handle the kids and anything else while you're gone."

She was quiet a moment, and the million things I wanted to say floated in my head.

I'm sorry.

I miss you.

I love you.

Do you still hate me as much as I hate me for what happened to Auggie?

But we Colburns had learned how to keep our emotions buried six feet deep—the price of growing up with a hard-ass, military, all-gruff-no-bluff father, who believed that children were to be quiet, obedient, little soldiers. So I said nothing and hoped she would keep talking.

"You'd actually do that?" she asked, sounding stunned. "Take the kids for a week? Are you insane?"

"Yes. And probably." When I heard a suspicious sniff, my heart sank. "Are you…crying?"

"No!" she said soggily, definitely crying. "I've just got something in my eye." She blew her nose. "I'm sorry. I didn't expect you to be sweet. I was just kidding about the week. Well, mostly. I love my wild, feral wolf cubs with everything I've got, I really do. It's just that some days are harder than others. I just want an hour alone at Costco."

"Tonight?"

"No, I'm too tired."

"Okay, how about this? I'm coming in tomorrow morning to take the kiddos to breakfast—do you want to go then? I can also do any evening."

"Yes! Our Costco opens at seven, and they have a bunch of really great breakfast samples."

"Whatever floats your boat."

"I can't wait," she said, the words warm and genuine. "And Ryder?"

"Yeah?"

"Thanks."

My throat tightened. "Any time. Maybe we could pick a day for us to hang out—"

"Alex just put a crayon up his nose, gotta go."

Sounded about right.

Caleb ambled into my office, dropped into the chair across from my desk and leaned back, kicking his feet up onto the wood, the picture of indolence plus a shit-eating grin.

"What?" I demanded.

"Nothing."

"Spit it out."

"You're less grouchy since you started seeing Penny."

"You know I'm not...*seeing* her," I said.

"Have you told that to your tongue?"

I rolled my eyes. "Does anything you say actually make sense in your head before you say it?"

He smirked. "Tell me you're not into her, I dare you. Can you even say it with a straight face?"

I let out a breath. "I've got no idea what I'm doing."

"No kidding."

"This isn't funny."

"Oh, but it is," Caleb said. "My big, bad, tough brother, brought down hard by a cute slip of a girl who—"

"She's not a girl."

His smile widened.

"Shit." I swiped a hand over my face. "I just proved your point."

"Yeah. But it's a good look on you, man."

I shook my head. "No, I mean it. I don't know what the hell I'm doing. It's not like I'm any good at being emotionally available." I tilted back in my chair and stared at the ceiling. "And then there's the fact that she's way too good for me."

When Caleb didn't say anything, I straightened and looked at him.

He was staring at me with a mixture of grief, regret, and a rare bad temper. "Wrong," he said tightly.

"You're biased."

"Of course I am. But you still deserve *all* the good things." He said this fiercely, all good humor long gone. "And if you want me to beat that shit into you, I'm game." He stood, palms on my desk, eyes intense as he leaned over me. "If you keep yourself emotionally unavailable, you let Captain Asshole win. If you allow what happened to Auggie take you out, you let the tragedy win. You gotta fight that bullshit."

"Why do you sound like the older brother right now?"

A humorless laugh rumbled out of him. "Again, happy to beat that shit into you." And then, as if he knew I needed to move on from this conversation, he plopped back into his seat. "Did Bill tell you he found out what happened with the missing materials?"

"Yes."

"Do you believe it was a simple inventory mistake?"

I opened my mouth, and then closed it.

"You don't," Caleb said, straightening.

"I don't know what I think yet."

"Well, I know what I think. It smells bad."

I nodded.

He studied me. "You have a plan."

"I do. I started this company with just a few people, and we all had access to everything, but things have changed. The business has changed. We've got too many hands in the pie." I paused. "People aren't going to like the changes I have in mind."

"Tough shit," Caleb said.

I nodded. "First up, new levels of access, depending on the employee. Project managers don't need direct access to inventory, they can go through material acquisitions. Foremen don't need direct access to the accounts, they can go through bookkeeping."

"How about an internal audit?"

I nodded. "That's happening too. An in-depth audit by our accounting firm from top to bottom. Next, we'll revisit our current tracking system, which is clearly flawed. And finally, we're going to update our software, which I've been putting off for two years. We become Fort Knox."

"We?"

I met my brother's gaze. "If you were serious about picking up more responsibility, then yeah. We."

Caleb smiled. His kick-ass, gonna-win-this-game smile.

"All of this is need-to-know only," I said. "No one without the last name of Colburn is in on any of it until we're finished with the internal audit."

My brother paused. "No one? Not even Bill?"

"No one."

He let out a slow breath. "You think someone's doing this from the inside?"

"I don't want to think that, but I need to eliminate the possibility without making anyone here feel like I don't trust them. So far all I know is there's been too much blurring of the lines between jobs—and that's on me. It was nice having things more informal, and knowing that most of us can pick up the slack here on multiple trades as needed, but…"

He nodded. "But…we need to batten down the hatches."

"Yeah."

"Damn."

"It could be nothing more than simple errors and genuine mistakes," I said. "But until we know for sure, we're on our own."

Caleb shrugged, unbothered by that. "Nothing new there, man."

True enough.

He headed to the door, then stopped, his hand on the handle, head bowed. Swearing softly, he turned back.

"Forget something?"

"You missed our staff team-building rock climb last night. I wasn't going to say anything, but…"

But I hadn't been able to rock climb since losing Auggie, even though it'd been a favorite pastime since being a kid. "I was busy."

His knowing eyes never left mine. "You're the one who set up the exercise, using the twelve-story side of the Adams Center as a climbing wall to celebrate finishing the job. The owners were thrilled to host us, by the way. A great time was had by all."

"That's good."

"You were missed."

"I was busy," I repeated.

"Yeah." Caleb stood there for a beat, hands on hips, giving me the look of frustration I usually gave him. "You're the fearless leader, man," he finally said. "You're the one who pushes us to take risks and step out of our comfort zone. We've always followed you without question because you walked the talk and lived the dream." He paused, took a breath. "But you don't do that anymore."

Kill shot.

"We're not talking about this now."

"Then when, Ry? Ever since Auggie died, you stopped living. You just stopped." He shook his head. "I know how much you worry about Kiera. But do you have any idea how much we worry about you?"

I forced myself to meet his gaze. "No one needs to worry about me. We done here? We've got a meeting."

"Shit. Yeah." Caleb hesitated. "But Ry?"

"What?"

"We already lost Auggie. Don't you dare make us lose you too."

"You're not going to lose me, *drama*."

"Damn right we're not going to lose you. And for the record, *you're* the drama." On that, he shut the door behind him.

CHAPTER 23

Ryder

JERKED AWAKE AT FOUR a.m., heart pounding. It didn't happen nearly as often anymore, but sometimes a nightmare about Auggie all over again hit hard.

I was still on shaky ground when I showered and woke up Hank by flipping on the light in his bedroom. The bedroom that used to be my at-home office.

As a kid, we'd had an unspoken rule: never, *ever* wake up Dad, not if you valued your life. But if you absolutely *had* to, you'd best just throw a two-by-four at him from the doorway and then run like hell, praying you got out of the house before he got a hold of you.

This morning, just like every morning since his second stroke and subsequent craniotomy, the old man smiled at me happily.

"Ah," he said.

"Gotta get a move on."

Once upon a time, Hank could be ready in four minutes flat with military precision, including making his bed so tight that a quarter could bounce off the linens. We kids were expected to be able to do the same. But these days, it took me forever to get him ready for the day. First up was the tricky dance of getting him out of the shower and dried. Even more tricky, getting him into his boxers. I crouched before him where he sat on the bed, holding out a navy pair for him to stick a foot into one of the leg holes like always.

Instead, Hank raised a hand.

I barely caught my flinch, a reflex from childhood, one I hadn't had in years. Apparently my nightmare had stirred up some serious shit, having me running on instincts rather than conscious thought.

Hank blinked at me, as if he'd seen the gesture I'd nearly made. Confusion flitted across his face. And not for the first time, or even the millionth, I wondered...*what did he remember?* The doctor had doubted he'd retained much from recent years. But the memories from years and years ago? Some might've stuck. No one had any way of knowing.

Hank put his heavy hand on mine and squeezed. He...he was holding my hand, as if he knew I was on shaky ground this morning. I lifted my head, thinking I'd see something on his face. Maybe his own sorrow and guilt.

But nope. Nothing but that cheery smile as he pointed to the dresser.

He didn't like the color of underwear I'd blindly grabbed. "Dad. Not this again."

"Ah."

Grinding my teeth, I went to the dresser and pulled out the stack of boxers folded in the top drawer, dutifully holding each up for his approval. Yellow. Black. Red. Green—

"Ah," he said.

Green it was then. Because no matter how much the old man had changed, some things remained exactly the same. He didn't care what he ate, or that he'd been a horrible father—just that he got his way on what color shorts to wear.

After dropping him off with Nell, I made my way to Kiera's to pick up the twins. I took a moment on her porch, feeling way too raw to be social.

But I refused to let down anyone inside this house, not ever again.

The house was a small, quaint American Colonial Revival. She and Auggie had bought it cheap years ago, and we'd renovated it, updating the symmetrical façade and side-gabled roof, enclosing the back porch, turning it into a sunroom. Now that there were two toddlers living inside, the place was almost too small, but I knew Kiera would never leave it, not when it brought her so many happy memories of Auggie.

My sister opened the door in leggings and an NYU sweatshirt—Auggie's—sweating and breathless. Behind her, I could see the TV in the living room playing a Pilates class.

As always, when she laid eyes on me these days, she didn't seem particularly happy to see me. Not that I blamed her. After all, I'd encouraged Auggie to go broaden his horizons, and he had.

And now he was gone.

"Hey."

"Hey." She gave a very small smile. "Thanks for the peanut M&Ms delivery yesterday. I'm sorry I snapped at you. That's what I do now. I snap."

"Gee, that's brand-new information," I said blandly.

"Hey, if you can't snap at your brother, who can you snap at?"

"The rest of the world, apparently."

Her eyes narrowed. "If this is about me yelling at Tucker and Caleb for buying Abi and Alex those massive squirt guns, they deserved it. They nailed sweet old Mr. Cooper in the face. His dentures fell out and his dog ate them."

"How about snapping at people you *aren't* mad at?"

She blinked.

Right. The question didn't compute because she was mad at the world. And I hadn't meant to ask in the first place, but I'd slept like shit and my filter was gone.

"Look," I said quietly, still way too close to the proverbial emotional edge of a cliff for comfort. "Push me away all you want, okay? I get it. I deserve it. But your employees are hardworking and loyal. They *don't* deserve it."

"What are you talking about?" she asked.

"I overheard you on the phone with Penny when…" Well, right after I'd had my tongue in her mouth, but best to keep that part to myself. "When she was stocking my kitchen. You were harsh, Ki. She's a great cook. People love her."

Me being one of those people. I had a brief flash of the sight of those three falling stars arching in unison across that moonless sky. Damn, I really hated it when Tucker was right…

Kiera narrowed her eyes. "Penelope's not supposed to socialize on the job."

"My employees like her, so sometimes they stop to talk to her. You can't control that. *She* can't control that. All I'm saying is that you don't want to lose her."

She angled her head, a tell I knew meant she was itching for a fight. Which was a step up from shutting me out. "Maybe you should look in the mirror before telling me how to run my business."

I paused. "What's that supposed to mean?"

"Look, you know I'm not great at advice. Can I interest you in a sarcastic comment instead?"

"Since when do you ask?"

She crossed her arms over her chest. "Okay, fine, I'm not even going to try to be gentle. Why haven't you hired someone to run the day-to-day business side of things to replace Auggie?"

I sucked in a breath. *I couldn't replace Auggie, no one could.*

"I'm bringing Caleb in."

She raised a brow. "*Our* Caleb?"

"Yeah, I didn't see that coming either."

Cocking her head, she studied my face. "But…you love the idea of it."

"I do." I would lose Tucker's presence here once he got hired on with the city. He knew this world, loved building and working with his hands. But as it turned out, there was something he loved more—helping people. Being powerless and vulnerable as a kid had stuck with him, and he wanted to be the one to save others. I understood that. I'd miss the excuse to give him shit every day, but I was happy for him.

Caleb, on the other hand, had lived and breathed hockey for most of his life. When he'd had to give up the game, he'd landed here in a bad head space. I'd always figured when he was ready, he'd go back to the world of sports in another capacity. Coaching, maybe. Or broadcasting.

But he was going to stay here.

Kiera's eyes softened at my expression, but then she rolled them. "You always did have to be in control and the boss of all of us. But at least you're finding a way to get outside of that building and back to what you actually love. Took you long enough." Again she just studied me, the most observant of all of us. "But something's still wrong. What is it?"

I shook my head. "You first."

"Mine's easy. My husband died."

I put a hand to my chest to hold in the ache, but she gave me a very, *very* small, genuine but wan smile. "Too soon?"

I let out a breath. "Little bit."

"I'll apologize by handing you over the world's cutest, sweetest little dictators who ever lived." She moved aside to let me in. "They're supposed to be getting dressed, but I hear a lot of heckling and giggling on the monitor."

I nodded and started toward the stairs.

"I'm sorry I didn't meet you guys at the gravesite last week," she said to my back. "Or anywhere. I've been…"

I turned around to find her expression open for once. "I know," I said quietly. "We get it. The last thing any of us wants is to push you too hard or rush you through your grief. But we don't want to leave you alone either. You could start coming to breakfast again."

"You still do that?"

The Colburn siblings had a long-standing weekly breakfast. It used to be dinner, and always at Kiera's, but she'd stopped wanting anyone over or even hanging out with us. So we'd switched it up to breakfast at Al's Diner—me, Caleb, Tucker… and Hank.

If and when Kiera expressed interest in joining us, we'd have to come clean about Hank first. But that was a problem for another day.

"You don't have to talk or even smile," I said. "We'll handle the kids. You wouldn't have to do a thing, except be surrounded by people who love you."

She looked away, but nodded. "Soon." She paused. "Ish."

I'd take that.

"And I'll work on being nicer," she said softly, the faintest glimmer of a smile in her eyes. "At least, to everyone but you."

With a rough laugh, I climbed the stairs. At the twins' bedroom door, I heard giggling, so I knocked, and using a Cookie Monster voice, yelled, "Fe, fi, fo, hum..."

Squeals. Then a rushed gasp to "Hide!" This came from Abi, who of course had never been forced to learn that hiding wasn't always a game, that sometimes it meant the difference between being safe...or not safe. God. I hope she never learned that.

More giggles...

This, I thought, briefly pressing my forehead to the door as my heart swelled against my ribcage painfully. *This* was what I needed, some unconditional, and probably sticky, love. Letting myself in, I eyed the twin lumps under the blankets in the bottom bunk. With four little feet sticking out.

Stealth was not their strong suit.

"Well, shoot," I said to the room. "I must have missed them. Bummer, I was really looking forward to breakfast."

Suddenly the four feet were in wild motion, cycling the air as two little kiddos with matching wild brown curls and bright eyes and sweet, soft smiles escaped the comforter and flew right for me.

Catching one under each arm, I sank into the massive beanbag in the center of the room.

"Unca Ry Ry," Abi said, smacking her palms to my cheeks,

staring at me, nose to nose. She smelled like forgotten dreams and strawberry shampoo. "Guess what?"

"What?"

"I found this in my nose." She proudly held up her pointer finger with something on the tip.

I tried and failed to squelch my grimace. "Is that a booger?"

"Yep!" she yelled cheerfully.

"Guess what?" Alex said, squirming closer.

I eyed him warily while grabbing a tissue from the box on the nightstand and confiscating Abi's booger. "What?"

"Jeez Louise isn't a bad word."

"Very true," I agreed, relieved he didn't also have a booger. Or worse.

"So I can say it whenever I want?" Alex asked.

"Yep." The beanbag was warm and cozy, and I wondered if I could talk the heathens into going back to sleep for a few. "You can say jeez Louise whenever you want," I said on a yawn.

"But not fuck," Abi said.

I choked on my yawn.

"Or fucker," Abi went on. "Or fuckwad."

"No," I managed to say evenly. "None of those." I eyed her. "Where did you learn them?"

"Unca Tuck Tuck," Alex said. "He was driving us to the park and someone took his parking spot."

Abi chimed in. "And then Mama said Unca Tuck Tuck can't take us to the park for two weeks and he has to put money into the swear jar."

I swallowed a laugh and met their matching hazel eyes, so like Kiera's, like mine too. Except theirs were still guileless and truly innocent. Had mine ever been? I didn't know.

HE FALLS FIRST

"I'll take you to the park this week."

Twin *yay*s followed and they snuggled in. Warm and cuddled, I held them tight and closed my eyes, trying to shake off the melancholy that had chased me here.

Two slightly sweaty palms were still cupping my face. "Unca Ry Ry tired?" Abi squeezed out from under my arm to cover me with her blanket, so gently and carefully, I wasn't sure I could take it. Then she climbed back on top of me, nose to nose again, her big eyes full of the love that I tried to soak in.

"You has a sad?"

I felt the sharp sting of tears behind my eyes, and my throat burned. "I do," I whispered.

Wrapping her arms high around my neck, she set her head on my chest, scooting over so her brother could do the same. I hugged them hard, burying my face in Abi's hair, blotting the few tears that I couldn't hold on to any longer.

CHAPTER 24

Ryder

IT WAS NINE WHEN I walked into my building. Grif, as always, appeared like magic. "Hey, boss, how you doing?"

"Great." Lie number one, although I was feeling *much* better after pancakes with the twins, and then an hour at the park behind the Colburn Restorations building, playing tennis with Hazel, where she'd handed me my own ass. But I'd rebuilt my inner crumbling walls and hopefully at least *looked* like I had my shit together.

But apparently not enough to fool Grif, who handed me a smoothie. "Drink this."

I stared at it. "Again with the green."

"Yep, and again, you'll feel solid as a rock after."

"Great," I said again. Lie number two. Even though I appreciated his fueling me up, I still had to force them down. "Thanks."

Next he handed me an iPad loaded with all my messages, my schedule for the day, and probably my blood pressure and sugar levels. Grif was nothing if not thorough.

In the office that was never supposed to have become mine, I stood at the floor-to-ceiling windows and let out a slow breath. I knew it was the nightmare bringing everything to the surface, but I couldn't help but remember how much Auggie had loved it in here. Loved the way the early morning sun cast the entire room in gold. Loved the view of the cliffs and bluffs. Loved that he could hear the hustle and bustle in the building from here. I tried to find the comfort in that.

"Hey," Caleb said from the doorway.

I turned to face him and Tucker, and both of their easy smiles faded.

"What's wrong?" Tucker asked, voice low and calm, body braced for anything.

"Nothing," I said, lie number three. Look at me go.

"Lie," Tucker said in that same I'm-prepared-for-anything voice.

"It's nothing."

"Another lie," Caleb said. "Something definitely crawled up your ass this morning. Spit it out."

I blew out a breath. "Hank…held my hand."

They both blinked.

"I'm sorry," Caleb said. "What?"

"He held my fucking hand. And then he patted me on the head."

Caleb dropped into a chair. Tucker, also looking stunned, remained upright.

I shook my head. "He's never…"

"Touched any of us for anything remotely related to comfort?" Caleb asked.

"Yeah."

Caleb looked unsettled. "What a mindfuck, huh?"

Tucker didn't say anything, just stood there, shields up as always when it came to dealing with Hank, never revealing his feelings on the matter. Or on anything, really.

I shook it off. "Why are you guys here? Aren't you two supposed to be walking the new Henderson job?"

At the subject change, Tucker stirred. "It's in the center of the area that flooded during last week's rains," he said. "Apparently, the road to the property is closed this week for repairs. Caltrans is on it. Didn't you read your texts?"

Caleb shrugged. "Maybe he's been busy planning how to get injured on the job so he could play doctor with Penny again."

I drew a careful breath instead of wrapping my hands around his neck as I wanted. "If you're not in the field, then spend the day taking that online course on the new inventory system we're going to implement. I need an expert. You're it."

Caleb, who'd hated school, grimaced. "You know that I can figure out the inventory system on my own once we get it."

He was excellent on the fly, going through life by the seat of his pants. He'd actually turned it into an art form, but he didn't always think everything through.

"It's also a cert program. It's good for your resume, it's good for us, and it comes with a pay hike."

"Well, damn. You should've led with that."

The guy was full of shit. He wasn't motivated by money, never had been. He wanted to be valued, craved a challenge, and needed to know he mattered. He'd found all of that here, and I was grateful. All I wanted was for him to be happy. Same with Tucker and Kiera.

So far, it'd been an uphill battle.

Tucker stepped out to take a call, and Caleb headed to the door after him, stopping to casually say, "Oh, and she's in the kitchen."

"Who?"

He snorted. "I hope that smoothie has ginkgo biloba in it, old man."

"Oh, it does. Make sure you go see Bill. He's got a permit problem. Apparently he and Scott at the city office got into it. Bill told him he's an idiot."

"Because he *is* an idiot."

"Irrelevant," I said. "Scott said you're up. He'll get you through in a timely manner."

"Yeah, well, his sense of timely and the rest of the world's sense of timely are two different things."

"This is a you problem. *Fixer.*"

Caleb handed me his coffee, taking my smoothie instead. "For your attitude problem."

"I don't have an attitude problem." I sniffed his coffee. "Decaf?"

"Hell, no. Decaf only works if you throw it at people."

I took a tentative sip and nearly gagged. "This isn't coffee. It's sugar with a drop of coffee."

"And?"

I swapped back for the smoothie.

He shrugged and, sipping his sugar, walked out.

I eyed the clock and told myself it was the perfect time to grab my own caffeine—from the staff kitchen. This made lie number four.

It wasn't caffeine I sought.

I stopped in the doorway, taking in the sight of Penny singing and shimmying as she unloaded her cart, her tone so horrifically and endearingly off-key that I couldn't even place the song.

"Morning," I said.

Nothing. She was wearing earphones, continuing to shake her groove thing. Moving into her line of sight, I waved.

With a squeak, she dropped into some sort of kung fu pose, similar to that morning all those weeks ago in Nell's dark hallway.

"Ohmigod," she gasped when she realized it was me. "What are you doing?"

"Watching you dance like no one was watching."

"Because I thought no one was watching!"

"I couldn't look away," I admitted.

"Creeper." But her face softened, and she moved toward me.

And then right into my arms like she belonged there. "You were smiling," I murmured, "looking so carefree and beautiful."

As always, uncomfortable with a compliment, she blew it off. "And *you* took five years off my life." Slipping out of my arms—after giving me an affectionate squeeze—she went back to work, pulling leftovers from her last load, of which there was precious little since everyone here loved her food, and then replacing with new.

"You are, you know," I said quietly. "Beautiful."

She snorted, and as she brushed past me, I snagged her hand and reeled her in, using my other hand to stroke the hair from her face.

"Why do you always do that?"

I smiled. "For the excuse to touch you." I did it again. "Love your wild hair. Love the color of your eyes too, and how they lighten and darken depending on your mood. Like right now for instance, they're darker than normal because you think I'm full of shit."

She laughed. "You are."

"Love your voice too," I told her. "When you're happy, it's light and musical. When I kiss you, it goes all thick and throaty. *And*," I said while she stared up at me, "when you're pissed off..." I smiled when her eyes narrowed. "It comes out low and husky with a tinge of I'll-kick-your-ass. That's my favorite."

"You're ridiculous."

"And then there are your moods."

"I only have two," she said. "Working my ass off and fast asleep."

I hated how hard she had to work, the long hours. "You're missing a few. Like...sassy and feisty." I smiled. "I especially love when either of those are aimed at me."

She rolled her eyes.

"*And* smart-assery," I murmured.

"That's not a mood."

"It is, and you've turned it into a fine art." The pad of my thumb ran lightly over her bottom lip, which I wanted to nibble more than I wanted my next lungful of air. As if she felt the same, she drew a shaky breath.

And then bit my finger.

I hissed in a breath while laughing at the same time. "See? Sassy, feisty, and smart-assery."

"You think you've got me figured out, huh?" She shook her head, and began stacking the now empty trays, sliding them into big insulated bags and setting them back onto the cart. When she was completely done, she turned to me, then cocked her head. "I think I missed something."

"What?"

"You tell me," she said, coming close again, studying my face. "You okay?"

"Of course." I'd lost track of what number lie that was.

Her gaze held mine for another beat, humor gone. "Do you always get away with deflecting like that?"

"I'm pretty good at it," I admitted. "As are you."

She dipped her head in acknowledgment.

My fingers entangled with hers. I wanted past her walls, which felt…dangerous. A woman like Penny would deserve—and expect—me to reciprocate, but after burying my emotions out of self-preservation since I'd been a kid, I was shit at it.

"Fact," she said. "I'm good at making believe people whatever I want them to believe about me. But…" She held my gaze. "You're different. I don't know what it is, but something makes me want to let you in."

"I'm irresistible."

"Or annoying."

I laughed. "Also that." I held her gaze. "And you make me want to let you in too, which I'm not even sure I know how to do."

She nodded and surprised me when she reached up and slid a hand to my jaw, her fingers gliding over the stubble there like she enjoyed the feel of it. "I'm not good at this whole opening up thing, so maybe we could start easy."

"Your pace," I said, not quite sure what we were doing. It didn't matter, I was already 100% in. "How do you want to start?"

"I don't know." She bit her lower lip. "Maybe…maybe we tell each other something that no one else knows. Just one little thing, and since we both have to get to work, we don't have time to discuss or overthink. Easy peasy, right?"

I laughed. Easy peasy. "Right."

"You first," she said. "Tell me why your eyes are sad today."

I almost joked it off, giving her a flip answer, but she was leaning in a little, eyes warm and curious and sweet. She really wanted to know. And in return, she'd give me a nugget of her own, and I wanted that. Badly.

So I said, "I had a nightmare about Auggie."

Her eyes widened. "Oh," she breathed. "How awful." And then she stepped in close and wrapped herself around me in a full body hug. I was so stunned it took me a moment to react, but then my arms closed around her, soaking up her warmth and the way she tightened her grip on me like I was something she cared deeply about, and I felt my throat burn for the second time today.

How long had it been since someone had hugged me like this, as if all that mattered was giving me comfort and letting me know I wasn't alone? I honestly couldn't remember the last time. She didn't rush me, so it was several moments before we pulled back and stared at each other. No awkwardness, no regret.

"Your turn," I murmured.

She drew a deep breath, eyes revealing some nerves, and then the words rushed out of her. "I sort of, secretly, maybe, a little bit want to have that 'just dinner' with you."

I'd been expecting…well, I don't know what. Not this. But my heart took a good running leap against my ribcage in excitement because that would be solely about just us, nothing to do with a favor. "I'd *love* to secretly, maybe, a little bit take you to that just dinner."

The nerves vanished and her eyes sparkled. "Okay then."

"When?" I asked, halfway expecting her to name a date far down the road.

"Tonight?"

I had no idea what was on my schedule. I didn't give a shit. I'd cancel God Himself if I had to. "Where would you like to go?"

"Can I surprise you?" she asked.

"You've been surprising me since day one—no need to change that now."

She laughed, the sound music to my ears. "Remember," she said. "It's just dinner."

"Just dinner." Possibly, most likely, yet another lie...

CHAPTER 25

Penny

THE CLOSER THE CLOCK got to six, the more butterflies took flight in my belly. Hank and Grandma were playing cards. Tucker, who'd apparently volunteered for Hank duty tonight, would be picking him up shortly.

As for me, I was just trying to keep my cool. Especially since I hadn't admitted to Grandma or Wyatt that I was going out with Ryder tonight. I hadn't wanted to make a big deal of it—which they would. I wanted to ease myself into this, so I'd told them we were going to run renovation errands.

It was the best I could come up. Especially since I couldn't believe I was doing this. I *shouldn't* be doing this. *Why was I doing this?* Before I could so much as pull out my phone to be a chickenshit and cancel, a knock sounded at the door.

Wyatt opened up to Ryder, who held out a fist.

My brother bumped it with his own.

"Ah," Hank said to his son.

"You good?" Ryder asked him.

"Ah."

Ryder nodded. "Tucker's stuck in traffic on his way back from a job in Marine Headlands, but he'll come straight here for you." He started to turn to me, but someone sighed exceptionally loudly.

Pika-boo.

"What's up?" I asked the bird. "What could possibly be bothering you, my little unemployed freeloader?"

"I asked him to stop talking," Wyatt said. "He's mad at me."

"Why did you ask him to stop talking?" I asked.

"*Pooping matters*," Pika-boo whispered.

Wyatt thrust a hand out in the bird's direction, like, "see?" Then he turned to Ryder. "I cleaned up the jobsite just like you asked."

"Nice job. Make sure to keep track of your hours on the time sheet I gave you."

"I will. Can't wait to get to the tile work."

"This weekend."

Wyatt looked so happy that my heart expanded. I could've kissed Ryder for putting that expression on my brother's face, but, oh right, I already had.

And more...

"We could start now," Wyatt said with more animation than I'd seen in a long time. "I'm done with my homework."

"I'm sorry, man. How about tomorrow after work instead? I've got plans tonight. Penny and I are—"

"Going on errands, like I told you," I quickly said. "All related to the renovation. Like the hardware store, and..." My mind went blank. "The hardware store."

Ryder looked amused.

Grandma just sighed wistfully. "I miss...errands."

Wyatt divided a look between me and Ryder, and I held my breath because the kid was smart as hell, but he said nothing.

"Me want banana," Pika-boo said in a Minion voice.

Wyatt looked at me. "You know what pet doesn't talk? Iguanas."

I pointed at the three of them—Wyatt, Grandma, Pika-boo—a silent request to please behave themselves. Then I grabbed Ry by the hand and tugged him toward the door.

"Lock up behind us," I called.

Wyatt beat us to the door, eyes on Ryder.

Ryder smiled at him. "What's up?"

"You going to hurt my sister?"

I nearly gasped in shock and surprise. "Wyatt—"

"No, I'm not going to hurt your sister," Ryder said, smile gone, holding eye contact with my brother, solemn and genuine. "*Ever.*"

Wyatt stared at him for a beat, then gave a single nod.

I drew a shaky breath and, unable to help myself, tugged Wyatt into me for a hug.

"Gross," he said.

I managed a slightly soggy laugh. "Don't forget to—"

"Shower with soap? Brush my teeth? Empty the rain bucket?" he asked dryly. "I know. I'm not a baby anymore."

And it was true, I realized, meeting his too-grown-up-for-his-age gaze. His limbs were gangly, his hair a wild mess. He was growing like a weed, already needing the next size up in clothes. I could see very little of the boy he'd been, and much more of the man he would become.

We headed out and I climbed into Ry's truck. He waited until I'd put on my seat belt to ask, "Where to?"

"South on River Drive." I swiveled in the passenger seat to face him. Tonight he was yet another version of Ryder Colburn I hadn't seen before. Not Corporate Ry. Not Carpenter Ry. Nope, in his sexy guy jeans and a green Henley that brought out the jade streaks in those hazel eyes, I was meeting Casual Night Out Ry.

"You're staring," he said, sounding amused.

Yes, because he had his sleeves shoved up, and I'd melted into a puddle at his tanned, corded forearms. "Just wondering which version of you is the real Ryder Colburn. The suit, the tool belt, or the jeans."

"Funny." He drove with focus and an easy confidence, dark lenses covering his eyes, several days of stubble on his sexy jaw. "I'm always just me."

I was starting to think that might be actually true. That unlike the men I'd previously allowed in my life, there was no hidden agenda. What you saw was what you got with him.

The narrow, curvy highway wound along the sparkling Russian River. I directed Ryder to turn off onto a quiet country road that took us to the far north end of Star Falls city limits. Here, the land softened into gentle rolling hills dotted with grazing cattle and sheep, and fields of vibrant green vineyards snaked across the landscape, their rows disappearing into the horizon. We turned again, onto an even smaller, lesser-known road that took us to a pocket of ancient redwood forest. Three-hundred-foot tall behemoths, reaching up to the clouds.

"Turn right," I said, pointing to a dirt parking lot filled with other cars.

He did as instructed. "Do I get a hint about what we're doing?"

"Is Mr. Adventure nervous?"

He grinned. "Do you want me to be?"

"Might be nice to have us on even ground for once."

His smile faded. "We are on even ground, Penny. Always."

"Uh-huh."

He parked and swiveled to face me. "We are."

"Ryder..." I shook my head and laughed. "It wasn't an insult. It's just...truth. You're CEO of a successful business. I cook and deliver food."

He slid a hand to my jaw, rubbing the pad of his thumb lightly over the scar. How he'd figured out that touching the new skin there softened any lingering stiffness, I had no idea.

"You're an amazing cook—"

I put my finger over his lips. "Thank you, but I wasn't fishing."

One side of his mouth quirked. "You don't like compliments. They make you uncomfortable."

"Yes, so you can stop trying."

"Or you could get used to hearing good things about yourself."

I rolled my eyes. "You going to let me feed you or what?"

"Can you both feed me and also give me the 'or what?'"

I laughed and we got out of the truck and stood in that beat of time between daylight and nightfall. Above us, the endless sky stretching overhead, a canvas of pinks and reds in the west, and deep velvety purples and blues in the east. We were surrounded by a woody terrain alive with movement: birds singing, small squirrels scurrying amongst the foliage, as if bustling to finish their business before nightfall. Even the trees and lush green plants seemed to take on a bright and more vibrant quality than normal in the fading light of dusk. A fairytale setting.

In the distance, muffled through the majestic madrones, came the faint sound of people and music.

"It's Star Falls's first ever food truck night," I said quietly. "Come on, I'll show you." I led him through the trees and into a large clearing beautifully lit with strings upon strings of lights. Haloed in those lights were a bunch of food trucks in a large circle, all open and operating. In the center of the circle were picnic tables filled with people eating, talking, laughing. Off to the side sat a line of fire pits, a babbling brook, and games like dartboards, life-sized chess and checkerboards, a massive Jenga set, and corn hole boards. Music played, drowning out the sound of the truck generators, and a few brave souls were already dancing.

As the sun continued to sink slowly toward the horizon, casting a golden glow on everything, the heavenly scents coming from the trucks had my mouth watering.

Ryder was taking it all in with a look of wonder. He'd shoved his sunglasses to the top of his head and inhaled deeply. I got the feeling he was rarely surprised by anything, and I felt a surge of pride at offering him a new experience.

He turned to me, eyes lit with interest, smile warm, easy. "So...what do you want to eat first?"

You.

I realized it must be all over my face because he gave a low, sexy laugh and leaned in, his mouth ghosting over my ear. "Just say the word."

"Falafels," I said quickly. "I want falafels. And Tex-Mex. But I also want some noodles. Oh! And ice cream..."

HE FALLS FIRST

"A smorgasbord." He nodded. "Let's do it."

The lines moved along, but it was still a decent wait. Remembering Vi's temper test, I kept a close eye on Ryder for signs of annoyance. But he easily conversed with the people in front and behind us, and with me. Always with me, maintaining eye contact, smiling like he was enjoying himself.

Twenty minutes later, we were at a small table in a corner out of the way and had enough food for ten people. I'd been bringing home work leftovers or cooking every night, so I was in heaven eating things that I hadn't had to make for myself.

Ryder dove in as well, like maybe he hadn't eaten in weeks. I watched him down three fish tacos and then look at his plate like he couldn't believe they were gone.

"You can lick the plate," I said with a straight face. "I won't tell anyone."

Unabashed, he grinned—a slow, mischievous one. "You jest, but those were the best tacos on the planet."

"Only because you haven't tasted *my* tacos yet." The minute the words were out of my mouth and hit my ears, I felt myself flush beet red. "I didn't mean—"

His smile was filthy.

"I meant I actually *make* tacos, and—"

He was full-out laughing now, the sound rich and full and joyous, the light brown and green of his eyes interspersed, like forked lightning through chocolate.

I crossed my arms and glared at him, and he worked at controlling himself. Then he leaned in and put his mouth to my ear. "I'd love to taste your taco, Pen. *Again.*"

"I'm talking about *real* tacos! Chicken tacos, carne asada tacos, shrimp tacos!"

He exhaled a soft laugh, his lips dancing over the sensitive flesh beneath my ear. "How about this? I'll eat *any* taco you offer me."

I could tell my face was red as a tomato as I put my hand on his chest and nudged him back. Actually, it was probably closer to a shove. "I changed my mind," I said loftily. "No tacos for you. Ever."

"Forever's a long time," he said, eyes so smoking hot I was surprised I hadn't gone up in flames. I grabbed my water and drank it down, earning me another low, sexy laugh.

"Dance," I said desperately. "We're going to dance." I stood, and then so did he, pulling me into his arms right next to our table.

"The band's on a break," he said, his rough jaw against mine.

I nearly moaned in pleasure. "So?"

He laughed with so much delight that I couldn't help the twitch of my lips. And then, music or not, he began to move against me, easy and confident. When the band came back a minute later and started with something slow and haunting, Ryder pulled me in tighter, his eyes on mine as we moved to the beat in unison, pressed tight from chest to knees. It was possibly the funnest, sexiest moment of my life. Maybe later I'd feel pathetic about that, but in the moment, up against his sinewy body, my usual reality seemed far away.

Our eyes met. His mouth curved as he leaned in close again so I could hear him. "I love how you feel against me."

Just a few words, simple words, and I melted. "You mean a hot, sticky mess?"

"I love it when you're a hot, sticky mess."

I laughed, but I also blushed.

"I love your laugh too." His mouth made its way to that spot beneath my ear. "And the way you look at me." A little nibble had my toes curling in my sandals. "It makes me feel…special," he murmured, "as if you see all of me, and accept me just the way I am."

I stared at him. Had anyone ever felt this way about me?

"I love being with you," he said, a low rumble of words from his chest to mine, and something deep inside me shifted into place, almost like I was a puzzle, one that had been missing a key piece for a very long time.

And that piece was him.

CHAPTER 26

Ryder

I COULDN'T REMEMBER WHEN I'D last allowed someone else to choose what I'd be doing for an entire evening. Nor could I remember the last time I'd been truly surprised by…anything.

But this woman, whom I'd done my damnedest not to yearn and burn for, surprised me at just about every turn. I had no idea where the night was going from here, and for once it was like the good old days, before I'd needed to consult a schedule, an admin, and at least one brother before doing anything that hadn't been planned out ahead of time. It felt like such a luxury.

Tonight, I was going old-school by allowing Penny, one of the most fascinating, achingly special women I'd ever met, to take me wherever she wanted, to do whatever she wanted.

After our impromptu slow dance, we made our way back to the table and ate…everything. We went for dessert next, and I watched her inhale an empanada while moaning in pleasure, and by the time she sucked a finger into her mouth to get the last little bite, I was a goner.

She paused, then slowly pulled her finger free with a little *pop*, her eyes locked on mine. "It was good," she whispered.

I leaned in. "I wanna taste."

She had another one on her plate. She could've handed it to me or held it up to my mouth. Instead, she slid her hands up my neck, fisted her fingers in my hair and kissed me, tasting like the empanada and hopefully my future.

She pulled back and smiled, probably at the dumbstruck look on my face. "Good, right?" she asked softly.

I lifted my gaze from mouth to meet her eyes, which tended to tell me things her mouth didn't. "Best I've ever tasted."

She snorted, not taking me seriously, which I secretly loved. "I bet you say that to all the women you go out with. Do you redo everyone's kitchen as well?"

"No," I said on a laugh. "I do not."

Cocking her head, she studied me. "You're a good man, Ryder Colburn."

"Don't tell anyone."

She smiled. "Your secret's safe with me. But you're not giving us enough to help you with on the kitchen. Don't take on all the work yourself." She lifted her hands, wriggling her fingers. "I'm willing and able. I get most of the stuff is technical and I don't have the skills, but there's got to be something more I can do to help."

"I'm nearly done with the first coat of the cabinet doors. I just have to sand them down and then do another coat."

"I can sand!" She grinned at me. "Let's do that after this!"

"Anything you want." A risky sentence, but I meant it.

"I'm so glad you said that." She stood up, dragging me with her. The band was going strong now, and she pulled me right into the middle of the dancing. The crowd was rowdy, everyone on the floor singing along to the music.

Thunder clouds had rolled in, blocking out the stars and darkening the night, but under those fairy lights, it was like we were out of time and place. We danced through a bunch of songs, with Penny belting out the lyrics, singing to her heart's content, making me sing along with her, each song heating me up because though this woman could absolutely *not* hold a tune—which I loved—she could dance.

"I like the way you move."

She grinned, and kept going, a little out of breath, laughing, leaning into me, trusting me to keep her upright while she let go. All I wanted was to watch her, take her in, absorb even a fraction of her ability to give one hundred percent to absolutely everything she did, whether that was work, her family, or this, tonight, with me.

A slow, cool mist hung in the air now, a warning that it would soon rain, blurring the woods around us. Penny looked upward, eyes shining, smile warm and sweet, the fluidity of her beautiful body as she moved making my heart roll over and expose its underbelly. When I hadn't been looking, she'd somehow obliterated the brick wall around my heart—the one that kept my emotions safe, the one that hid that scared little kid I'd once been, existing only to keep my siblings safe, leaving me feeling exposed and vulnerable, but also…happy.

The source of that happy smiled up at me. "What are you thinking?"

"I'm thinking that I've been hiding myself for a long time." I slid my hands to her hips. "I'm thinking I've just been going through the motions. I'm thinking I'm glad you walked into my life, because with you I don't do any of that. I think I'm falling for you, Penelope Rose."

Her eyes flickered with surprise, like she couldn't imagine that I might want her in my life, much less tell her so. "You are?"

My heart cracked even as I chuckled. "I am."

She stared up at me, letting out a shuddery breath. "I'm falling for you too, Ryder Tate Colburn."

I raised a brow at being middle named. My brothers were dead. "Caleb or Tucker?"

"Caleb," she admitted.

I groaned, even as the thrill of her saying she was falling for me rushed through my veins. "Remind me to kill him later."

"How dare you. I'm going to marry that man someday."

I growled and she was laughing when I caught her against my chest, my heart kicking hard as she cuddled into me like she belonged there. *Because she did.* My eyes drifted closed of their own volition. How was it that having her in my arms made all my problems seem so, so, so very far away? Maybe because she was like sunlight, warm and life-affirming, giving. She could wrap me up in her without so much as a touch. Her warmth, the vibrancy of her...

A slow song came on, and in the next beat, we were plastered against each other again, so close I could feel her heart thumping in rhythm with mine. Her mouth curved and I thought of what else she might do with that mouth. Unable to help myself, I leaned down and took a little nibble of her lower lip.

With a moan, she tried to climb me like a tree. I had one hand at her nape, my fingers curled into her hair, the other at the small of her back, balancing her as she rocked against me. My world shrunk to this, with her. Unable to resist, I blazed a trail of kisses to the hollow of her throat, pulling another breathy moan from her that burned deep in my core and fed my soul. When my tongue flicked out to taste her skin, her fingers tightened in my hair.

"More," she demanded.

And though I was inclined to give her whatever she wanted, especially if that was me, I slowed down, lifting my head to meet her gaze.

"You're teasing me," she murmured.

I dragged my mouth to her ear, biting the lobe, tugging gently. "Am I?"

Her eyes flashed, and she turned, swaying to the music as she pressed her back and sweet ass into my front, smiling at me upside down.

My fingers tightened on those dancing hips, and I was cross-eyed with lust as I put my mouth to her ear. "If I'm teasing, what are you doing?"

"Giving as good as I get."

Definitely going to be the death of me.

It was fully dark outside now, and undeterred by the mist turning into a light, drizzly rain, more people kept showing up. When it was too crowded to hear each other, she took my hand and led me off the dance area.

We walked in comfortable silence back to the parking lot. With no city lights out this far, the wet night was lit only by the retreating ambient glow of the food square.

At my truck, I gently pressed her against the passenger door. "Thank you for bringing me here tonight," I said. The rain was still so light it barely touched us but felt good on my heated skin. Felt even better when Penny fisted her hands in my shirt and yanked me down for a kiss.

CHAPTER 27

Penny

I DON'T KNOW WHAT IT was about Ryder, but the second his mouth was on mine, my mind calmed. A small part of me still reeled at the fact I'd been slowly opening up to him, telling him things I'd never shared before. I'd shown him my darkest past, and he hadn't offered me empty platitudes or condemnation. He'd given me simple understanding and an easy affection I'd come to crave. I felt safe and comfortable, and most shocking of all…happy. He thought the best of me, and because of that, I could as well.

So I let go as the rain hovered in the air all around us. Visibility had diminished enough that we were in a bubble of our own. I couldn't see much more than the man in front of me, which left me to feel everything a hundred times over. The weight of his body pinning me against the truck. The cool mist covering us. Ryder's warm hands on me.

"Here comes the rain," he murmured.

Only seconds later, it started to come down, soaking into

our clothes, clanging on the roof of the truck. Even then, we didn't move, letting it sluice off us. One of Ryder's legs pressed snug between mine and his fingers tangled in my hair, keeping it out of my face.

The nearly unbearable pressure built between my thighs... And the sure but honey-slow movement of his lips against mine as he kissed me was overwhelming, his hard body driving my own crazy. When he groaned softly against my mouth, I felt the sound all the way to my toes.

"You smell amazing," he whispered, the tip of his nose lightly grazing along my jaw. When he got to my throat, he took a nibble. "And taste even better."

I felt boneless, like I might die if he stopped touching me, but when I shivered, he lifted his head, sanity coming back into his eyes.

"You're cold." Pulling me away from the truck enough to open the door, he helped me in, then a few seconds later, slid behind the wheel.

Dripping wet, soaked to the bone, we stared at each other.

I had no idea who moved first, but in one blink we'd somehow met in the middle, kissing, touching, moaning. Or maybe that was just me. I still didn't understand how I could want him at this magnitude, utterly without reason, especially since I'd always so fiercely claimed I no longer wanted any attachments. But I did.

I wanted him more than I wanted that dream café.

I wanted him more than I wanted to be able to pay the bills.

I wanted him more than I'd ever wanted anything in my entire life.

And the feeling of his hands on me, the warmth in them over my chilled skin, the way he touched me—like he was just as helplessly thrown by this as I was and *needed* to get closer, closer, closer. Every movement of his hands, his lips, his body dragged me nearer to oblivion. I couldn't breathe, couldn't think. I'd never felt sexier, and never felt more out of control at the same time. I wanted this never to stop. My entire body vibrated with desire, but the console between us kept getting in the way, until with a growl of annoyance, he hauled me over it and into his lap, maneuvering me so I straddled him.

"Did I tell you how gorgeous you look tonight?" he asked in that low, husky voice. "I can't keep my hands off you. I want… God, the things I want to do to you, Pen."

"Tell me." Was that really my voice, all wobbly?

"I want to touch you for hours, taste you, breathe in those breathy little whimpers of yours when I make you come over and over—"

I kissed him, *hard*, sliding my hands beneath his shirt, touching heated wet skin over hard sinew. His abs, his chest, up and then down again, slowing as I reached the waistband of his jeans.

"You're hot."

He chuckled. "Thank you."

"No, I mean your body."

"Again, thank you."

With a snort, I dropped my face to the crook of his neck. "Temperature wise! You're always so warm! It's clearly your fault that we've fogged up all the windows…"

And they were fogged up, completely, leaving us cocooned in a whole world all to ourselves. Ryder's warm palm encircled my neck, his thumb tipping my face to his, holding my gaze captive as his free hand skimmed up my thigh, taking my sundress with it, his rough fingers feeling incredible on my skin.

The heat in his eyes burned with an intensity that made every part of my body pull taut with anticipation, and then we were kissing again, slow and deep and delicious. When we broke apart to breathe, his mouth simply shifted southbound, down my throat, his teeth scraping over my collarbone as he nudged the straps of my dress to fall from my shoulders.

I touched every inch of him I could reach, my hips rocking the softest part of me into the hardest part of him. It was a thrill to feel what I could do to him, that I wasn't alone in this, and my only goal became to get him inside of me.

"Don't stop."

"Never," he said, his lips finding mine once more to seal the promise while I worked at his shirt, which I needed off. Yesterday.

He pulled it over his head in one easy motion and my fingers immediately slid over his shoulders, over the tattoos inked into his skin and up into his hair, eliciting a very rough, very male sound of pleasure.

He was way ahead of me, tugging the cup of my bra down so he could get his mouth on bare skin. He teased my nipple with his tongue, sucking little kisses, and then gave a light tug with his teeth that had me gasping. The sound seemed to pull his focus back to my mouth. Sealing his lips against mine once again, he cupped my ass, using the hold to rock us against each other, setting a rhythm that made me desperate for more. I popped open the buttons on his Levi's and reached in, finding *exactly* what I wanted.

"Oh fuck," he rasped when I wrapped my hand around him.

My sentiments exactly. I gave an experimental stroke, and he swore again, still managing to get into my undies.

For a single heartbeat, I lost concentration, trying to

remember which pair I was wearing, hoping they were something sexy. But then he stroked the pads of his fingers over me and I stopped thinking. Stopped breathing too, and on his second stroke, I rocked to meet those fingers, quivering, already on the very edge—

His phone rang, but he ignored it. When it went off again, he swore, tugged the thing from his pocket, and tossed it somewhere behind us.

I gaped at him. "What if it was important?"

"It's Caleb. He'll figure it out…" Turning his full attention back on me, his eyes promised all sorts of wicked, dirty, wonderful things coming my way.

I shakily said his name and gave him another stroke. He groaned, his eyes drifting shut, head falling back. Leaning in, I pressed my mouth to this throat.

His hands slid down my body and into my undies as he rumbled out, "Going for my jugular?"

With a low laugh, I sank my teeth into him, then laved the spot with my tongue. "I can't believe Mr. Always In Control of Himself let that happen."

He squeezed my ass with both palms, then slid his fingers lower. Then lower still…

"I can't seem to control myself around you. Believe me, I've tried." Lifting his head, he flashed a smile, then kissed my shoulder as he gave a targeted swirl of those long, diabolical fingers, eliciting a shockingly needy sound from my lips.

"Love how you melt for me. Love watching you come," he breathed, bringing me close to doing just that.

"Ryder…"

A hard rap sounding against the driver's side window

startled me so hard I nearly leapt right out of my skin. We both swiveled to look out, but the window was still completely fogged over, little drops of condensation running in rivulets down the glass.

I scrambled back into my seat, fumbling to right my clothes, shoving my hair out of my face, my heart pounding hard in my ears. "Who's out there?"

"I don't know." Ryder was buttoning his jeans when the rap came again.

Not a hand hitting the window, but something harder. Ryder put a hand on my thigh to calm me and gave a quiet *we're okay* smile. With his other hand, he powered down the window.

And came face to face with a cop.

Instantly, I was transported to a different time and place, to that night in Seattle when Mitch had shown up, aggressive and tense. I'd mistakenly thought I could talk him down. When he'd gotten loud, a neighbor called the cops. They'd hauled us both outside to sit on the curb for the world to see and judge. I'd held a dish towel to my bleeding face while Mitch yelled at everyone that it'd been all my fault.

At first, I'd been relieved to have the police there, thinking I'd be safe, but the abrupt, aloof way they'd questioned me had been almost as scary as the incident itself. I'd never forget how helpless and very alone I'd felt.

Now, through the rain, the cop leaned in and eyed us both for a long moment. "License and registration, please."

Without a word, Ryder leaned into me, reaching to pull the paperwork from his glove box. He then retrieved his license from his wallet and handed both over.

While I was trying to stave off heart failure.

"Stay put," the officer said, and then turned and walked back to his squad car.

My heart pounded in my ears. I hadn't had a panic attack in a very long time, but it barreled down on me like a freight train. What would happen? Would Ryder get a ticket? Would he blame me? Would he—

His hand squeezed gently on my thigh. Then he frowned, leaning in to see me better, stilling at whatever he saw on my face.

"Penny? Hey, it's okay—"

Trembling from head to toe, I shook my head. He didn't know that, couldn't know what might happen. What if he made us get out of the truck and—

"Penny, I need you to take a deep breath for me, okay? In like this…" He demonstrated by taking in a deep inhale. "Now slowly let it out."

So I breathed, feeling like an idiot. "I never did this," I managed. "I never got caught doing anything wrong when I was a teenager."

A small smile tilted his lips. "Better late than never."

I shook my head. "What if he arrests us for indecent exposure?"

"We're not getting arrested," he said. "He couldn't see in the window, and nothing was exposed when I rolled it down." Again, he gently squeezed my thigh with warm, strong fingers. "It's going to be okay."

I let out a shuddery breath. "I can't believe we almost did it in your truck."

His smile was wry. "Been a long time since I've been caught with my pants down."

I choked on a disbelieving laugh. "This has actually happened to you before?"

"Well, yeah, but in my defense, I was sixteen and, as we've already established, really stupid. But I'd rather have you in my bed tonight, with lots of time." His voice was pure wicked sin. "Lots and *lots* of time, Penny."

Another knock came at the window, and once again, I nearly climbed out of my own skin. Would have, if Ryder hadn't kept that grounding hand on my leg.

"I'm letting you off with a warning," the cop said sternly, handing over Ryder's license and registration as he slid a gaze between us both.

I shrank back, hating myself for it, but all he said was, "Get a room."

And then he walked away.

I waited for Ryder's reaction. I'd been waiting for it since the knock on the window. But all he did was turn to me with a smile. "You're a fun date."

And then he took us on the road.

The night was dark and still stormy. The only thing visible through the driving rain was the outline of the rolling hills and the tall, militant shadows of craggy trees. As we drove, he reached for my hand and glanced over at me.

"I'm good," I said with faux calm, keeping my face to the side window, trying to get myself together. I was doing a shitty job of it—still trembling, still having trouble drawing a deep breath, still a little lost in that long ago memory.

The moment we left the woods and turned onto the curvy two-lane road that would lead us back through Star Falls, Ryder pulled over at a lookout point and turned off the engine.

"Come here," he said softly.

"Isn't this how we got into trouble in the first place?" I'd tried to sound glib, tried to infuse laughter into my voice, but I knew I'd failed.

He didn't reach for me as he had the first time. This time, he simply held out his arms, making the choice mine. Which made it no decision at all. I climbed over the console and crawled back into those waiting arms. I sighed in relief, soaking up his warm, steady presence for a long moment, neither of us talking, just Ryder running a hand up and down my back.

"You're still shaking," he murmured, dipping his head so he could meet my gaze. "You cold?"

Unable to form actual words, I just nodded and burrowed in.

He cranked the heater and directed all the vents my way, then tightened his grip on me, sharing his body heat, warming me up as I took a deep breath and slowly let it shudder out of me. I hated the feeling of being out of control, but surrounded by Ryder, it was quickly dissipating.

"Better?" he asked, his jaw pressed to mine.

As I was beginning to understand, when I was with him, everything was always better.

CHAPTER 28

Ryder

IT DIDN'T TAKE A genius to know Penny had been triggered by the cop, and *shit*, I was so stupid. I'd brought her right back to that dark place she'd worked so hard to leave behind.

"I've got you," I whispered, holding her close until finally she started to relax, her face still smashed into the crook of my shoulder.

"It was just an overreaction," she whispered. "I'm okay, everything's okay."

She seemed to be talking to herself, soothing herself, not me, and it killed me. Had she been alone in the aftermath?

"Pen—"

"Let's go sand."

"What?" I shook my head. "No. You're—"

Still burrowed into me, she set a finger over my mouth.

I kissed that finger before I spoke around it. "It's okay to need a moment, to give yourself some—"

"If you're going to say *time*, don't." She hesitated, then finally lifted her face, eyes stark, mouth grim. "I've given myself time. Too much of it. What I want is to be...*normal*. So please, let's just go sand. Unless you've changed your mind, which I would understand."

A shot right through the heart I didn't like to acknowledge. She was one of the strongest women I'd ever met, and even though she didn't need me to, I still wanted to slay her dragons for her.

"I've meant everything I've ever said to you." If nothing else, I needed her to believe that. "My woodshop's in the barn behind my house. Are you sure—"

"I like your house," she said quietly. "It's warm and safe. Take me there."

So I did.

CHAPTER 29

Penny

TWENTY MINUTES LATER, RYDER had parked in his driveway, and the beautiful farmhouse was lit only by his truck's headlights.

Around us, the world was dark, rain coming down in sheets now, the drumming of it on the roof accented by the occasionally violent flash of lightning and booming thunder that reverberated in tune to my heart.

We were both dripping wet, and yet I wasn't ready to leave the warm cocoon of the truck.

"Can you talk to me?" he asked quietly.

I shrugged. "It's nothing."

He reached for my hand. "Since when do we lie to each other?"

Fair enough. I stared down at our entangled fingers. "I want to be done with this feeling." I pressed a hand to my belly. "I want to be done looking behind me."

"I hear that," he said softly.

I knew he did, that he felt the same way about his own past. "I realized something tonight," I said, turning to meet his gaze in the ambient light from the dash. "Somehow when I wasn't looking, I let my guard down with you."

"And that's a bad thing?"

His eyes were dark and concerned, and I knew he deserved the truth. "I made a promise to myself that I wouldn't do that, not ever again, unless I'd gotten to know the other person."

He cocked his head, his manner mild, still calm, if a little confused. "And haven't we? Gotten to know each other?"

"Yes." Too much, maybe.

"Is that what upset you?"

"No. *No*," I said again at his concern. "I…had a panic attack. I'm sorry—"

"No, you don't apologize for that, are you kidding me? I'm the one who's sorry, that I couldn't prevent it, that I couldn't help—"

"You did help." I'd still be freaking out if he hadn't hauled me into him and held me tight. I shook my head. "I thought you might be…mad. Or at the very least, irritated."

He blinked. "What? Why?"

"I ruined the night."

"You didn't." Reaching out, he took my hand and pressed it against his chest. "Penny, I'd never get mad at an honest reaction. Never." He paused. "You expected me to blame you for your reaction tonight?"

"No." I paused. Grimaced. "Maybe." I felt my face heat, unable to understand why this was all coming out of me now, when it'd been such a lovely night. "Ignore me."

"I'd do just about anything you asked of me. Except that. Please talk to me."

I let out a long, slow breath and met his gaze. "What *would* you get mad at me for? What would bring out your temper? Please, be honest."

Something like grief flashed across his face and his eyes softened. "Full honesty. I do occasionally lose my temper. Everyone does one way or another. But for me, it takes a lot. I've got a very long fuse. But there's a big difference between getting angry and taking that anger out on someone. It's a line I don't cross."

I shifted to fully face him.

His expression was quiet, reflective. "I grew up with a man who lost his temper at the blink of an eye and had no problem taking it out on his wife and kids. For most of my growing-up years, we walked on eggshells. We learned early on to be fast and how to vanish in plain sight. So you have to understand, I was incredibly young when I swore I'd never be that guy."

He drew a breath. "And then after losing Auggie, very little seems worth losing my shit over. So if you're waiting on me to blow up at you for something, you're waiting in vain. I'm not that guy. I'll *never* be that guy."

There was a feeling in my chest that I couldn't name, the sensation that my heart had been peeled wide open. "I'm sorry for what happened to you when you were a kid," I said. "And then Auggie's death. It's awful and tragic, but still not your fault."

He squeezed my hand. "And I'm sorry for what happened to you. Which wasn't your fault either."

We stared at each other for a beat, the only sound that of the rain hammering the truck roof and my unsteady heart thumping away.

Finally, I gave a small, tremulous smile. "So now what?"

"Your call. We could go to the barn and sand. Or...we could go into the house and I could make you cookies, since I'm a pro now. Whatever you want."

There was something in his gaze that said he'd meant that last sentence literally, and my heart began to race—in a good way now.

"You do realize I'm a hot mess, right?"

"Not any more than the rest of us."

I snorted and turned my attention to the house, which was dark. "You don't leave a light on for yourself?"

"I have them on a timer..." He frowned. "The porch light should be on." He pulled out his phone, accessing his home system. "Huh. Power's out. Storm must've caused an outage."

"Do you have a generator?"

"Not a hard-wired one. The house is too old for the electrical load, so I sacrificed certain modern conveniences. I do have a gas run generator to plug a few things into if needed. But I rarely bother for myself."

And why did the prospect of not having power actually seem...cozy?

"Maybe I should take you home—"

I found a smile. "You're afraid you left your tighty-whities on the floor, aren't you?"

He snorted. "I don't wear tighty-whities."

I already knew that, but it still took my mind to a very dirty place, which in turn, lifted me from the anxiety that had been swirling in my belly ever since the cop had banged his flashlight on the truck window.

"The last time I was here, you had some good wine. Still have some?"

He smiled, exited the truck, and came around for me as if the rain wasn't pelting him with every passing second. Hand in hand, we ran through the downpour to the front door, laughing breathlessly as he got us inside. His wet hair clung to his forehead and had fallen into his eyes as he dripped all over the small mud room floor.

I wasn't in any better shape.

Kicking off his shoes, he pulled a large flashlight from a small closet and flicked it on. I slipped out of my sandals, then stepped into the dark living room.

Ryder came up behind me as he lit the room up with the flashlight, his chest brushing my back, and immediately, a sense of warmth and calm hit me. The house was basically an extension of him. I already knew the calming effect it had on me—the cream walls with wide oak trim, the high, open-beamed ceiling, the wood floors and big, comfy furniture, all of it clearly masculine and comfortably broken in. I knew the shelves were stuffed with books on everything from architecture to travel to Stephen King, that there were two plants bookending the glass slider, both thriving, and that there was a pile of battered sneakers and work boots littered around to trip over.

Still shivering, I pulled my wet sundress away from my skin with a suctioning *pop*.

"I'll make a fire," Ryder said. "There's also probably enough hot water for a quick shower."

"Pretty forward of you to offer me a shower on our first date," I quipped, even though it sounded like the *second* best thing I could wish for right now.

He cupped my face with his warm hands. How they were so warm when mine were frozen was beyond me.

"This isn't about getting you naked," he said softly. "It's about the fact you're still shaking and your skin is like ice."

I'd rather it be about getting naked... "I'm fine." I immediately ruined this statement by giving a full body shiver. Dammit.

His mouth quirked. "Humor me."

"Humor this." I slid my icy hands beneath his shirt, resting them on his abs.

He hissed in a breath but manfully sucked it up.

Smiling sweetly, I dug my fingers into those muscles.

He just raised a brow.

"Not ticklish?" I asked.

"Not there."

A challenge, but it'd have to get in line. "I'm not here to be pampered, Ryder. That's the last thing I want right now."

"Then name it." His eyes darkened. "Anything."

I'd never been particularly bold or brave, but something about this man brought it out in me. So I stepped into him, nudging him up against the wall, which, let's be honest, he allowed, because if he hadn't wanted to be moved, I wouldn't have been able to budge him.

But...he did want to be moved. At least according to those fiery eyes. He wanted other things too, because as I pressed into him, I found him hard.

But he didn't make a move, just waited me out, because...he was all about choices, and he wanted this to be mine, wanted me to have all the power, knowing I hadn't always had that. I wanted him for that alone, but also for far more. For so long, there'd been a hole in my heart, and a lingering ache of loneliness I hadn't been able to shake. But Ryder seemed to chase away that aching loneliness, leaving me filled with excitement, anticipation...*joy*.

More than anything, I wanted to do the same for him. I smiled, and he returned it. Honestly, I could drown in the way he looked at me, like I was worth something to him, like in this very moment there was nowhere he'd rather be and no one else he'd rather be with.

"What do I want?" I repeated, and when he nodded, my smile widened. "You." Something flared in his eyes as I went up on my tiptoes and slid my hands into his silky, wet hair to brush my mouth over his.

And then again…

A very rough, sexy male sound escaped his throat as he dove into the kiss. His hand slid to my nape, fisting in my hair as his other cupped my jaw, stroking his thumb across the pounding pulse point at the base of my throat. All of it ignited a wildfire in my chest as he lowered his mouth to mine. The kiss instantly went nuclear as I touched every inch of him that I could reach, and believe me, I already had my favorites. Panting, I opened my eyes and found his fixed on my face.

"Hurry," I whispered. I meant to sound soft and sexy, but it might've been more of a demand.

Not that he listened. Or if he did, he wasn't taking requests. His gaze darkened as he took me in. I knew my hair had for sure rioted, but I hoped the sundress clinging to my body maybe offset that a bit. Given the deep growl that escaped him, he most definitely enjoyed the view as he finally leaned into me, hands flat on the wall at either side of my face now, mouth inches from mine.

"We are not going to hurry."

At the implication that he intended to draw this out, I couldn't seem to draw a breath. But who needed air? Not me, not when he kissed me again, slow and deep, like he was trying to convince me of something.

It was a very compelling argument. I had one hand under his shirt, the other on his face, enjoying the scratch of his dangerously alluring stubble as he teased kisses along my jaw, beneath my ear, down my throat, making me break out in goose bumps from head to toe. By the time his mouth found mine again, his teeth gently tugging at my lower lip, I was nothing but a puddle of desperate need and hunger.

"But hurrying can be fun, right?" I panted, reaching for the button on his jeans.

His hands caught mine. "I've been fantasizing about all the things I want to do to you," he said. "There's a list, Penny. A *long* list."

Could one get goose bumps on top of goose bumps? Could one have an orgasm from simply thinking about what might be on his list?

"You've given this a lot of thought then," I managed.

"You've got no idea." His hands let mine go to slide past my hips, down the sides of my legs, and then began the return trek, taking the hem of my sundress with them, the material pooling on his forearms.

"I started the list the day I got hurt at work. You were so fiercely determined to take care of me." His smile was filthy. "Bossy, too. I liked it. Playing doctor made the list, but next time it's my turn."

I snorted.

He shook his head, getting serious. "That morning, on the floor in the kitchen… No one's ever done anything like that for me before. I think I knew right then what you'd mean to me."

My head reeled from that as he ran a hand down my body, his fingers catching on the scrap of lace masquerading as panties, tipping his head to the side to better see what he was doing.

"I like this dress, especially wet." Lowering his head, he kissed his way along my collarbone, letting his tongue slip beneath the bodice, heating my skin. "Mmmm. You're still so wet. Where else, I wonder..." He took his mouth on a tour, seemingly a personal mission to sip the rain from my body, urging the spaghetti straps off my shoulders with his teeth, groaning when the bodice slipped to my waist. He palmed one breast while his tongue rasped over the other. Then he took a nibble, and I swore that my knees vanished into thin air. Luckily he had a good hold on me, so I didn't hit the floor.

"Is this on your list?" I asked breathlessly.

"You being all drenched and revved up for me? Oh, yeah. I dream about it."

"Do you talk this much in your dream?"

His warm breath danced over my skin as he laughed, the sound wicked and naughty as he turned us, switching our places before pinning me against the wall, lifting me up by the backs of my thighs, wrapping my legs around his waist. Hands freed, he fisted them in the fabric of my dress, rucking it up to my waist. Holding my gaze captive, those talented, deliciously calloused fingers scraped my panties aside and glided over me.

"Fuck, Penny..." His voice was so low it almost didn't register. "You're drenched."

"This is a shock."

His wicked laugh danced over my skin as his fingers worked me into a desperate wreck while I whispered, "Please, oh, please," on repeat, which made him smile against my neck.

"Now who's talking?" he murmured as he kept up the torture, teasing me with diabolical glee.

Pressed to the wall, I could do nothing but writhe and beg, utterly beyond the ability to joke. I was rocking into him rhythmically, moaning his name, my hands fisted tightly in his hair as he slowly, purposely drove me wild. When he nibbled at the spot between my shoulder and neck at the same time his fingers finally gave me the pressure I needed, I came so hard I saw stars. Sweaty, panting, *marveled*, it took me days and months and years to catch my breath. When I finally did, I tore at the buttons on his shirt, parting the fabric in the same careless way, peeling the wet material from his shoulders.

"Still in a hurry?" he asked mildly, mouth gliding up and down my throat.

"Yes." I tilted my head back to give him more to work with. "Join me, won't you?"

He was laughing when I tugged open his jeans and slipped a hand inside, seeking treasure—and I found it.

He abruptly stopped laughing and groaned.

I'd learned his body too, and I stroked him just how I knew he liked, smiling in triumph when he swore and rocked his hips into me. I started to taunt him, saying, "Turnabout's fair play—" Only to break off on a ragged moan when he entered me in one smooth motion, burying himself as far as he could go.

Our gazes met, his hooded, dark, erotic. Just looking at him sent another tremor through my body, little aftershocks I couldn't control. He filled me completely, until I thought I'd shatter from the sheer joy of it. Every nerve in my body was on edge, sensitive to every sound, every touch.

When he began to move, I gripped him tightly, whimpering, panting, trembling…barely holding on as he relentlessly took me apart again, piece by aching piece. It took me a moment to realize he was gripping my hips, shaking. He was close, I knew he was, but…holding back. No.

Needing him as wild and out of control as he'd made me, I kissed my way to his ear, nibbled the lobe and whispered, "Let go."

My name rumbled from deep in his throat as he came unglued, unmoored, wild, taking me right along with him.

When I found my senses again, he'd sunk to his knees, still holding onto me, head bowed, forehead pressed to my shoulder. We stayed like that for long moments, gulping air.

"I need to get you off the floor," he finally said, voice hoarse. "Give me a minute." He didn't move a muscle. "Maybe an hour."

I tried to snort but didn't have the breath for even that.

Somehow, we made it to his bedroom. He wrapped a fuzzy throw blanket around me, then pulled a battery-operated lantern from somewhere, casting everything in a low glow. I hadn't gotten a good look at his bedroom last time I was here, having been utterly consumed by the man it belonged to, but the room was large, mostly dark woods, cream walls lined with a massive bookshelf.

On his dresser was a series of pictures. A teen shirtless Ryder and his siblings, all knee-deep in a river fishing, looking like wild savage hooligans. Another of a much younger Ryder, holding hands with a young woman who had his smile—his mom. But the photo that melted my heart was the Ryder I knew, stretched out on a couch, arms curled protectively around two babies on his chest, all three of them fast asleep, looking utterly relaxed, contented, at peace.

I sat on his bed and listened to the rain drumming the roof, feeling far more relaxed than I could've thought possible. Ryder came back from the kitchen with two waters, handing me one. He drank his in one go, then plopped to the bed, propping his head up with a hand, utterly, perfectly naked.

I wanted him again.

As if I'd said it out loud, an arm snaked out and pulled me down to the mattress. A smile flashed and he rolled, tucking me beneath him, one hand braced by my head, the other at my hip, his knees between mine, nudging them apart. His movements were so sensuous and purposeful that I didn't even track what he was up to until his weight settled over me, both calming and revving me up at the same time.

His broad shoulders blocked out the glow of the lantern. Not being able to see much left me to *feel* everything a hundred times over.

The weight of his body pinning me down on the mattress.

The pull of his fingers tangling into mine above my head.

The hard heat of him pressed between my legs.

And the sure but deliberately unhurried movement of his lips against mine, one lush kiss sliding into another. When he groaned softly against my mouth, I felt the sound all the way down my spine. The first touch of his tongue had me arching up off the pillow, unable to reach for him because his hands still held mine.

"Again?" I whispered.

He simply lowered his head and demonstrated his answer. With his body.

A long time later, he cuddled me into him. Conversation flowed between us with shocking ease. He told about his family, and how they still needed to tell Kiera that Hank was living with Ryder.

I told him how I still missed my dad but was selfishly glad my mom kept herself busy and mostly out of our lives.

He talked about the complicated balance it took for him to keep both Bill and Hazel in his life, the worry he'd alienate one and lose them both.

I shared my concerns about Wyatt and raising him when I had no idea how to raise a teenage boy.

We talked about the wild adventures he used to take and how many international hospitals he'd seen as a result of those adventures. I mapped the scars on his body with my fingers.

And then my mouth.

We were serious and flippant, then back to serious, balancing the scale, always respectful of the delicate trust we'd handed each other.

"You wear a lot of hats," I murmured. "Ryder Colburn, restorer and protector of historic things, caretaker, badass boss, and newly minted baker of cookies…"

Pulling me over the top of him, his hands went to my hips as he smiled, clearly enjoying his view. "*And* lover of a certain smart—and smart-*ass*—woman named Penny." He smiled when I rolled my eyes, then kissed the tip of my nose. "I like the way you say my name," he whispered.

"You mean with sarcasm and attitude?"

This time he kissed one corner of my mouth, then the other corner. "With feeling. Say it again."

"Ryder," I said in the tone I used when annoyed. "Ryder,"

I repeated, but this time with humor. And finally, "*Ryder,*" I whispered breathlessly, with hunger and need. With a groan, he kissed me again, and I lost myself.

And then, like always when I was with him like this, I found myself again.

CHAPTER 30

Penny

IT WAS WELL AFTER midnight when Ryder drove me home and parked in front of Grandma's house. He'd asked me to stay the night, but I knew that would add all sorts of complications.

"Thanks for...just dinner."

His smile was filled with trouble of the very best kind. "I should be the one thanking you."

I found a laugh and slid out of his truck, blinking in surprise when he came around and offered a hand. "Oh, um, you don't have to walk me to the door—"

He smiled sweetly but also with unmistakable steel. "I'm walking you to the door, Penny."

It was old-fashioned and protective, and yet somehow I felt myself flush over it. "Okay."

He brought our entwined hands up and brushed a kiss to my palm. "Okay."

On the porch, he kissed me quickly, though with no less heat than usual, but didn't let go of me. "Tonight was just what I needed. And in case that wasn't clear, I mean being with you was what I needed. I'm sorry about what happened in the parking lot, but please don't let that scare you off."

I stared at him. "I was thinking it might be the other way around."

"I hate to break it to you, but you're not that scary." His smile quickly faded. "And I meant what I told you. I'm falling for you. Falling hard."

My stomach bounced around a little, but not in the *I'm going to throw up* way. More in an *I'm in deep and shockingly okay with it* way. "I meant it too."

He ran a finger along my temple, tucking a wayward strand of hair behind my ears. "Afraid?"

I thought about it and was shocked to find the answer. Vulnerable, yes. Nervous, yes. Afraid? "No. You?"

"Petrified." He gave a crooked smile. "Be gentle."

When he looked at me like that, like he'd opened the window to his soul to let me see everything he was, I felt my heart roll over in my chest. "I got your six," I whispered.

The corner of his mouth quirked. "You've got to stop hanging out with Caleb."

"But he's my future husband."

He snorted, and I wasn't sure who leaned in first, but suddenly we were reaching for each other, and—

The porch light came on. We both blinked at the jarringly bright light as the front door opened.

"Hello, kiddos!" Grandma said happily. "How did the date go?"

I started to tell Ryder not to answer that question but pivoted back to Grandma. "Wait. How did you know this was a date?"

"You told me."

"No." I shook my head. "I said we were running errands."

Grandma slid her dentures around. "You sure?"

I narrowed my eyes. "Very."

"Huh," she said, then lifted her finger as if she'd just had an "aha!" moment. "You're wearing nice clothes and mascara. Dead giveaway. And my goodness, would you look at the time? I've got to get to bed—"

"*Wait*." I knew her tells, she was shifting on her feet and not making eye contact. She was up to something. "What am I missing?"

Grandma slid Ryder a quick look. "Nothing."

I turned to him as well.

He opened his mouth, but Grandma beat him to it. "It's not his fault. I was just trying to help."

Ryder grimaced. "Nell, this wasn't that."

And just like that, I knew. "Oh my God. Tell me you didn't somehow make him take me out."

"Well, not *make* him, make him," Grandma said. "I asked nicely."

Stay calm, stay chill, don't waste the orgasms you just had... I eyed the man who'd given them to me. "*And you said yes?*"

"Well, to be fair, he really didn't want to," Grandma said for him.

Something in my chest caved in. "That makes me feel all better."

Ryder winced at my sarcasm. "Penny—"

"It's not his fault," Grandma said quickly. "I laid it on pretty thick and wasn't going to take no for an answer."

"Why?" I asked her, horrified. "*Why* would you do such a thing?"

Grandma's eyes went shiny. "You were down, and I wanted to help pick you up. I thought if you could go out and have a good time with someone, someone who'd never hurt you—"

"Oh my God."

Ryder reached for my hand, but I crossed my arms.

"And anyway, you turned him down," Grandma said. "So I don't see why this is a problem—"

"You don't see why—" I turned to Ryder. "Is that why you didn't mention it? The whole please-take-my-pathetic-granddaughter-out-on-a-date because I turned you down?"

"Amongst other things, yes."

"What other things?"

"Namely that I'm an idiot."

I couldn't hear this right now. I shook my head, flooded with humiliation that Ryder had asked me out…as a *favor*. "You know what? I need a minute. I'm going upstairs. No one follow me."

Grandma, suddenly looking very small, nodded. "I'll be inside if either of you need anything."

Ryder snagged my hand before I could follow her in, waiting until I met his regretful gaze. "It's not what you're thinking," he said.

"Good, because what I'm thinking is that you asked me out because you pitied me."

"No," he said, his tone soft steel. "It had nothing to do with pity." He ran a hand over his face, like he was sincerely rattled that I would think so. "I've been drawn to you from the beginning, more than I've ever been drawn to anyone. I get that this looks bad but, Penny, my feelings are very real."

Something sparked in my chest at that, but I couldn't deal with it now. "Look, I'm trying really hard not to do what I normally would, which is use this as an excuse to walk away."

He drew a deep breath. "I appreciate that, but does it really matter how we figured out we like each other? Isn't the important thing that it's real?"

I gaped at him. "I think that's the most guy thing you've ever said."

He opened his mouth, then closed it. Shoved his fingers through his hair. "Look, yes, I asked you out because Nell asked, but the truth is, I wanted to be with you even then. When you said no, I was torn. Bummed you weren't ready, but also relieved because that took Nell out of the equation."

He met my gaze, his own filled with something that kicked my heart into gear. "Everything that came after that, getting to know you, sharing things that I hadn't shared with anyone, even just laughing and goofing around, it all meant something to me. *You* mean something to me, Penny. And that's all organic, just you and me. It has nothing to do with anyone else."

I understood what he was saying. I did. But I needed to think without pressure. "It's late…"

He nodded. "I know. And I understand. But please promise me that we'll talk. Because I'm willing to fight for this, for you."

I stared into his eyes and saw he meant every word, so I nodded. "Good night, Ryder."

He dipped his head to brush a kiss to my temple, running a hand down my hair, yearning and care in every movement. "'Night, Penny."

I watched him go, the door shutting quietly behind him. I drew a deep breath and headed to the kitchen.

Grandma pushed a mug of hot tea across the table to me.

I was mad at her, really mad, but also thirsty, so I took the tea. "I know you thought you were doing something nice for me." I met her wary gaze. "I get that. You love me. And I love you back. But, Grandma, you need to stop worrying about me. I'll figure things out in my own time, in my own way. Okay?"

She let out a slow breath and nodded. "Okay."

"No more meddling."

She nodded again.

I gave her a long look, and she sighed. "I mean, I'll try."

It was all I could ask for. I took the mug and headed straight to my bed, crawling under the covers, where I planned to remain until I was either old and gray or my alarm went off.

CHAPTER 31

Ryder

TUCKER OPENED HIS FRONT door the next morning, looked me over, and said, "You look like shit."

Ignoring that, I peered past him. "He about ready? I'm in a rush this morning."

"I know you didn't oversleep, not with those bags under your eyes."

Hank came up behind Tucker, dressed and ready to go. "Ah." This was in a slightly petulant tone.

"Let me guess," I said. "Tucker wouldn't cave on letting you pick what color underwear you put on."

Tucker didn't have many tells. If he didn't want to share something, not even God Himself could get him to. But he actually ran a hand down his face. "He's free-balling it."

I could've sworn Hank smirked. I stared at Tucker. "He's commando?"

"We couldn't come to terms."

It was then I realized that I wasn't the only one who looked tired and out of sorts. It seemed wearing people out was Hank's superpower. "Awesome." I eyed Hank. "You ready?"

He rubbed his belly. "Aw."

Tucker sighed, another huge tell. "He didn't like my oatmeal."

"Because you don't use sugar, you control freak weirdo."

"Processed sugar's bad for you," he said. "Especially for stroke victims. I put in some berries."

"Yeah, not the same thing." I looked at Hank. "Nell will feed you."

Hank beamed and pushed past the both of us, heading to my truck without looking back.

"Guess we know where we line up against Nell," I muttered, then followed Hank, who was struggling to get into the passenger seat. "You're supposed to wait for me." I gave him a boost, then walked around to the driver's side, but before I could slide in, Tucker was there. He gestured with his chin for us to step aside.

"How the fuck do you manage living with him?" Again he swiped a hand down his face. "Twelve hours. I had him twelve hours and I'm losing my shit."

"I pretend he's a golden retriever. He can't mouth off, he doesn't have opposable thumbs, and he's got the intelligence of a three-year-old."

Tucker blinked, then gave a rough laugh, shaking his head. "Brilliant. As always." He sighed and met my gaze. "Sorry. You do this daily. I need to step up more and help you out."

"I'm fine."

"You don't look fine. What's going on?"

Well, let's see. I'd started the internal audit process with my accountant, and I was pretty sure someone was stealing materials from the inside. I worried about Kiera. And yeah, I had Hank living with me, and though he'd done nothing wrong, I still felt raw and exposed around him. And then there was the best date I'd ever had, up until Penny had found out about Nell asking me to ask her out.

And now I had no idea where we really stood. "Nothing's going on."

"Uh-huh." Tucker crossed his arms. "Try again."

I blew out a breath. "I made a mistake and don't know how to fix it."

He eyed me for a beat. "With Penny?"

"How did you know?"

"Because you're in deep with her, and I figured you'd do something stupid to mess it up because you think you don't deserve to be happy."

"You're one to talk."

He rolled his eyes. "I've seen you go through a lot of shit and remain steady as a rock. Nothing much has ever gotten to you, except her. You'll fix it."

"How do you know?"

"Because you're my big brother. All my life, you've always fixed everything." He stepped back to let me leave. "Love you, you stupid dumbass."

I felt my throat tighten. "That's Mr. Stupid Dumbass to you."

Tucker laughed and flipped me off before going back inside.

A few minutes later, I parked at Nell's, staring at the house that was filled with warmth and love and had given something back to me that I'd been missing.

I felt sick with worry that I'd lose Penny. I should've known

I'd mess it up, that you couldn't catch sunlight, couldn't hold it in your hands. Sunlight was only to be looked at, never touched.

"Ah?"

I didn't take my eyes off the house. "Everything's fine. You ready?"

"Ah." This was said with more than a slight bit of doubt, and possible sarcasm as well. When I looked at him, he seemed… worried. For me. Which *still* felt like a mindfuck.

I sighed. "Okay, so everything's not fine. But I don't know how to fix it, so let's just drop it, okay?" And when I'd started having conversations with my dad, complete with understanding all the difference nuances to his various "ah" sounds, I had no idea.

But I couldn't think about that now, not with my heart pounding uncomfortably in my chest. "Let's go."

Hank tried to get out of his seat belt and couldn't. But he didn't lose his ever-loving shit—a visceral reminder that I wasn't doing myself, or him, any favors by hanging onto the past. I helped him out and up the walk.

When Penny opened the door, I stood there like a tool. She was already dressed for work in her usual black trousers and white blouse, with her hair knotted on top of her head and a few loose strands framing her face. And then there were those mesmerizing eyes I could never look away from.

"Hank," she said with a soft, genuine smile. "Come in." She stepped back, gently taking his arm, leading him to the couch, covering his legs with a throw blanket and handing him the remote. "Grandma will be right down."

"Did you poop?" Pika-boo asked Hank.

"Don't answer that," Penny said, glaring at Pika-boo.

Hank made a sound that might've been a laugh.

I shut the door behind us, then hesitated. I'd spent most of my life following my instincts, which had saved my ass many, many times over. I'd always trusted myself to figure shit out. Except now, with this woman.

I had no idea what to do.

Finally taking mercy on me, Penny tilted her head ever so slightly to the kitchen. I nearly collapsed in relief. She was willing to talk to me.

The kitchen was still a construction zone, so we stood on one of the tarps, her looking at me, me trying to access the right words. And damn, was it hot in here? I unzipped my sweatshirt and began to pull it off.

"About last night—"

Her lips twitched, clearly to fight a smile, and I stopped, confused. "Is this funny?"

"No, but that is." She pointed at my chest.

I wore the shirt Nell had insisted on giving me. It was a match to the woman's own shocking pink one, and just like hers, it read: STAND ASIDE BOYS, THE EXPERTS ARE HERE.

It was an unfortunate size too small, so it stretched tight over my chest and was short enough to reveal a strip of my stomach. And if I was being honest, I'd worn it hoping to score brownie points.

Penny was biting her lip now, unable to hide her amusement.

Brownie points achieved. "I'd pretend to be insulted that you're laughing at me," I said. "But I'm just so damned happy to see you smiling."

"It's amazing what a bowl of Cap'n Crunch can do for

morale." She gave me a long once-over. I was pretty sure she lingered on the strip of stomach my shirt exposed, but that might've been wishful thinking. But she was standing in front of me, willing to talk. Or at least, listen. Go time.

"Penny, I—"

"Wait." She grimaced. "I'm sorry. I need to go first before I lose my nerve."

"It's just us," I said quietly. "You can tell me anything, always."

"About last night…" Her cheeks went rosy. "I don't want to be that girl who uses a fight or misunderstanding as an excuse to doubt everything, when it's really because…" She broke eye contact. "She got scared that she'd opened herself up to more hurt."

Is that why she'd shut me out last night? Not because I was a dumbass, but because she was scared? I stepped closer, not daring to touch her, but needing to be in her orbit. Heart pounding, I said, "I swear, I never meant to hurt you. The opposite, in fact. I wanted to take away your pain. Only, when I wasn't looking, you took away mine." I could hear the emotion in my voice, but I didn't even try to temper it.

"After I dropped you off last night, I told myself that if, after thinking about it, you decided you wanted to be just friends, I'd find a way to be good with that. I'd take whatever part of yourself you shared with me because I knew…"

"Knew what?" she whispered.

"That being with you is the easiest thing I've ever done."

I was holding my breath when she let out a shaky one of her own. "Same," she said softly. "Which doesn't change the fact that when it comes right down to it, neither of us wanted this." Her face was carefully blank, not giving me much of a clue as to her thoughts. "I mean, we both know I'm a hot mess inside."

If it was reassurance she was after, I wanted her to know I understood and that opening myself up to possible hurt wasn't easy for me either. Not that it would stop me. She was more than worth it.

"If you're talking about last night, everyone has moments like that."

"I don't see you panicking about anything."

I let out a rough laugh. "Should've seen me after I left your place."

Her gaze searched mine. "Tell me your most embarrassing panic attack."

So we were going to open up a vein and maybe bleed out. What the hell. For her, I'd probably do anything. "It has to do with cafeteria food."

She went brows up. "Cafeteria food."

"Yeah. I actually gag every time I see meatloaf." I swallowed thickly. "Even thinking about it now, I'm gagging on the inside."

She couldn't have looked more surprised if I'd tossed her out the window. "*Meatloaf.*"

"Meatloaf," I confirmed and caught her mouth twitch. "You want to laugh at me."

"I'd never. But what did meatloaf ever do to you?"

I lifted a shoulder. "Certain things remind me of my childhood, of Hank when he was a very different person, of a life I don't like to think about."

Her eyes softened. "I see."

"I've just ruined my tough guy reputation, haven't I?"

The very small smile on her beautiful face made my knees

weak. "I don't know," she said. "Meatloaf can be absolutely petrifying."

With a snort, I pulled her into me and set my forehead to hers. "I'm sorry I didn't tell you that your grandma asked me to take you out. She meant well. And I should have told you. Are we okay?"

She was quiet for long enough that my heart stopped beating. "I want us to be," she finally said. "But—"

I tensed and she pulled back to look into my eyes. "If I learned anything from last night," she said, "it's that I need to take this slow. I need to give myself the grace to be a hot mess as I heal."

Knowing her as I did now, the things she'd been through—the death of her dad at a young age, a remote mom, an ex I'd like to get my hands on—I really did get it. And since having her in my life was immeasurable compared to losing her, I nodded.

"Your pace. Always."

She gave me a grateful look that reminded me of how few times she'd been given the driver's seat to her own life. Fuck that. I'd go at whatever speed she wanted, glacial if that was what she needed.

So it was a hell of a time to realize exactly how much more I wanted. I wanted her heart and soul. I wanted her to be mine, but more than that, I wanted to be hers. Whenever she was ready.

Even if I didn't deserve it.

CHAPTER 32

Penny

IT WAS LATE WHEN Vi called to ask me about a new recipe she was working on. Hearing something in my voice, she and Renee showed up fifteen minutes later in their pj's with a bottle of vodka.

Grandma and Wyatt were asleep, so we claimed the living room.

"Shhh," Pika-boo said. "I'm sleeping."

We gave him a cracker to keep him quiet, then added a splash of Grandma's cranberry juice to the vodka while I recounted everything that had happened between me and Ryder. When I finished, the sisters exchanged a long look.

"This is where you tell me I did the right thing by slowing things down," I said.

"Look," Vi said, "I get that one, you had a little freak-out, which was embarrassing, and two, Grandma played matchmaker—which bee-tee-dub, I adore—and you got upset at both. Understandable. Truly. But I also but think

Ryder gets huge points for not being scared off by either of those things."

Renee nodded.

"I like him for you," Violet said.

Renee nodded emphatically.

I blew out a sigh and leaned back. Because the truth was, somehow, when I hadn't been looking, my life had fallen into two categories: Before Ryder and After Ryder. AR.

Before Ryder, I'd been in a rut, stuck in a lane I couldn't get out of.

Now, AR, I'd not only changed lanes, but I was out of traffic. I felt...*alive*. Was I still afraid of getting hurt? Yes. But wasn't it much better than being numb? Also yes.

"I like him for me too," I admitted.

Vi shrugged, like that was the answer. Period. The end.

I held my breath, then let it out, along with a truth I hadn't intended to share. "I told him I was falling for him." I waited for them to react like they were watching a horror show, but all they did was smile and nod. "*Falling* for him," I repeated.

Vi patted my knee. "Honey, we already knew that."

"Like way before you did," Renee added.

I sighed. "I'm pretty sure he already knew too. I drool every time I even think about him taking off his clothes."

"To be fair, we *all* drool when we think about him without his clothes," Vi said.

"I don't," Renee said.

"Renee doesn't," I said.

"Oh, wait..." Renee's eyes had gone soft and dreamy, like she was just now picturing it. She swiped at her mouth. "Am I drooling?"

The next morning was rough. I took more than my fair share of ibuprofen, but my head still drummed like I had someone standing on my brain, whaling at it with a sledgehammer.

Note to self: too old for vodka.

I managed cooking just fine, and also loading up the Hungry Bee van. But then all too soon, I stood in front of Colburn Restorations, staring up at the building. Everything would be fine. I'd go in there and do my job. Ryder and I were still close. The only thing that had changed was the pace of our relationship. All was well.

But myself was a big, fancy liar because all was *not* well. I missed him. My heart hurt far worse than my head.

"You okay?" a woman asked.

Turning, I came face-to-face with a petite redhead. Hazel, who I'd met several times now. She was pretty in that girl-next-door way, wearing a tennis skirt and a t-shirt that showed off an enviably fit figure, her gorgeous hair pulled back in a ponytail. She was eyeing me worriedly, phone in hand, like maybe she planned to call Ryder.

"I'm fine," I said. "Thank you. And you?"

A small smile crossed her face. Her slightly sweaty face. And that coupled with the tennis gear and battered athletic shoes, it wasn't a stretch to realize she'd probably been playing her weekly game with Ryder.

"Who won?"

She smiled. "He was easy pickings today. You have anything to do with that?"

I bit my lower lip, and Hazel laughed softly before saying,

"One thing about Ryder, he's got a hell of an armor. Hard on the outside, but it's to protect his—"

"If you say creamy center—"

She grinned. "*Heart.*" Whatever she saw on my face had her good humor fading, replaced by genuine caring concern. "Listen, if it helps to hear it from someone who grew up with him, he's a really good guy."

"I know."

"Not that it makes him easy." She laughed. "I wouldn't call any of the Colburns easy." Her eyes went sad for a beat, like she was somewhere else, somewhere in the past, but she shook it off. "They're definitely worth the trouble though." And with that, she walked off.

It'd only been two days since I'd told Ryder I wanted to slow things down, and already there was a hole in my heart where he used to be. I stood there drawing some deep breaths, knowing I'd overreacted and hating that. I'd pushed away the best thing to happen to me in a long time.

Making matters worse, I'd promised to have Ryder's back. I'd told him I was falling for him. And I'd meant both of those things, to the depths of my soul.

And yet, at the first opportunity, I'd used a mistake, a misunderstanding, as an excuse to back off, even when I'd told him I wouldn't run scared.

I didn't know how to come back from that, or why he'd even want me to.

My phone rang. Ryder. Staring at the screen, I stopped breathing. I tilted my head up to eye his office window as I answered with a shaky, "Hello?"

"You okay?"

I could see him, just a shadowy outline, one hand in his pocket, the other holding his phone to his ear.

"Why do people keep asking me that?" I asked.

"Maybe because you've been standing there talking to yourself for seven minutes. I've gone downstairs and then back up again twice, unable to decide if you wanted to see me."

Because he'd heard me when I'd asked for time and space and was trying to give me what he thought I wanted. "Are *you* okay?" I asked.

"Now who's answering a question with a question?"

I had to laugh. "Fine. I'm working on being okay, okay? And for what it's worth, I'll always want to see you."

There was a beat of silence. I'd surprised him. "Then please come in," he said softly. "I'll stay out of your way—"

"No—" I shook my head. "Please don't." I was done holding my cards close to my chest. "At the very least, we're still friends. Right?" I tried to get another look at him, but he was no longer in the window.

"Penny, I'm anything you want me to be."

The front doors opened, and Ryder stood there, hair damp and curling around his ears and collar like he'd immediately showered in his office bathroom after tennis with Hazel.

"Hi," he said into the phone.

"Hi back."

"Want a hand?"

"Yes, please," I said, still holding my phone to my ear.

He moved close, and the two of us stood there like chronic idiots, still holding our phones against our faces.

"I was half convinced you'd trade this account away and I wouldn't get to see you."

I gave him a small smile. "And I thought you'd make sure not to be here."

He disconnected the call and slipped his phone into his pocket. Then he gently pulled my phone from my hand and dropped it onto my cart. "Glad we were both wrong," he said.

Then he pushed the cart through with one hand, the other settling warm on my back, guiding me inside. When we entered the kitchen, Caleb and Tucker were there, cackling over what I'm guessing was a dirty joke, since they refused to repeat it.

"You know I've heard dirty jokes before," I said. "I even have a few myself."

"Tell us one," Caleb challenged.

Tucker clasped his hands together under his chin, the face of hopefulness.

"Ignore them," Ryder said.

"It *has* to be dirty," Caleb said. "The dirtier, the better."

Tucker nodded like a bobblehead.

Ryder sighed, probably because he knew I wasn't going to pass up a challenge.

And he was right. "Okay," I said. "What's the difference between a snowman and a snow-woman?" I paused for dramatic effect. "Snowballs."

Caleb paused, then laughed so hard he had to bend over at the knees. Tucker just shook his head. "Weak."

Ryder looked pained. "Snowballs?"

"I said what I said."

He shook his head and smiled at me.

It made me ache.

Caleb tossed Ryder an energy drink from the fridge. "I drank your green smoothie for you. You're welcome. We've got a crazy schedule today—drink up."

While I unpacked the food, Caleb regaled us with the story of being stood up last night by a blind date, with Tucker poking fun at him.

Ryder was quiet.

I could tell his brothers knew something was wrong, although they didn't call him out on it. I knew they wouldn't, not in front of me. Instead, they joked and bullied him out of his shell. Another tug on my heart, because they loved him.

And…so did I.

At the shocking realization, I found myself standing in the center of the kitchen, surrounded by boisterous testosterone, my hand to my chest as if I could hold my heart inside. Sounds and sight and my emotions all froze while the world around me kept going. I could hear the guys—Caleb reminding Ryder that he had five minutes until his meeting, Tucker hyping them up for some touch football game they were going to play later. Ryder responded, his voice melting me, his words escaping me.

Then Ryder got a call, sending me an apologetic glance as he left the room. Caleb and Tucker followed.

I stood there, trying to catch my breath and figure out how to make my world start revolving again.

CHAPTER 33

Ryder

AFTER SLEEPING A TOTAL of zero minutes, I gave up before dawn and stood in the shower, head bowed, letting the water beat over me as I tried to relax my tense muscles. When I was done, I grabbed a towel and stared at the guy in the mirror.

He looked hollow and empty.

Half an hour later, I dropped Hank off with Nell. It was the first time we'd had a moment to speak since my date with Penny.

"I'm sorry my mouth never knows when to shut up," Nell immediately said, unusually subdued.

"Your heart was in the right place."

"So's yours." She looked at me for a long moment. "I might be old as dirt, but my eyes work just fine. I know what's real and what's not. For example, I know the sun rises every day. I know that by seven p.m. my right knee's going to ache like a son of a bitch. I know that Hank's belly is going to rumble within twenty minutes of him getting here without fail, and that two minutes after he eats, he's going to let one loose that clears the entire living room."

I grimaced.

"But," she went on, "most of all, I know my granddaughter's sweet, damaged heart is slowly coming around. I know that she's healing here in Star Falls, and that you're a big part of the reason why. So please, *don't give up on her.*"

"Never."

Her eyes filled. "So it's...real for you too?"

"*Very.*"

She threw her arms around me and held on tight.

Pika-boo made some smoochy, kissy noises. "Me too, me too!"

With a chuckle, I pulled back. "I'll be back after work to put a few hours in. I need to get the electrical upgrade finished before the appliances come in next week." I couldn't talk about it anymore or I'd lose my mind. I got back into my truck and ten minutes later, parked at Kiera's house.

But then I realized it was barely dawn, and Kiera might kill me if I woke her.

"Why are you standing out here in the dark, you creeper?"

Caleb. I didn't even hear him drive up behind me.

He frowned. "You look like shit."

"Aw, thanks. I did it myself. And don't you have an early Caltrans meeting?"

"Tucker's handling it."

"You think he knows what he's doing?"

"I wouldn't go that far." Caleb shrugged. "But he'll figure it out." He gave me a meaningful look. "We Colburns always do, don't we?"

"What's that supposed to mean?"

"Like you don't know."

I didn't have time for bullshit games. "Just spit it out." No one could stand on my last nerve like any of my siblings. Especially this one.

"You're in a bad mood." He eyed me carefully, and for good reason. The last time we'd both been in a bad mood, it'd ended with us rolling around in the mud during a rainstorm, trying to beat the living shit out of each other.

"You're in a bad mood," he repeated. "Because you still haven't figured out how to fix the best thing that ever happened to you."

"Tucker has a big, fat mouth."

"Well, yeah, have you met him?"

"There's nothing to fix," I said. And wasn't that a shitty feeling. "Penny slowed us down. She needs some time."

"Then give it to her."

"I am."

Caleb nodded. Clasped my shoulder in silent commiseration, and it drained my annoyance at his busybody-ness.

"So what are you doing here?" he asked me. "It's my turn to take the kiddos to breakfast."

I shrugged. "Thought I could tag along." I could use a toddler hug. Or two.

He eyed my truck, then moved closer, his voice low. "Where's Hank?"

"Dropped him off at Nell's."

He relaxed a bit, but not much. "Good. Kiera doesn't need to find out like this."

"You know we're going to have to tell her eventually, right?"

"But not yet. She's just starting to let us in again."

The front door opened and Kiera gave us the exact same raised brow look Caleb had just laid on me.

"Two brothers at the same time. That's against the rules."

"We promise not to gang up on you with all that love you hate so much." Caleb started to push past her and into the house but she stopped him.

"I'm not in the mood for an intervention," she groused.

"Interesting," he said. "You're at least admitting you need one."

"I'm not admitting a damn thing. And great, now I need to put a dollar in the swear jar." Kiera glanced at me. "Why are you here? It's not your day."

"Is there a quota?"

She put her hands on her hips and eyed me in disbelief. "Let me get this straight. You're *choosing* to spend extra time with the two feral wolf cubs I birthed."

"Yes."

"Actually, it's *three* feral wolf cubs if we count *you*, Ki," Caleb said, and then took a healthy step back because we all knew she'd been kickboxing for years and had no problem using her skills on her brothers..

But Kiera just let out a surprising laugh and stepped aside.

Caleb and I eyed each other warily, then shrugged. She must've had her caffeine already. In hopes she had some for me as well, I started to follow Caleb in, but she slapped a hand on my chest.

"What?" I asked.

"You look like shit."

"I just told him the same thing," Caleb said over his shoulder.

Kiera looked me in the eyes for a beat before her gaze skittered away.

Right. She really didn't want to see me more than necessary. Couldn't blame her. "You know what, I'll just…" I turned to go, but she caught my hand.

"Don't be stupid." She drew a deep breath. "Caleb told me you're still blaming yourself for what happened to Auggie."

I sent a glare at Caleb, who was lounging in the doorway between the living room and kitchen. Our resident mother hen in stubble and work boots.

He shrugged. "You know I hate conflict." He waved a hand at us. "So I need everyone to get *unconflicted*."

"That almost made sense," Kiera said, then shooed him. "Go away. I'm about to tell my dumbass oldest brother that guilt doesn't look good on him, nor does it belong with him." She turned to me. "Listen, I need you to get this through your thick skull once and for all—what happened to Auggie wasn't on you. It wasn't on me. It wasn't on anyone who's still alive, so you have to let it go. Trust me…" Her eyes were solemn, serious, and anguished. "Stop punishing yourself, Ryder. It's no way to live."

I let out a shuddering breath. Was that what I was doing? Punishing myself?

She sighed, muttered something about stubborn-ass men, and scrubbed a hand down her face. It was the same tell I had. We'd both gotten it from Hank, not that I intended to say so. I liked my face the way it was.

"I know I'm not one to talk," she said. "I know I've fallen apart. I mean…" She shook her head. "I haven't taken a deep breath for two years."

My heart pinched, hard. Caleb, who hadn't followed her

request to go into the kitchen, looked like someone had just kicked a puppy.

I opened my mouth to say something, even though I had no idea what that something might be, but she shook her head.

"Just listen, okay? Two years. Two years, during which time I cried daily, once even over soggy cereal. So…" She tapped my chest. "Trust me when I say it's okay to take all the time you need to grieve. But let go of the guilt. You weren't at fault for what happened, and you're not stepping foot into this house until you look me in the eyes and say it. Say that you know it wasn't on you, and that you'll stop letting it eat you alive."

"I will if you will."

She drew a slow, deep breath and reached for my hand. "Together then, okay? Together we let it go."

"Together," I said. I knew it wouldn't be that easy, but I let her pull me into the living room, and as always, was slapped in the face with memories of Auggie. I wasn't sure I'd *ever* walk into this warm, comfortably lived-in house and not think of him. I took in the large photo over the fireplace of Auggie, Kiera, and the twins, one each on their parents' laps, taken on their first birthday. Alex reaching for his mom's hair, Abi chewing on one of her dad's fingers. Kiera looked to be in the middle of an eye roll, and Auggie, the center focus of the picture, had his head tipped back, laughing. It was a single beat in time that perfectly captured the essence of the family.

And less than three months later, Auggie would be gone.

Kiera had hated the photo on first sight. But Auggie had loved it, and she'd loved Auggie enough to cave in and hang it in a place of honor.

She was at my side, studying the picture as well. "I was so mad at him for secretly getting this one printed," she said. "I'd picked out one where we were all looking at the camera and smiling. But he loved it so much..." She let out a small smile. "I'm ridiculously attached to it now. Besides, if I took it down, he'd probably come haunt me about it."

Hard to believe I could laugh about such a thing, but I did. "I'm sorry if we woke you."

She snorted. "I'm owned by two toddlers. It's safe to assume I'm always awake. They jumped on my bed an hour ago. Abi gave me a cannonball knee to the uterus, and Alex licked my face. It was great."

I snorted, causing her to turn to face me. She frowned. "Something's still wrong. What is it?"

"Nothing."

"Lie." This from Caleb, still mother-henning from the doorway.

Kiera stared at me. It'd been two years since she'd taken a good look at any of us, much less reached out and touched. I wanted to smile. I wanted to cry. Instead, I closed my eyes.

"Why is he lying?" she asked Caleb.

"Ask him."

I rolled my eyes.

"He's in love," he said casually, like one plus one equals two.

Kiera gasped.

I nearly gasped too but managed to swallow it. "He doesn't know what he's talking about."

"Deny it then," he dared me.

All I had to do was say, *I'm not in love.* So I opened my mouth and said, "I'm in love." *What the...*

Tucker strode in the front door just as I said it. "We already told you that," he said.

"No. I meant..." I drew a breath. Ah, hell. The gig was up. I couldn't hide it from myself anymore, much less them. I just shook my head helplessly, so out of my league I couldn't even see the league.

"Cute," Caleb said. "You ever going to tell *her*?"

"This isn't funny."

"If you could see the look on your face, you'd think it was a little funny," Tucker said.

"How did this happen?" Kiera asked. "I'd have laid down money you'd be the last of us to fall."

"Well," Tucker said, "when a man and a woman—"

Kiera elbowed him in the gut. "I meant because he doesn't easily engage."

"Takes one to know one," I muttered.

"Hey, my husband died."

Caleb slid her a look. "How long do you get to use that excuse?"

Anyone else might've been horrified or taken offense, but Kiera grinned. "As long as it works," she said and laughed. She laughed so hard she had to sit down, which she did, right there on the floor. Then she went from laughter to sobs.

Shit. Aching for her, for us, I sat next to her, and when she didn't punch me in the nose, I slid an arm around her. She slumped against me, shaking from head to toe.

Tucker sat on her other side and reached for her hand.

Caleb vanished down the hall and came back a moment later with a box of tissues, which he dropped in Kiera's lap before sitting on the floor in front of her.

"The kids are watching a show on my phone." He drew a breath. "I'm sorry, I shouldn't have asked you that."

She made good use of the tissues, then sighed, seeming... lighter. "No, it's okay," she managed past what sounded like a ragged throat. "I think..." She shook her head. "I think I needed that. I must be in my Caleb-Meltdown Era."

"Hey," he said.

When Caleb had gotten hurt in the NCAA's Frozen Four tournament, he'd been stoic. When he'd gone on to have three subsequent surgeries, he'd been stoic. When he'd been told his hockey career was over, losing out on being the nation's number one draft pick, he'd remained stoic—for a full year.

Which I knew because he'd been living with me at the time. He'd been quiet. Unflappable but also unreachable. No one could get him to talk about what was happening to him—not me, not Kiera, not Tucker.

Then one day the four of us had been sharing a pizza and nachos at the Cork and Barrel, and some drunk idiot had called out in passing, "Hey, No Hands, how ya doing?"

Caleb had ignored him, but Tucker had asked, "What does that even mean?"

"It means I've seen better hands on a digital clock!" the guy had yelled and jabbed a finger at Caleb. "I lost two large when you tanked that championship game because you got a little boo-boo and were too pussy to go back in!"

Caleb had erupted. One second, he was drinking a beer, the next he'd taken a flying leap over the table and tackled the guy to the floor.

When we were bailing Caleb out of jail a few hours later, we learned that the guy had gone to college with Caleb, had spent a lot of time heckling him during games no matter how Caleb had played, and had also slept with someone Caleb had been seeing.

Turned out Caleb had *not* been quiet and calm during that period between getting injured and the bar incident—he'd been a volcano building pressure, and he'd finally burst.

Now he looked at Kiera, rubbing a rueful hand over his jaw. "At least during your meltdown you didn't get arrested."

Kiera shrugged. "Day's still young." She turned to me. "So who's the woman?"

A direct question, and I knew it'd only cause more trouble down the line if I didn't tell her. "Penny."

She blinked. "The Penny who works for me? My Penny?"

"Yes."

"You're seeing Penny…" she said slowly. "One of my employees."

"If it helps," Tucker said, "I'm pretty sure he got himself friend-zoned."

I gave him a shove that knocked him over. "She didn't start it," I said to Kiera. "Which means your problem, if you have one, is with me, not her."

She just shook her head. "Why didn't you tell me?"

Caleb and Tucker slid me a quick look and I knew we were all thinking the same thing—that there were a lot of things we hadn't told her over the past two years, all to protect her. One of them a six-foot-tall, ex-military man who'd had a personality transplant via stroke.

"Oh my God." Kiera drew a deep breath. "What else don't I know?"

Just about everything…

"To be fair to Ry," Tucker said into the awkward silence. "You haven't wanted us to tell you much since..."

She grimaced. "I get that. But I didn't mean to make you feel like you had to keep things from me."

He cleared his throat. "I believe your exact words were 'All of you go away and forget about me.'"

Kiera went still, looking stricken. "I said that, didn't I..." She closed her eyes. "I'm sorry. I take it back." She turned to me. "But...you and Penny?"

"I mean...maybe," I said. "Tucker might be right about the friend zone."

"No," Caleb said. "No way are you two just friends. I saw her patch you up after you got hurt. I've seen how she looks at you. She gets all flustered, like they do in those porn books."

She looked at me. "You got hurt?" Then turned back to Caleb. "They're not porn, they're romances. Not that I expect you idiots to understand."

"It was nothing."

"He only says that because he and Penny got to play doctor," Caleb said. "It looked very cozy."

"It's like you *want* to die," Tucker said to him.

"Hey, I meant it in a good way," Caleb said in his defense. "Like genuinely, it's obvious how much she cares for him."

"How could she not," Kiera said softly. She shook her head, like she was surprised at herself. "I hope you're wrong about her just wanting to be friends. She's...special." She held my gaze. "Like you. She'd be lucky to have you."

I waited an extra beat for the punch line, but it never came.

"Maybe she just needs time," Tucker said, then shrugged when we all looked at him. "I mean, Kiera's the only one of us who believed she could be loved. The rest of us..." He shrugged. "We don't," he said bluntly. "Maybe she's like that."

I thought that was way more optimistic than I could've managed to come up with, but I couldn't deny that I wished with all my might that he was right.

"I'm realizing I've missed a lot," Kiera mused, letting out a long, slow exhale. "I know I've taken pain-in-the-ass-baby-sister to new heights these past two years, and I'm sor—"

"Do not apologize," I said. "Not to us."

"No, I have to," she said quietly. "Because I'm sorry, so very sorry for pushing you all away. I know it's words, but I'm ready to show you." She paused. Gave a tiny smile. "Also, if I'd known Caleb was stupid enough to give a couple of wild, feral three-year-olds his phone, I wouldn't have avoided you guys for so long."

Caleb looked confused. "What's wrong with letting them play a game on my phone?"

"They know what the Amazon app looks like and how to work it," she said. "Yesterday, Amazon delivered three Candy Land games."

"Shit." He jumped up and vanished down the hall.

He was back in ten seconds. "I put it in airplane mode." He looked at Kiera. "No more apologies. I mean, unless you want to apologize for this..." He parted his hair and bent his head to us. "Do you see it?"

"Your brain?" Kiera asked. "No. It's too small."

Chuckling, I held out my fist, and she actually fist-bumped me.

Caleb flipped off both of us. "I'm talking about my gray hair."

"As in one singular strand?" Kiera asked.

"Yes." He pointed at her. "And it's got *your* name on it."

She leaned in. "Let me see again."

He lowered his head again, waiting for her to sift through his tousled mop.

"I see it," she said and yanked it out.

Caleb yelped, then straightened and glared at her. "You can't do that! If you pull it out, it *multiplies*."

"Uh-oh."

"Uh-oh? What uh-oh?"

"I pulled out three," Kiera said.

"Liar."

She held the strands up for his inspection. Three. All gray.

Caleb had his hands on his head as if protecting the rest. "Where did you learn to be so mean?"

"You lot!" Her smiled faded. "But thank you," she said more seriously, to all of us. "For waiting me out, giving me the time I needed without smothering me—even though I know damn well you were on rotation to watch over me, stealthily filling my fridge with food and my car with gas." Her eyes went suspiciously shiny again. "You never gave up or left me."

"Never," I said.

Caleb stopped messing with his hair and laid unusually solemn eyes on her. "Never *ever*. Even if now I'm going to have a full head of gray hair before I turn thirty and it'll be all your fault."

Her eyes filled and she sniffed.

"Again?" he asked, pained. He'd never known how to act in the face of tears.

I squeezed Kiera's hand and she sniffed again. "I missed you boneheaded morons." She then shocked the hell out of me by grabbing us all, hauling us in for a hard hug.

"Ouch," Tucker said when his head knocked into Caleb's with a *thunk*. "Why does your love always hurt?"

Kiera rolled her eyes and stepped back. "I gotta go to work." She looked at me. "You're in charge."

"Hey," Caleb said. "It's *my* day."

"What the hell," Tucker said. "They love me best."

"She picked me," I said. "But whoever wants Al's pancakes can come along."

Caleb and Tucker raced to the door like they were little kids, shoving and yelling, "Shotgun!"

Just then a tornado ripped into the room. Two of them, actually—one named Abi and one named Alex—and took a flying leap at us.

Kiera gasped, but by some miracle, I caught them both.

My sister put a hand to her heart. "We've talked about this!" she said to the twins. "You can't just expect to be caught!"

"Unca Ry Ry *always* catches us," Abi said proudly, wrapping her tiny little arms around my neck with the strength of a boa constrictor. She smiled at me and set her head on my shoulder. My heart would've swelled with love and affection, but she'd cut off my air supply.

Ten minutes later, we were at Al's Diner. Everyone scrambled into the big booth in the back. Our order was massive. Apparently emotional confrontations made people hungry.

Fifteen minutes, and three toddler tantrums later, the food arrived on two very full trays. I was halfway through eating when someone said my name.

I turned and came face to face with the one ache still left in my chest—Penny, flanked by Wyatt, Nell…and Hank.

CHAPTER 34

Penny

MY HEART POUNDED SO hard that I could barely hear myself think as I took in the sight of Ryder and his family sharing breakfast—my boss included.

Caleb and Tucker greeted me warmly, but it was Kiera I was worried about. Shockingly, she gave me a small but genuine smile, which faded when she realized who stood next to me.

Her father.

"Morning," Ryder said to us. His smile, aimed at me, was also warm and genuine, if a bit strained.

Wasn't hard to figure out why. I knew they hadn't told Kiera about Hank.

Ryder had the twins on his lap, who were oblivious to the sudden tension between the adults, happily munching on pancakes. Alex shoved in his last bite and eyed Ryder's plate.

He put his hands over it protectively.

Alex stuck out his lower lip.

Ryder sighed and handed over his last pancake, then nudged

the twins off his lap so he could stand. He nodded to my grandma and Hank, then turned to me.

Before he opened his mouth, Kiera spoke, face expressionless. "I'm guessing there's something you all forgot to tell me."

"Oh, right." Tucker smacked the side of his head. "Dad got kicked out of his retirement home."

"Actually," Caleb said. "he got kicked out of *all* the retirement homes within a hundred miles. Then he had two strokes and a craniotomy, and now he's nonverbal. I think that's it."

"Except none of those places will take him back," Tucker added. "There. That's everything."

Hank was still smiling, and I couldn't tell if he understood they were talking about him or not.

"He's living with me," Ryder said. "Nell, Penny's grandma, is his caretaker during the day while I'm at work."

"He's just as sweet as can be," Grandma said, putting her hand on Hank's arm. "No trouble at all. As long as you don't feed him dairy, if you know what I'm saying."

Kiera looked at Ryder.

"It happened shortly after Auggie died," he said.

She just kept looking at him.

He sighed. "You had enough on your plate."

"You should've told me." She eyed her brothers. "You *all* should've told me."

"You're absolutely right," Ryder said. Paused. "You okay?"

"I'm trying to decide." She shook her head. "I want to be furious, but I can't hold on to it. I've been a disaster and I know it." She eyed Hank, who was still smiling at her. "He really doesn't talk?"

"No," Ryder said. "And we have no idea how much he

remembers, but his demeanor's calm and…affable, so I'm guessing he doesn't remember much."

Not for the first time, I wondered just how incredibly difficult it must've been for the guys to take care of this man who'd once been the source of their nightmares. Especially since Hank stood there, looking happy to see so many people he actually knew.

Kiera drew a deep breath and looked at Hank. "Do you remember who I am?"

"Ah."

Kiera shoved Tucker. "Move."

Tucker shoved Caleb. "Move."

Everyone shuffled so Kiera could get out of the booth to stand in front of her father. "Do you remember me?"

Hank tilted his head to one side, the smile never faltering.

"Do you remember what kind of a dad you were?"

Hank just kept smiling.

Kiera turned to Ryder. "He really doesn't."

He gave her a small sympathetic look that pretty much broke my heart for all of them.

"Huh," Kiera said. "Karma really is a bitch."

Ryder winced. "I'm so sorry, Ki."

"You're sorry you got caught, you mean." She let out a long exhale. "Don't worry, I get why you did it. You were just trying to protect me, like always." She looked at her dad again. "So he's really…nice?"

"And sweet," Grandma said. "God's got some sense of humor, huh?"

"Nice. And sweet," Kiera repeated softly to herself. "Wow."

Hank reached out and gently patted her shoulder.

Kiera let out a half laugh, maybe half sob, but patted her dad's hand in return. Then she looked at her brothers. "So what was your plan? Were you ever going to tell me or just hope I never found out?"

Tucker, Caleb, and Ryder looked collectively guilty.

"Door number two then," she said and shook her head. "What's the deal, you all taking turns taking care of him?"

"Mama," Abi said. "Alex's looking at me again."

"Not now, baby, I'm watching the season finale of Idiots On Parade." Kiera shook her head at her brothers. "Morons, all of you." She gave Tucker, who'd sat back down and had resumed shoveling pancakes into his mouth, a shove. He sighed and stood up again so she could scootch back into her spot.

"Put me on the schedule," she said to Ryder. She pulled Abi onto her lap, then held out a hand for Alex across the table.

Ryder scooped the boy up by the back of his Paw Patrol sweatshirt and dropped him into Kiera's lap.

Hank turned to Grandma. "Ah."

"You're hungry," Grandma said. "Gotcha." She smiled at the group. "I'm going to take Wyatt and Hank to the counter. We're getting ours to go." She turned to me. "Your usual?"

"Yes, please." And when they walked away, I realized I was just standing there, so many emotions coursing through me that I couldn't keep up.

Sadness that I'd sidelined my relationship with Ryder out of fear. Frustration that I'd ignored how my heart beat for him. Adrenaline from just looking at him. And last but definitely not least, a bone-deep affection watching him love his family so deeply. They seemed to always have each other's backs, through thick and thin. Yes, maybe they fought as loud as they loved, but they *did* love, even after all they'd been through. It was amazing.

So was how they never gave up on each other.

Never.

I could learn from that. I knew I needed to say something, but all I could seem to do was stand there, both aching and yearning, knowing what I wanted, but unsure how to get it.

The Colburn brothers were all looking at Kiera. She let out a long exhale, then said, "I reserve the right to be messed up about this later, but for now, I'm fine so stop looking at me." And then she hugged the kiddos and accepted a massive bite of pancake dripping with syrup from Alex.

Everyone dove back into their food as well. Except Ryder. His gaze locked on mine. "Sorry about the drama," he said quietly.

"Don't be. Your family's amazing."

He stroked a finger along my temple, doing that sweet, affectionate thing where he tucked a stray strand from my face.

I gave him a shaky smile. "Can we talk?"

"Of course." Leaning in, he brushed a kiss on my cheek, then lingered, taking a deep breath like he'd missed me.

My heart skipped a beat. Skipped all the beats.

"He never kisses me like that," Caleb said to Tucker.

Ignoring this, Ryder took my hand in his.

"So she *didn't* dump you," Kiera said with a small smile in my direction. "Not that any of us would blame you if you had."

"Oh good," Ryder said dryly. "You really are doing better."

"I didn't dump him," I said, then turned to him. "I didn't dump you. Or I didn't mean to… I was wrong—"

"*Whoa.*" Caleb looked around. "Did you all hear that? A

woman just admitted she was wrong. Quick, someone check to see if hell froze over—"

Not taking his eyes off mine, Ryder said in a dangerously low voice, "Tucker."

Tucker put his hand over Caleb's mouth.

The only other empty booth was next to this one. Ryder tugged me to it, turning our backs to his family.

"What were you wrong about?" he asked me in a tone so gentle my eyes stung.

I'd had it all planned out in my head. I was going to track him down after work and tell him everything, starting with how stupid I'd been to give into my fears, but then I'd seen him sitting here and I knew I couldn't wait.

"I—"

"What's happening?" Grandma asked, having come back with Wyatt and Hank and a lot of food. She handed me a cup of orange juice and a to-go bag with pancakes.

"Over here, Grandma," Caleb called out and scooted over, patting the bench.

And just like that, Grandma and Wyatt sat with the Colburns, our mismatched families seamlessly blending together like sprinkles on a cupcake. The waitress brought over some plates and silverware, Grandma started opening up the to-go bags, and transferring the pancakes out of the containers. Caleb and Tucker fist-bumped Wyatt. Grandma cut up Hank's pancakes and poured his syrup.

I closed my eyes to the chaos and looked at Ryder. "I'm not sure you know this, but when we first met, I was pretty closed off."

"It's okay," he said. "Like recognizes like."

Hard to believe I could find a smile when I felt so anxious, but I did. "I'd locked my heart and soul up tight and thrown away the key. I didn't see that ever changing. I didn't want it to."

"I know." He ran his fingers lightly over my hair. "It was months before I even got to see your smile, but once I did, I was done for."

"True story," Tucker called over to us around a big bite of pancakes. "Last week, he walked right into a wall while he was talking to you on the phone. Made a huge dent in it too. It was pretty great."

"Hey," Caleb said. "Why do you get to talk?"

Our families laughed, and I didn't know how to explain the feeling that came over me, but I felt like I was a part of something. I'd opened the door to my heart and soul, and Ryder had walked right on in. And not just him, but the people he loved and cared about as well.

Once again, Ryder turned us away from the other booth. He kept his eyes on me, calm, patient, waiting for whatever I wanted to say—which gave me the courage to do it, in a soft, just-for-us voice.

"I once told you that I couldn't open up my heart, not ever again. But that was before you. Before all those mornings at Colburn Restorations, before all the late nights fixing up grandma's kitchen, laughing, talking. You let me in, Ryder, and it was…" I searched for the right word. "*Everything.* If you could do that after everything you'd been through, surely I could do the same." I shook my head with a little laugh. "I think it was how you accepted me, hot mess and all. I never saw that coming. I never saw *you* coming."

He squeezed my hand. "Right back at you."

He'd been brave enough to face it head-on from the start. And now it was my turn to be brave. "I said I was falling for you, but that wasn't the whole story. I *wasn't* just falling. I'd *already* fallen. Irrevocably. Face-first."

Ryder's mouth dropped open.

"Wow," Caleb said across the booth's divider. "Never seen him speechless before. But don't worry, he's in love with you too. So...welcome to the family. The sarcasm's strong and the fucks given are few."

The table gave a collective snort of amusement. "You're all assholes," Ryder told his family, then cringed and slid a look at the twins. "Except you two."

"Is asshole a bad word?" Alex asked.

"Yes, but not as bad as fuckwad," Abi said.

Kiera glared at Ryder. "Seriously?"

"Hey, that one they learned from *Tucker*."

Tucker winced at the truth of that.

Ryder held out a hand to me, which I took. He then led me out of the diner to the sidewalk, where we stood blinking in the bright morning sun. He tipped my face up to his.

"You're in love with me?"

"Irrevocably," I whispered.

A look of wonder and marvel crossed his face, and he shook his head, like he couldn't believe it, before cupping my jaw. "Say it again."

His smile was contagious. I felt it all over my face as I set my hands on his chest to feel the comforting, steady, slightly too fast beat of his heart.

"I'm in love with you, Ryder Colburn."

"Irrevocably," he said. "Don't forget that part."

As if I could. "Irrevocably."

"Penny." He seemed gobsmacked, like he hadn't dared see this coming.

And my heart broke for him. "How do you not know that you deserve every good thing on this planet?" I asked. "You deserve the love of your family, the respect of your employees, and all your success." Going up on tiptoe, I pressed my forehead to his. "And us."

His eyes shuttered closed. "Us. There's an us—"

We both turned at the sound of someone knocking on the glass and found everyone's faces pressed up against the window. Well, except for Hank. Hank was stealing a sausage off one of the plates.

Grandma gave me a thumbs up.

Caleb was waving like a lunatic.

Tucker took a pic with his phone.

Wyatt was eating my pancakes.

"Ignore them," Ryder said and yanked me in closer. One hand slid into my hair at the nape of my neck, the other to the small of my back. "I love you, Penelope Rose, with everything I've got."

My heart swelled against my ribcage. "You're sure?"

"*Irrevocably* sure." His smile was brighter than the sun. "I'd convinced myself I didn't need anything more in my life. That it was as good as it got, even though I *knew* a piece was missing. And then you came along, not needing anything either, least of all from me." His eyes held a quiet promise. "Crazy smart, feisty as hell, willing to challenge me at every turn. You had me *baking cookies*."

His smile faded, replaced by pure affection and pride. "You'd been through so much, and still had so much courage and spirit. I knew you were my missing piece."

We heard some murmuring from all those faces pressed up against the glass, though we couldn't make out what they were saying.

"*And* you accept the craziness that is my life," Ryder said wryly. His phone buzzed an incoming text.

And then another.

"You should look," I said. "Maybe there's an emergency."

He pulled out his phone and I leaned in. The text was from The Annoying One.

"Tucker," Ryder said.

The text read: **It's the Legend.**

I looked at Ryder.

He sighed. "The Legend of Star Falls."

"You…you believe in the Legend?"

"Believing isn't the same as seeing three falling stars. I saw three falling stars. And so did those idiots." He jabbed a finger in the direction of his brothers.

I'd never known anyone to actually see the three falling stars, so I'd never given the Legend much thought. Especially since the notion of soul mates had always seemed so farfetched, at least as it pertained to me. But here I was, undeniably connected to Ryder, heart and soul.

Then and there, I knew I'd believe in the Legend for the rest of my days. My heart felt so full I thought it might burst.

"Want to get out of here?" Ryder asked.

"Yes, please."

He led me to his truck.

"How will your family get home?"

"Kiera drove her car here." He smiled at me. "Trust me?"

For once in my life, I didn't hesitate. "Yes."

The roads were quiet, the houses on either side of the curvy two-lane road peaceful, beautiful. We were in an older part of downtown, a beautiful oak-lined street with glorious architecture stretching for two short blocks filled with kitschy-cute antique shops, art galleries, bars, a few inns, a fire station, and touristy shops.

Ryder parked in front of the Devereux Building.

Through the windshield, I stared up at what had been his first big job, the building cast in a golden glow by the early morning sun.

"There's something I'd like to show you."

I smiled. "Right here? Where anyone can see us?"

He snorted. "Come on, smart-ass."

The ground floor had four retail spaces that held a florist, a gift and clothing boutique, and a local-made jewelry shop. The front one with the massive picture windows sat empty. The sun had everything aglow in there too, highlighting custom woodwork, the open layout.

"It's beautiful here."

"The building's for sale," he said quietly, watching me take it all in. "I'm buying it back."

I laughed. I'd gone to the store that morning and bought fresh fruit and veggies, bemoaning the cost. But Ryder was buying a building... "Full circle?"

"Full circle."

Music spilled out of the boutique, and chatter and laughter from the florist, all of it mixing together perfectly. It seemed so quaint and intimate, like somehow even surrounded by life, we were alone.

Ryder took a deep breath. "That space..." He pointed to the empty unit. "Needs something."

"I can see that."

"The large windows provide ample natural light and a stunning view of the valley. Makes it perfect for a café."

My head whipped to him. "What?"

He was still just watching me. "Can you picture it?" He pointed to the windows. "Tables lining those windows, the big glass doors wide open to the outdoor space, where more tables invite visitors to relax and take in the views and chow down on the most amazing food, prepared by the most amazing woman..."

My biggest dream, dangling in front of me like a carrot.

For so long, I'd been afraid of failing my family, afraid to trust again, feeling like it'd never be my time to have a life. And here it was, all of it, ripe for the taking.

"You're...serious?"

"Very." One corner of his mouth quirked with good humor, but his eyes were quiet, thoughtful. "I happen to know the price is right." His gaze continued to hold mine, sincere and warm. Calm and patient.

"I..." My mind was whirling, my heart so full I felt like I could burst. "I don't know what to say."

"Say yes."

I stared at him, knowing I wore a stupid, goofy smile. "And what exactly would I be saying yes to?"

His smile matched mine. "Only everything."

EPILOGUE

Penny

MY HEART THUDDED IN my chest so loudly that I couldn't hear my own chaotic thoughts, which was probably for the best. I stood in the arched doorway between the dining area and the kitchen.

Of my new café.

It'd been six months of hard work, figuring out a business plan, a layout that suited me, creating menus, hiring staff... Sunlight streamed in through the windows, dappling the wood floors in a warm glow. The exposed brick walls were adorned with local artwork, landscapes of rolling vineyards, ocean bluffs, and towering redwoods. Mismatched vintage furniture and potted plants created a cozy feel.

I'd named it Redwood Roost, and it was exactly what I'd always wanted.

"How's Wonder Woman?" Ryder asked, his arms sliding around me.

"Shaking in my boots," I admitted.

Lowering his head, he rubbed his stubbled jaw to mine. Calm. Quiet. Patient, as always. "And?"

"*And*...so excited I can hardly contain myself."

I felt him smile against my neck. "Will it make things worse if I tell you that you've got a line of people waiting for you to open?"

My stomach jangled with nerves. "Did you have something to do with that?"

"Everyone's here because they love you."

"And?"

He chuckled. "Kiera put up a social media post that said if they wanted to taste the best food in town, they should run not walk, because it'd be first come first served, and you were going to have to turn people away."

A warm, fuzzy emotion settled over my nerves like a weighted blanket. Behind us, I could hear the hustle and bustle of the kitchen, with Vi—my kitchen manager—giving orders.

"Five minutes," I whispered, eyeing the time. "I open the door in five minutes."

"Which means I have just enough time for this." He turned me to face him. "Do you have any idea how much I love you?"

I smiled. "It's the breakfast casserole we shared this morning. It makes people crazy. Remember that time Caleb ate it and then asked me to marry him?"

"Let's say it's *not* the breakfast casserole." His mouth was smiling even as his eyes remained serious. Cradling my face in his hands, he looked into my eyes. "Let's say it's that having you in my life has made me a better man, that I'm so in love with you I can no longer remember what it was like without you. That my present and future are yours."

My heart skipped a beat. "How much of that future?"

"Let's just say I want to still be holding your hand at eighty."

My throat tightened at the beautiful words that meant so much more to me than I could ever say. "That's a long time."

"I want it all, Penny."

I gave him a watery smile. "Me too."

"I was hoping you'd say that." He dropped to a knee.

I gaped at the sight of him holding a little black velvet box. "*What are you doing?*"

"Asking you to share breakfast casserole with me for the rest of our lives."

I blinked. "Well, Caleb's going to be very upset."

Ryder choked out a laugh. "Is that a yes?"

"Yes!" Vi called out. She'd come out of the kitchen and was jumping up and down, a huge smile on her face. "She says yes!"

There was thudding on the window closest to the front doors. Turning to look, I saw Ryder's entire family *and* mine, all noses to the window.

"Yes!" they chanted.

"I'm feeling déjà vu," I stage-whispered.

"Did she say yes?" Grandma asked, squinting, Hank at her side. "I can't see a damn thing."

"If she's smart," Kiera said. "She's considering running for the hills."

"She hasn't had the chance to say anything," Ryder grumbled, still on a knee. "I should've pulled the shades first."

"Ask me," I demanded.

He smiled up at me. "Penelope Rose, will you do me the honor of being my wife for the rest of our days, in spite of the family I'm shackled to?"

I smiled down at him. "There's nothing I want more."

He opened the box, and I gasped at the beautiful platinum diamond ring nestled inside. "Oh, Ryder, it's beautiful."

"He's had it in his pocket for months," Caleb said. "The chickenshit was afraid he'd scare you off."

"I was afraid *they'd* scare you off," the "chickenshit" muttered.

Heart melted, I held out my hand for him to slip the ring onto my finger.

The clock chimed the hour. I stared at Ryder. "Best sixty seconds of my life."

Nervous all over again, I headed to the front door, but Ryder reached out, snaring my fingers. His free hand brushed my hair away from my face and bent to kiss me.

"Just sealing the deal," he murmured.

Laughing and tearing up at the same time, I flung my arms around him as my entire world fell into place.

ABOUT THE AUTHOR

New York Times and *USA Today* bestselling author Jill Shalvis writes contemporary romance and romantic comedies filled with madcap adventures and shenanigans and sexy times. She's sold twenty million plus copies worldwide to date and lives with her family in a small mountain town near Lake Tahoe full of quirky characters. (Any resemblance to the quirky characters in her books is mostly coincidental.)

Website: jillshalvis.com
Facebook: JillShalvis
Instagram:@jillshalvis